The Z-Papers

The Z-Papers

B Y

GEOFFREY S. SIMMONS

ARBOR HOUSE
NEW YORK

TO ARTHUR C. FIELDS

Chapter I

The Secretary of Defense and now, of course, vice-presidential candidate, should be coming into sight any minute. Despite the dreariness of this autumn day, police have estimated that nearly a hundred thousand people have lined both sides of State Street. Many are shoppers or people on their lunch breaks, waiting for a quick glimpse or possibly to shake his hand . . . he often walks among crowds, in the pressing-of-flesh tradition of the late Lyndon Johnson and Bobby Kennedy.

He's not had much time for campaigning, and this is his first trip to Chicago in over three years. As you know, this is his hometown, and many here have shown their local pride in a favorite son by turning out today. If you asked most of them they'd probably say they'd have preferred he ran for president rather than vice-president.

Secretary of Defense Kramer, along with such other notables as Hugh Hefner and Kim Novak, graduated from Steinmetz High School. He got his law degree at Loyola University Law School. Many consider him the most effective DA this city has ever had —tough but also fair-minded, a man who believed the law should be strictly enforced but not without humanity. This reporter recalls a case in which he actually abandoned his prosecutor's role when he became convinced a defendant was innocent and worked to clear

7

him—hold on, I think I see the first car coming . . . that should be the mayor. The crowd seems to be getting more excited, they're piled up along the sidewalk.

We're just south of Marshall Field's department store, but you can barely make out the entrance over there. I'd say that ticker tape's seen better days . . . the drizzle's bringing it down in little clumps.

There's the mayor, all bundled up as usual, scarf, hat, overcoat and gloves. They say that he never gets a cold, and looking at him you can see why. Earlier today there were a few demonstrators, but the police managed to clear them away.

I think that's the candidate's car, a Continental with a small American flag on the hood. Yes, it definitely is. We can see him getting out of the car to shake hands. The Secret Service men have made a small ring around him. The people are pushing all around him to touch him. They must be ten deep in some places. He should be coming in front of our cameras in just a few minutes. There's a big reception planned for tonight at the Palmer House, over four hundred guests, many are old friends—something's happened! . . . I can't see. The Secretary appears to be falling backwards. He's holding his hand . . . something's definitely happened but we can't see well from here. He seems to be slumping. They're taking him back to the car. I can see he's talking. I didn't hear any shots. Looks like there's blood on his hands. I don't understand. Hey—I think I see someone breaking out of the crowd, just a flash of him. It's hard to be sure, though, with so many people milling around. The Secret Service men are having trouble getting through the crowd. Everyone's in hysterics. People are blocking the way. Now the candidate's car is going off. Two men are hanging on the side and three motorcycles are chasing behind. This is awful. The area's screaming with cops now. No one seems to know what they're doing. Damn it, didn't anyone see him? He must have gone into Field's, they should have the place surrounded by now. God, I hope this isn't another assassination. I don't think the country could take it. But I didn't hear any shots. They must be taking him to Presbyterian-St. Luke's Hospital. It's only a few minutes away. Let me repeat, Secretary Kramer has been . . .

WOS-TV, 12:09

We interrupt this program for a very important news bulletin. While shaking hands with a record crowd on State Street Secretary of Defense Kramer may have been shot. It's not certain at this time what his exact condition may be, but he definitely is alive. He's being rushed to one of the hospitals in the area, Michael Reese or Presbyterian. Please stay tuned.

WIND radio, 12:10

Here is a bulletin. During a parade down State Street the Secretary of Defense was attacked by an unidentified assailant. His condition is unknown, but several eye-witnesses describe seeing blood on his hands and across his jacket. Stay tuned for further developments . . .

As part of the routine planning for any campaign trip one or more hospitals in the vicinity were always placed on standby alert and the candidate's chauffeur given specific instructions in case of emergency. Before Kramer's departure from Washington the Secret Service had considered alerting three different hospitals near the Chicago Loop—Michael Reese on the South Side, Weiss Memorial on the North Side and Presbyterian-St. Luke's on the West Side; but two days before his arrival only Presbyterian was notified. It was felt at the time that this hospital was ideally situated, sitting as it did next to the Eisenhower Expressway two miles from the downtown area and less than a mile from the intersection of two other major arteries, and therefore notifying the other two hospitals would be superfluous. With the exception of the few minutes spent at O'Hare International Airport, the vice-presidential candidate would always be within a five-minute radius of the hospital's doors.

Presbyterian was considered by some to be the Midwest's answer to Boston's well-known Massachusetts General. The atmosphere at Presbyterian was purposefully academic—a modern, well-equipped hospital prepared for nearly any sort of emergency except perhaps serious burn victims. These had to be rushed across the street to Cook County Hospital, a dilapidated row of discolored brick buildings maintained for the poor and uninsured, which unaccountably happened to have a good burn unit.

The two hospitals belonged to an enormous medical center that housed three other hospitals and three separate medical schools, all of which stood out like an island amidst an ocean of rundown tenement houses occupied mostly by poor Italians and blacks. Only the Eisenhower Expressway cut a swath of urban renewal; Presbyterian-St. Luke's, as well as many of its well-to-do clients, appeared misplaced.

This was not the first time the house staff at Presbyterian had been placed on alert for a visiting dignitary, so when the memo came down from the administration's office few showed concern. Such detachment changed to near panic when the radio call came in from Kramer's limousine to announce the estimated time of arrival would be less than three minutes.

Within seconds, two aides raced from the front office and began clearing out the crowded waiting room, referring the sicker-appearing patients to Cook County or Illinois Research Hospital. As one security officer ran into the nearby intersection to begin diverting the noontime traffic, another officer hurried toward the emergency loading dock to make sure the ambulances were out of the way. A moment later, a nurse joined him with a metal stretcher, which had wheels at the bottom of its long thin legs and a portable oxygen tank. The outside air was cool and the morning drizzle had turned to a steady downpour.

10

Dr. Nissen, chief of surgery, was scrubbing for an elective abdominal exploration on an eighty-year-old female with an unexplained mass when the phone rang outside the operating suites. The balding short physician of German descent was a few yards away, wearing his surgical greens and standing over a large sink with suds dripping from his elbow to his fingertips. He was about to complete the last rinse before entering the suite when one of the attendants rushed into the dressing room and called out the message to him. The surgeon immediately broke scrub, grabbing a discarded towel from a chair close by, and ran back toward the main desk, where the receiver was still lying on its side. The switchboard operator was waiting on the other end, and after she repeated the message that Kramer had been hurt and was on his way to Presbyterian, Nissen quickly gave her the names of two other surgeons to page and headed toward the nearest elevator. As he waited for the doors to open and finished wiping the yellow soapsuds from his arms, he could hear the page operator's voice echoing through the hallway, repeating the same two names, three times each, and directing them to report immediately to the emergency room.

Each month a rotating schedule placed two interns in the emergency room—one from the department of surgery and the other from medicine. When the call came, both men on duty were in the midst of routinely taking care of patients.

Dr. Wheelin, a youthful blond intern, was trying to suture a small laceration on a six-year-old boy's knee as two nurses, an attendant and the boy's father fought to hold the frightened child still. Despite the fact that Wheelin had to deal with a moving target, he managed to get the last stitch in place and quickly tie a surgical knot. He then instructed one of the nurses to take the boy into another room to bandage the knee.

Dr. Herbert was a few years older than his partner, having been in the army before college and medical school. He was also much shorter, with brown hair and a gloomy expression that seemed to match the patients he attended. Just now his patient was a forty-year-old housewife on her tenth visit to the hospital over the past six months for recurring headaches, a tingling sensation in her hands, nausea, swollen ankles, constipation and other vague complaints that were by now demonstrably psychosomatic. He was the only person who welcomed the alarm, which gave him an excuse to escape her clutch and show her to the door.

Three minutes was barely enough time to clear the area. Many of the patients were abruptly pushed out the door and, not unreasonably, were highly indignant. Some refused to go to another hospital and others demanded to see whoever was in charge.

As the inhalation therapist made last minute checks on the standby respirator and confirmed that the two oxygen tanks still had a reasonable amount of pressure, an EKG technician loaded a new roll of paper into her machine and then made certain the stylus was warm enough to record properly the heart rhythm.

Upstairs in the operating suites personnel were making last minute preparations. Although an operating room had already been set aside for Kramer, much of the equipment was being used elsewhere and had to be quickly retrieved. Next door in the blood bank, where Kramer's blood type was on file, four units of type A blood were moved from cool storage to an incubator so that any transfusions would be body temperature when used.

No one knew what to expect, and as the nurses began drawing up critical medications in the emergency room, the black limousine came into sight, its windshield wipers swishing back and forth and its tires slipping on the slick asphalt at the edge of the driveway. Just before the car came to a full stop, the back door swung open and one of the Secret Service men jumped from the back seat.

Both interns, Wheelin and Herbert, were waiting at the bottom of the ramp with the wet stretcher behind them. They could see Kramer slumped over the seat. Once the car's brakes were secure, Wheelin reached inside and with the help of a Secret Service man he moved Kramer to the waiting stretcher.

Kramer's lips were pale and they quivered when he tried to

speak. There were spots of blood smeared across his jacket, pants and—like a red gash—across the front of his white shirt. He kept his hands tightly clasped together, but blood continued to ooze between his fingers and began pooling on the wet cement beneath the stretcher. Mentally he was alert, complaining of pain in his right hand.

The two interns hurried the stretcher back through the automatic doors, almost striking the glass panels as they opened, and into the emergency room a few feet away. Everyone seemed poised and ready as the stretcher was pushed between two beige curtains. Dr. Nissen arrived simultaneously, out of breath, face flushed and hands drenched with perspiration. Just outside a small crowd seemed to appear from absolutely nowhere and had to be pushed back by the hospital's security police, who were just beginning to get themselves organized.

Although the house staff at Presbyterian was accustomed to handling life-threatening emergencies, the fact that they were dealing with a V.I.P. this time seemed to affect everyone concerned, including some of the veterans. Disaster training had been usually taken in a light vein, and the rubber dummies used as surrogates were often targets of something less than respect. In the classroom or on an actual practice alert, a misplaced electrocardiogram lead or an occasional mistaken diagnosis had only academic importance. This time it was for real, and no routine ambulance delivery. All were aware they were dealing with an important cabinet member who likely would be the next Vice-President, and they also knew the whole country would be keyed in on their management.

"What happened?" Nissen said, still gasping for air, looking first to the Secret Service man and then to Kramer. "Where were you hit?"

"It's my hand. It feels like someone set it on fire!" There was a film of cold sweat across Kramer's brow. His eyes stared at the older man, and he sounded indignant and pained all at once.

13

Despite specific instructions, there were too many people in the small emergency room; they were getting in each other's way, duplicating procedures and nervously echoing words somebody else had just spoken. Disturbed by the growing confusion and worried that time was against them, Nissen took command and in between his questions began issuing orders like a general in the army.

"Are you hurt anywhere else?"

"I don't think so."

"Somebody get his blood pressure. Cut that sleeve away if you have to. Tell the blood bank to stand by. Are you having any trouble breathing? Was it a gunshot?"

"No."

"Get an intravenous going." Nissen turned toward Wheelin and shouted even though the intern was only a few feet away.

Nissen's major concern was the source of bleeding. He immediately began cutting the jacket sleeve away from the injured right arm while a nurse cut the other sleeve to get his pulse and blood pressure reading. At the same time Herbert, the other intern, unbuttoned Kramer's shirt and slid his cold stethoscope inside to check Kramer's heart and lungs.

"Pulse 110, blood pressure 160 over 90," the nurse announced as she unsnapped the cuff to give Wheelin room to start the intravenous line.

Herbert came back to Nissen's side and began helping him expose the wound, which turned out to be a jagged gash at the juncture of the wrist and the base of the thumb. It was immediately obvious they were dealing with an arterial bleeder, which began spurting blood several feet into the air with each heartbeat and within seconds had managed to splotch Nissen's surgical gown and the floor beneath him. Kramer's arm was covered with blood that had traveled both up his sleeve and down his hand. Nissen quickly grabbed a sterile 4 x 4 gauze pad from a nearby surgical tray and hurriedly laid it across the pulsating wound as he simultaneously grasped the wrist to add pressure and elevated the arm, hoping to diminish the arterial pressure and thereby limit the bleeding

"This looks more like a knife wound," Nissen said in a surprised tone, and while still maintaining pressure he looked away from the heart monitor, which had just been hooked up, to check hurriedly the rest of Kramer's body, looking for other injuries. There appeared to be none.

"I don't know *what* it was. Everything happened too fast to see anything. It could have been some little old lady with an umbrella as far as I know." Kramer grimaced as Wheelin stuck his other arm with another intravenous needle. This came unannounced after the intern noticed that the drip in the first bottle was slowing on its own and might fail soon.

"You must have seen something—like a knife or an ice pick?" Nissen persisted.

Kramer shook his head.

After Kramer's vital signs were rechecked and shown to be stable, Nissen ordered an analgesic injection for the pain and returned to his questioning. "Don't you think it might have been a knife?"

"I don't think so. It was rougher . . . I had my hand out and something, someone grabbed it. I saw something white and then lightning shot up my arm." As the analgesic began to work, color was returning to Kramer's face.

"I don't understand. What was white?" Nissen said, keeping a firm hold on the gauze around Kramer's wrist.

"I don't know. It could have been a man's sleeve. I honestly don't know . . ."

Although a small amount of blood continued to soak through the gauze bandage beneath Nissen's grip, it now appeared that Kramer's life was not in jeopardy. Some of the personnel returned to their normal chores; most lingered, watching from a distance. The news of the assault had, of course, spread through the thirteen-story hospital, as had at least an equal number of rumors.

15

Patients, visitors, and house staff began piling into the lobby just to get a look or offer their own opinions, and soon the small waiting area was dangerously overcrowded—it also provided an unexpected opportunity for everyone to take an extra break.

Kramer's anxiety did not subside as quickly as almost everyone else's around him. Everything seemed to happen too fast. He remembered extending his hand into a smiling crowd, being struck from nowhere, thrown into a car and rushed to an emergency room. He thought about the blood spurting from his arm and how he couldn't stop it with the other hand. At first he assumed he had been shot, but he couldn't recall any gunfire. He was, in fact, damn confused . . .

Kramer was known for his equanimity, rarely flappable in court, controlled and composed in the heat of recent Congressional inquiries prompted by the opposition party, which had a special interest in him now that he'd become a vice-presidential candidate, as well as during the pressures of the campaign trail thus far, including some provocative remarks at rallies by militant pacifists—the Secretary's ironic designation for them.

Kramer was fifty-four, but could have passed for closer to forty. His dark wavy hair barely showed a hint of gray about the temples, and only the deep worry lines across his forehead and beneath his eyes more accurately suggested his true age. His features were lean and chiseled, with high cheek bones, prominent chin and a broad nose that had been broken twice during his career in college football and baseball. Until the campaign he had managed to keep himself in shape by regular turns in the handball court.

For the past three and a half years he had been a member of the Cabinet, first as Attorney General and then as Secretary of Defense, and if the incumbent Vice-President had not suddenly become too ill to run, he doubtless would have held, or been content to hold, his post another four years. According to the polls, the President, and therefore Kramer as Vice-Presidential candidate, appeared to be leading and gaining momentum. The shock of inflation and recession had had their impact, and the President, most seemed to feel, had if not solved all the problems at least made some forceful and courageous moves toward a solution. The public seemed to feel him an ally, not a fall guy.

As for Kramer, people tended to be impressed by his no-nonsense style, by his quiet manner and soft voice, not to mention the reassuringly rugged appearance. There were some, though, who were less than pleased with Kramer's policies—which he could argue determinedly and with conviction, especially in private councils. For Kramer, the true pacifist was the one who best prepared for peace, who helped his country maintain a full arsenal, without qualification, to offset and balance the opposition. No sabre-rattler or yahoo rightwinger, Kramer nonetheless felt that the best way to achieve and maintain such a delicate condition as détente was to keep the score even, not to let one fellow get ahead and feel encouraged to make a dangerously provocative move on the theory that the other side couldn't retaliate. In the days of the Cold War it had been a mindless race without international agreement. Kramer felt the current effort to keep the peace by mutual agreement on arms made more sense and promised more success—providing the U.S, didn't make itself the weaker partner in the arrangement.

Of course, on the other side, Kramer's position could seem tilted in the direction of guns instead of butter, and the Secretary himself might agree to that, claiming that it was difficult to maintain both equally, regardless of what the gentlemen on the Hill might say for the benefit of constituents. Kramer by no means underestimated, however, the importance of butter; indeed, he firmly believed that if another major world upheaval occurred, it would be over food, not ideology or even territory. And in line with such thinking, he opposed giving arms to starving enemies, preferring to give food and keep their bellies rather than their arsenals full. He also believed that countries with serious overpopulation should be obliged to undertake mandatory birth control before qualifying for

U.S. relief—another position that was considered too tough for many who took a less matter-of-fact approach. With few exceptions, though, even those who opposed Kramer and his policies respected him for his sincerity and decent intent.

"You sure had us worried, sir," Dr. Wheelin added with a loud sigh. "I expected to see someone in much worse shape than you are."

The young intern proceeded to wrap a rubber tourniquet around the candidate's left wrist, just below the new IV site, and as the veins on the back of his hand began to engorge, he sponged off a plump vessel with an alcohol swab and then gathered together a syringe and three vacuum tubes for routine studies.

At first Kramer seemed amused at the intern's comment, but his smile disappeared at the sting of the sharp needle as it penetrated his skin and popped into a dilated vein. A moment later bright red blood began flowing into the first vacuum tube.

As soon as Wheelin had collected enough blood to fill three tubes and made certain that the puncture site had stopped bleeding, his colleague, Dr. Herbert, took over, strapping the cold metal electrocardiogram leads to each extremity and placing six suction cups across Kramer's chest. The ten wires from each lead made him seem more like a puppet than a patient. The machine was already warmed up, only requiring the flick of a switch, and as the thin roll of paper began rolling across the recording screen, the tracing indicated that his heart, other than its rapid rate, had not been affected by the injury.

Over the next few minutes, Kramer's pulse slowly returned to a normal rate of eighty beats per minute but his blood pressure remained slightly elevated. Nissen immediately inquired if he had been having trouble with his pressure in the past and Kramer said no. For the moment, however, his vital signs could be considered stable and a note to that effect was sent out to the waiting press corps.

Dr. Nissen then called for 6-0 suture material, a sterile black thread that was as thin as hair and, using a special jeweler's eyeglass, began repairing the lacerated artery, fitting the tiny jagged edges together like a miniature jigsaw puzzle. Wheelin stood at his side and helped by keeping a tourniquet on just above the injury to minimize the bleeding. When the surgeon had tied the last stitch and the tourniquet was released, Kramer's hand immediately began to warm up and lose its bluish discoloration. The remainder was simple, requiring five skin sutures and some antibiotic ointment. Afterward, Kramer was given a tetanus booster and transferred to a special room on the fifth floor for observation.

Everyone's impression at that time was that a poorly calculated attempt on the candidate's life had failed despite the severed artery, and that the wound would not amount to any consequence. That feeling of security persisted until the first blood tests returned. At the bottom of the blue CBC or Complete Blood Count, which happened to be normal except for a slight anemia as measured by hemoglobin, they found a handwritten note.

Hematology Laboratory
CBC
Time Drawn: 12:20

Test	Result	Normal Values
Hemoglobin	13.0	14-18 gm/100 ml
Hematocrit	39%	42-52 ml/100 ml
Red Cell Count	4.2 mil	4.6-6.2 million/cu mm
White Cell Count	9,800	5-10,000/cu mm
neutrophils	60%	54-62%
bands	3%	0-5%
lymphocytes	31%	25-33%
monocytes	3%	3-7%
eosinophils	2%	1-3%
basophils	1%	0-1%
metamyelocytes	0%	0%
promyelocytes	0%	0%

MCV	92	82-92
MCH	31	27-31
MCHC	34	32-36
Platelets	290,000	2-300,000/cu mm
Sedimentation Rate	10	less than 15 mm/hr

Red Cell Morphology: Slight anisocytosis, slight poikilocytosis
Atypical lymphocytes: none seen

How much is Kramer's life worth? He has 24 hours to live. Next message at 4 pm.

WGN-TV, 12:57

This is Mike Stahl reporting from the front lobby of Presbyterian-St. Luke's Hospital, where Secretary Kramer was rushed a little over a half hour ago with an injury that has everyone baffled. We've just learned that his condition is stable and that he's being kept for observation purposes only.

Some of you might have seen the earlier coverage. Someone buried in the crowd along State Street struck out at Mr. Kramer, presumably with a knife—certainly an unusual and risky form of attack. No shots were heard by anyone. Officials have been reluctant to give out information, but we've been told by a hospital source that there is a deep cut somewhere around the wrist and that it hit one of the main arteries leading to his hand.

As far as the assailant is concerned, police are still searching the Loop area. Nearly every spectator within a two block area of the assault has been held for questioning, including one of our own camera crews and reporter Roger Thornton.

The same thing seems to be happening here now. A few minutes ago the entire hospital was cordoned off without any explanation, and we're told several of the hospital *staff are being questioned. There's no explanation for this, but one wonders if perhaps there's been another attempt or if one is expected . . .*

From State Street there are conflicting reports on the description of the assailant. We hope to get more information when they release Roger Thornton. We do understand the police think the assailant escaped into Field's and are still searching–anyone who lives in Chicago knows how easy it is to lose oneself in that store.

We repeat . . .

Reporter Mike Stahl was closer to the truth than he might have thought. The message at the bottom of the CBC may have been unclear as to details, but it was clearly a threat and indicated that the assailant or an accomplice had made his way into the hospital and might still be on the grounds. Two security men were immediately dispatched to the hematology laboratory on the second floor. An order went out to close all exits to the hospital, and Dr. Nissen, who was dictating a note for Kramer's chart in the emergency room, was summoned to the fifth floor, where Kramer had been taken for observation.

Chapter II

Kramer's campaign manager, J. L. Thomison, was working in the banquet hall at the Palmer House when the news of the assault reached him. His secretary, Sandy Duncanish, almost pretty, almost built, raced into the empty dining area and announced hysterically that Secretary Kramer had been shot. At that particular moment Thomison was arguing with a young assistant manager over the night's seating arrangement and at first seemed more stunned at her unexpected outburst than her actual words, but within seconds his face turned pale from shock. Forgetting the disagreement, he hurried across the room, using the open space in front of the podium,and demanded that she repeat everything she heard.

The girl's information came from the coffee shop and was sketchy at best. As he listened he recalled hearing sirens a few minutes before, but they seemed to be coming from the opposite direction of the motorcade.

His first concern was for Kramer, feeling as if a relative or good friend had been injured, and yet being a cold pragmatist, a quality necessary for his job, he was also concerned about the campaign and possible loss of revenue if the dinner had to be cancelled. He felt like calling New York for advice and the hospital for information at the same time. Thomison knew that Presbyterian Hospital had been designated for emergencies, having been part of the preliminary arrangements, and he immediately went to a nearby house phone, but when he reached the hospital switchboard the operator refused to transfer his call to the emergency room. He tried arguing, repeating his credentials, but the operator refused and finally, frustrated and angry, he slammed the receiver down. Forgetting his hat and coat, he hurried down the steps and caught a taxi waiting at the front entrance.

Meanwhile, the Secretary was moved to the Executive Suite, more like a hotel suite, at the far end of a carpeted and semiprivate hallway. There were two Secret Service men stationed outside his door and a third officer, Lt. Dan Woodsley, an ex-cop, ex-Marine, who had been with the Secretary since the beginning of the campaign, and had been in charge of security on this trip, stood at the elevators checking identification.

The lieutenant was a husky man whose muscles were slowly turning to fat because of disuse and his age, now close to fifty, and whose beer belly overlapped a lowered beltline. His manner was rough and callous. Although his comments were an occasional embarrassment to Kramer, he was extremely reliable and usually watched the Cabinet member like a hawk. Twice in the past he had been responsible for deflecting unexpected attempts on the Secretary's life. Both were initiated by crazed gunmen, one of whom had also used a large outdoor crowd as his camouflage.

At the time of the assault on State Street, Woodsley was standing next to Kramer, studying some of the faces toward the back of the crowd. The silent attack from the frontline took him by surprise. His attention naturally went to the ailing Secretary, immediately helping him back to the waiting limousine, and never focused on capturing the assailant. He was beginning to feel responsible and yet, remembering that he had warned Kramer not to walk among the people, where security was always at a minimum, he was able to rationalize away some of his guilt feelings.

When the threatening note had made its way to Kramer's chart, Woodsley was the first to see it and quickly issued orders to his own men to close the hospital. The administration was stunned by his actions, but there was nothing that they could do. It was the

23

Secretary who had Nissen paged after the lieutenant showed him the note.

While Kramer waited for the surgeon to arrive, he tried thumbing through some of the voluminous papers in his thick briefcase. Despite the lingering pain in his wrist he thought that he might take advantage of the observation time to catch up on some back work, but the note kept bothering him and he was too upset to concentrate. What had once been easily explained as a fanatic with a sharp weapon had changed dimensions and now it seemed there might be a collaborator and possibly another attack.

He had enemies dating from earlier criminal prosecutions to present-day subversive groups, who had made it known that his life was always in jeopardy. Everyday there was an anonymous threatening note, but they were never taken seriously. This time it was different.

Kramer lay in the midst of a king-size bed that was completely electric and included a vibrator with three different speeds. To his side was a floor-length window that opened onto a small wrought-iron balcony, across from him was an antique desk with a highly polished marble top. There was also a remote-controlled color television suspended from the ceiling a few feet from the end of his bed. The last person to use the room had been a banker's wife who wanted to have her hemorrhoids removed in secret.

The Secretary had just set down one of the pending congressional bills on defense appropriations when Dr. Nissen, closely followed by Dr. Wheelin, entered his room. Lt. Woodsley followed them inside, quietly closing the door. The CBC lay at the foot of the bed.

"What do you think of that?" Kramer pointed with his good hand. "I'm sorry. I hadn't planned on looking. As a matter of fact I wouldn't want to look. But now that I have, I want your opinion."

Years of habit made Nissen check each result slowly, and as he neared the bottom, where he was accustomed to seeing a handwritten description of the red cells, he shrugged his shoulders and said, "It's consistent with the small amount of bleeding. You might have lost—"

"I think this kook's going to try it again," Woodsley said, impatient with the older man, who only just then finally saw the note. "There's no way he'll get through our security again like that."

"Maybe he's not going to try," Wheelin said as he peered over Nissen's shoulder. "Maybe it's all some kind of twenty-four hour poison someone managed to inject—"

"I don't think that's *possible,*" Nissen quickly responded. "It could be a hoax. Besides, that wound looked much more like a cut than a puncture wound."

"But *could* he have injected something, never mind what the wound looked like?" Wheelin's persistence alarmed Kramer, and Nissen, noting it, took a moment before he answered.

"Anything's possible, I suppose. It would have to have been awfully quick, and I think we'd have had some hint of it by now. You look, I'm pleased to say, quite healthy."

"The note says twenty-four hours," Wheelin reminded his chief. "It might be too early."

Wheelin's comments were beginning to bother Kramer more than the note had. He repeated Wheelin's question. "*Could* he have injected something?"

Nissen walked to the window, stared at the dark clouds for a minute and then returned. "We'll run tests. But why would someone want to poison you over a twenty-four hour period? That doesn't make any sense to me. Why not just shoot you or—"

"Money," Woodsley answered from the back. "He said, 'How much is his life worth?' Plenty, I'd say. Son of a bitch!"

"No, I don't think so." Nissen glanced at the lieutenant, not expecting the last comment. "He could have picked a score of other wealthy men and not taken nearly the chance of being caught. He's after something else, if it really is a poisoning, but we'll start running tests. You're going to have to go back on the heart monitor."

Dr. Heinrich Nissen had just passed his sixty-fourth birthday and was planning his retirement at the end of this academic year. He had been the Chief of the Department of Surgery for almost ten years and enjoyed full professorship at both the Rush and University medical schools. He was nationally known for several radical innovations in the surgical approach to lung cancer and had published numerous well-received papers on related topics.

He was born in Ulm, Germany, studied medicine in Berlin during Hitler's early years of power and barely escaped the pogrom with his wife and two sons in 1939. They'd spent one year in Norway with forged papers, and then made their way to New York City on an old Danish freighter. For the first two years, their life had been very difficult. Language problems hindered employment, and money was scarce. At first he had to work as an attendant in a private hospital, despite his extensive training. As soon as he was able to pass the American medical examination for foreign graduates, however, he moved his family to Chicago and affiliated with the University of Illinois. At the end of the war he returned to Germany, but like many others in 1946, he was unable to find the remainder of his family.

He was a short man with a crisp but usually pleasant nature. His Teutonic accent was barely noticeable, occasionally confusing a V with a W, but his style was distinctly German, in the old tradition. He demanded a great deal from his staff, maintained a high level of discipline. There was always that slight bow of his head whenever he shook hands. Teaching seemed to be his forte and his students loved him. He'd been known to spend hours on any interesting case they brought to his attention, and often stopped in the middle of an operation just so that one of the students could get a better look. Socially he was a hermit, devoting his free time to his family, rarely attending hospital functions, and whenever he did, never discussing religion or politics. He managed to keep up with most of the new advances in medicine, but poisoning cases rarely came to his service—the last patient was a lye ingestion that needed his esophagus repaired—and so he planned to call an emergency staff

26

meeting. Meanwhile he would order the routine battery of screening tests.

As Nissen stepped from the Executive Suite, his mind pondering a list of other possible tests, he was confronted by Thomison, who was being detained by the two Secret Service men. The campaign manager had used his credentials to pass security at the front door, but he had to await pernission to enter Kramer's room. When he saw Nissen's white coat he came directly up to him.

"How is he, doc? How long you going to have to keep him? My name's Thomison. It was only a superficial wound, wasn't it? We've got a dinner tonight at the Palmer House. Thousand dollars a plate, you know. I'm his campaign manager. I have to see him . . ." Thomison's statements were fired in such rapid succession that they all seemed to run together.

Nissen didn't know what question to answer first, glancing from Thomison's frantic face to a nearby nurse and then back again. Somehow he didn't like him and yet knew that he owed him some explanation, which he didn't have. "Well, it's difficult to say," seemed to be the only thing that he could come up with.

"What do you mean, 'it's difficult to say'?" Thomison moved closer and almost put his face in Nissen's. "It's just a cut wrist, right? I've had cuts myself and stitches to boot and never had to stay in a hospital. Give him a tetanus shot and I'll make sure he gets to bed early tonight—"

"That's not quite it . . ." Nissen started to explain, but Thomison was overbearing. There was perspiration speckled across his forehead and a tense look in his eyes. He knew that there was more than he was being told. "What's *not it* ? I need to know what *it is*. There's a lot at stake here—"

"There's been a complication."

"What *kind* of complication?"

"Mr. Thomison, I think you're going to have to calm down. The Secretary is in excellent health. I think perhaps he should explain it to you."

27

Nissen stepped aside, as if giving the campaign manager permission to enter, which he quickly did.

"Well, let's pack up and get out of this place," Thomison said as he entered. Kramer was accustomed to his manager and had long ago become immune to his lack of concern for anything but the campaign. Thomison was not his selection. That came from the party members, who felt that his managerial sense and influential friends would be major assets.

"I feel much better now, thank you." Kramer's sarcasm flew over Thomison's head.

"That's good." Thomison carried on. "That was quite a scare you gave us."

"Sorry about that."

"New let's get down to business. Let the police take care of the rest. When they going to let you out of this place?"

"It's not going to be that easy." Kramer handed Thomison the threatening note.

The manager had a confused look on his face as he accepted the blue slip and made a disgusted look as he glanced down the list of meaningless words and their associated serum values. When he reached the bottom line, his face turned pale again.

"What the hell does *this* mean?"

Kramer shrugged.

"This must be a joke. Someone here in the hospital's getting it off. It must be. I wouldn't give it a second thought. Someone here just doesn't like the military. I'll take you back to the hotel and if you're not feeling well, I'll bring you back—"

"J.L., this time I don't think that I'm going to take your advice."

"But what about tonight?"

"That's five hours away. By then we should know. They're going to run some tests."

"What about television? Closed circuit TV?" Thomison's mind had wandered off to another idea. "We could hook you up from here."

"We'll see." Kramer wasn't particularly happy with the idea but was willing to give it some thought.

While Thomison began making his plans upstairs, two Secret Service men were in the hematology laboratory, questioning everyone who had anything to do with the CBC. The head technician, an Oriental girl, who also was the most experienced, had done the actual count. She denied writing anything other than her results, but did admit to leaving the slip unattended at the messenger station. Eager to help, she set her work aside and led the two officers to an old metal desk located just out of sight around the corner and cluttered with wire baskets for each ward, inter-hospital mail and unsorted lab results. Once again, when she arrived, the station was deserted. To be certain, however, her handwriting was checked against the note.

Reporters began crowding the lobby area, but no one was permitted to leave the hospital while an intensive floor-to-floor search for an undescribed individual took place. Wires from television cameras crisscrossed the waiting room. Intermittently a red light would flash on, a lacquered reporter would put on a smile and try outshouting his neighbors. Ashtrays began overflowing with crumpled cigarette butts and half-empty coffee cups, billows of smoke weaved their way among the bright fluorescent lights and mud was caked at every entrance.

Outside wasn't much better. Curious spectators and well-wishers were arriving by the carload, filling every parking lot, space and alleyway. Both freeway exits had traffic jams. Three huge television vans lined up along the northern perimeter of the yellow brick building, each with thick black cables that stretched along the sidewalk and into the lobby. Another eight cars from the newspapers lined the west side, and police cars blocked nearby intersections. While uniformed policemen stood guard at the three entrances, detectives just inside demanded identification from everyone who passed. Many of the people who came to visit their relatives had difficulty getting inside, and none could leave. The only place where passage was not totally obstructed was the emergency room, where business was beginning to pick up again. Altogether, three teams of investigators handled the floor-to-floor, room-to-room search for a missing messenger boy and a nondescript stranger who might have written a threatening note. No one knew what they were looking for, so everyone had to be checked, house staff and patients alike. All fire escapes, stairwells and elevator shafts were inspected. The detectives were refused access to the surgical suites, but were not caught in time on the Obstetrics Service, where they accidentally witnessed a breech delivery. Doctors were interrupted as they were examining their patients and patients were interrupted while they were sitting on their bedpans. Even closets were checked, in one of which four cleaning women were discovered playing canasta on the seventh floor.

It was over half an hour before they found the right messenger boy, first checking with administration and then some of his friends. They finally caught him taking his third coffee break of the day, devoted to flirting with a cute high school candy-striper who disliked most of the chores that she had been given. At first the boy was frightened, thinking that he was under arrest, but when they got him downstairs for questioning he denied seeing anyone at his desk and had not seen the note on the CBC. He said that he carried the CBC upstairs in a pile of other tests for other floors and that he rarely looked at anyone's results. He guessed that the laboratory slip had gone unwatched for less than ten minutes.

At 1:45 the other laboratory tests on the Secretary were completed. The sodium, potassium and chloride, measurements of vital serum electrolytes, were all normal, as was the BUN, which directly reflected kidney function. Although the blood sugar was slightly elevated, its value could easily be attributed to the release of adrenalin during stress and would not have to be treated with insulin or other drugs. Among the results in the liver profile the enzymes were elevated, but because they could come from a variety of sources including muscle, the injury could be incriminated and not a specific liver problem. If they were truly muscle and not liver, they would soon return to normal.

Routine Chemistry
Electrolytes
Time Drawn: 12:20

	Value	Normal
Sodium	140	132-142 mEq/L
Potassium	4.1	3.5-5.0 mEq/L
Chloride	101	98-106 mEq/L
BUN	10	10-20 mg/100ml
Sugar	131	60-90 mg/100ml

Special Chemistry
Liver Profile
Time Drawn: 12:20

	Value	Normal
Albumin	4.5	4.0-5.2 gm/100ml
Globulin	2.6	1.3-2.7 gm/100ml
Bilirubin, total	0.8	0.1-0.8 mg/100ml
Bilirubin, indirect	0.3	0.1-0.6 mg/100ml
Alkaline Phosphatase	1.0	2.0-4.5 units
SGOT enzyme	47	15-30 units
SGPT enzyme	25	7-24 units

At 2:00 the Secretary's temperature had risen slightly, to '99 degrees, but there was no concern. Tissue damage alone might be responsible. His pulse was still recorded at eighty beats per minute and his blood pressure continued falling to a normal value. His only complaint was pain, and Dr. Nissen had left orders for analgesics as needed.

It took less than a minute for Dr. Nissen's secretary, an attractive brunette, to place the three emergency phone calls. Her message was purposefully vague, but the urgency of the situation was made clear.

Dr. Robert Blackwell, the Chief of the Department of Medicine, also near retirement, was probably the most distinguished member of Presbyterian's staff. He was a stately old gentleman with shaggy gray hair that fell over his ears, much like Carl Sandburg, soft-spoken and highly respected for his medical acumen. He had once wanted to be a surgeon, but rheumatoid arthritis crippled his hands and it was now all he could do to rid himself of morning stiffness. The field of gastroenteritis was his expertise and he was internationally known for research work on small bowel malabsorption and subsequent malnutrition. His credentials included a B.S. in chemistry from the University of Chicago and a combined Ph.D. in human physiology and an M.D. from Harvard graduate school.

He was an honorary member of three international medical associations, a former officer of the A.M.A. and a frequent speaker at the Academy of Sciences.

When Dr. Blackwell received his call, he was lecturing a class of third-year medical students on the hemodynamics of shock therapy and had just finished the introduction. He was aware of the Secretary's earlier arrival, but like everyone else, thought that it was only a minor injury. After reading the message, his alarm became apparent. He quickly gathered his notes, to which he rarely referred, offered an apology to his students and hurried from the lecture hall.

The second physician notified was Dr. Harvey Dressner, Chief of Pathology. Although twenty years younger than Blackwell and considerably less well-known, he was also highly regarded and often called for consultation at other hospitals in the area. He was a wiry thin man with a sallow complexion, whose small face was easily buried behind thick, dark-rimmed glasses. Crowds bothered him and he was shy even among friends. To say Dr. Dressner lacked spontaneity would be an understatement. Everything was serious, his whole life was medicine. At the time of his call he was alone in his office preparing notes for a lecture in Seattle and had been so engrossed that he wasn't even aware that the Secretary was in town. It took him several minutes to organize his papers before he felt comfortable enough to leave.

Dr. Harold Stecker, a clinical pharmacologist with a Ph.D. in biochemistry, was an expert on drug therapy, including indications and toxicity. He came from Cornell University and had been highly sought, after publishing three major articles on the metabolic pathways of heart muscle under stress. He was in his early thirties and ambitious, with dark curly hair, deep brown eyes and a thick black mustache. It wasn't uncommon to find him dressed in blue Levis and a print shirt, only adding his white coat when dealing with patients. During the past six months he had computerized the pharmacy's complicated filing system, eliminated every drug of questionable potency and had revolutionized the department by assigning full-time pharmacists to the three special care units. In addition, he used a great deal of his free time for special research which he conducted in a small laboratory on the eighth floor.

Like Dressner, Stecker was unaware of Kramer's arrival, assuming the sirens he heard accompanied a routine city catastrophe. Two plainclothes detectives, near the end of their harried in-hospital security search, found him quietly rummaging through a back portion of a dimly lit storage room. As usual, he was working without his white coat, and his wallet happened to be upstairs in his laboratory. Despite some loud objections, he was taken for questioning. When he was finally cleared he quickly borrowed a white coat, a size too small, from an intern who was going off duty, and hurried back to his laboratory to retrieve his wallet. He couldn't imagine what was happening but en route he heard his name coming over the page system and immediately called Nissen's office.

While Nissen's secretary was answering the return call, Nissen stepped out of his office to find Donald Harrison, Kramer's press secretary, who earlier had been in a separate car on State Street and arrived at the hospital a few minutes after the limousine. The old surgeon wanted personally to call Kramer's family and assure them that the situation was not nearly as serious as the news media might have made it seem. After searching the first floor he returned upstairs and found the newsman sitting outside the Executive Suite. Thomison was with him, giving him explicit instructions, insisting on a low profile that would play down the injury, emphasize the Secretary's well being and ignore the threatening note.

33

There were only a few close relatives. Both of his parents were deceased and the Secretary had been a widower for almost thirteen years. His wife died when she was only thirty-eight from kidney failure complicating a rare disease called systemic lupus erythematosis. She'd had two miscarriages and one stillborn delivery prior to the time that her disease was diagnosed, and then spent seven miserable years in and out of hospitals. Just prior to the time that she became ill, however, they had adopted a three-year-old boy who had been orphaned by a car accident.

It took almost a full year for the boy, whose name was Robert, to adjust to his new environment, at first rejecting the Kramers and everything they tried to give him. Then about the time that the child was beginning to play with other children in the neighborhood and accept his new life, Mrs. Kramer's disease became more apparent. Her symptoms initially were a few vague joint pains, a faint rash on her face and an occasional headache, but the disease progressed to affect her blood vessels and cripple her hands.

By the time Robert was five and starting pre-school, Mrs. Kramer had been hospitalized a dozen times, and twice for extended periods. His age kept him from visiting and he could never understand why his new mother had to be away so often. After a while, they were forced to hire a full-time housekeeper, an elderly practical nurse by the name of Henrietta Nelson, herself the mother of seven children and bragging about her ten grandchildren. Despite her late years and bad back, which didn't seem to bother her when she really didn't want it to, she was able to care for the ailing mother and the child as well. Mrs. Nelson was a prime source of love and support for the boy, who was eleven when his mother finally died, too confused to recognize him and as thin as a cancer victim. Afterward he blamed his father for his misery, talking only to Mrs. Nelson. The Secretary, who was District Attorney then, tried everything he could but it was the housekeeper who finally managed to get them back together.

Now Robert was a law student at Harvard, following in his

adoptive father's footsteps, and interested in politics. Physically he was much taller, six feet four, lanky with straight brown hair and wire-rimmed glasses. He was extremely quiet, rarely dating, a kind of grind. He kept in constant touch with his father and had just seen him before he flew to Chicago. He was in a torts class when news of the State Street assault came. Nissen's call caught him in his apartment with a small overnight case packed and about to cab to the airport. The surgeon tried to offset his fears, but the boy, having experienced tragedy too many times before, was skeptical. He told Nissen he would be at O'Hare International in approximately three hours.

Nissen's second call went to Mrs. Cathleen Blankenship, the Secretary's sister. She was living in Santa Monica, married to a construction engineer, and had already heard about the attack on the news. Nissen was unaware that she had already spoken to the Secretary and was also packing. Again Nissen tried explaining that the wound was a minor injury, but she was too nervous to take it in and insisted on flying to Chicago.

Nissen's last call went to Mrs. Nelson, who was now in her eighties, confined to a wheelchair and living in a nursing home that Kramer paid for. It took several minutes for an attendant to bring her to the phone, but when Nissen tried explaining what had happened, he quickly realized the old nurse was too senile to understand. He cordially wished her well and hung up.

Meanwhile Secretary Kramer was alone in his room staring at the bandage on his wrist. He was trying not to think of the death threat and the possibility of being poisoned. He felt helpless, an uncharacteristic and hardly congenial feeling for him, as he also speculated on the possibility that the note meant something else. His mind drifted to his wife and how she must have felt when she knew that she was dying. He had tried to make her last days tolerable, but her pains were always present as a reminder. It seemed as though they were just married and their twelve years together were more like twelve days. He could see her joy when

35

she was first pregnant and the grief when the third died before
taking a breath of air. He loved her as much today as he had then.
He wished she was still there.

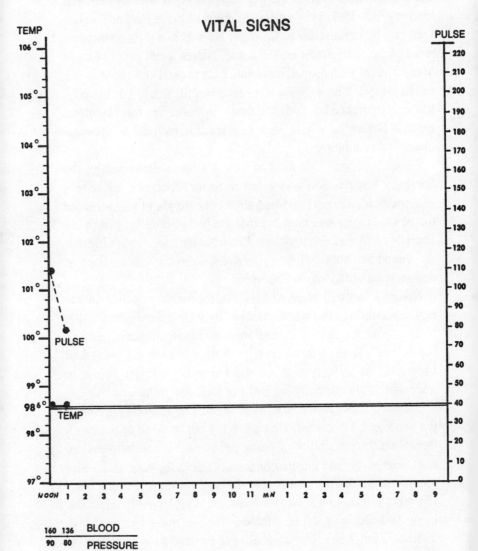

VITAL SIGNS

TEMP

PULSE

PULSE

TEMP

NOON 1 2 3 4 5 6 7 8 9 10 11 MN 1 2 3 4 5 6 7 8 9

160 136 BLOOD
90 80 PRESSURE

PATIENT'S NAME: A. KRAMER
I. D. No.: A3-15647

Chapter III

Dr. Blackwell, the chief of medicine, was the first to arrive and began helping Nissen drag two extra chairs into his small office. After moving four cartons of free samples, they squeezed the chairs along the window beside his desk, which was still cluttered with the day's mail, mostly advertisements, and several unfiled journal articles. The most prominent item on the dark walnut desk was a large photograph of his two boys when they were much younger. There were nine proudly displayed laminated plaques along one wall, and across from them were three black filing cabinets and metal bookshelves overflowing with bound textbooks and teaching manuals that went back to 1953.

"I thought that this was just a small wound. Something for your department," Blackwell said as he slid the second chair in place and sat down.

"That may be all that it is, but on the other hand we just might be dealing with some type of poison—"

Stecker, the pharmacologist, was next to arrive. Dressner of Pathology came in a second later, and Nissen began relating the sequence of events as he knew them. Dr. Blackwell sat back and filled a briar with a wine-cured tobacco, Dressner nervously fidgeted with his glasses and Stecker reversed his chair and laid his head on his folded arms, listening intently. No one interrupted until Nissen had passed the CBC slip around the room. After taking a fast glimpse, Stecker was first to speak. "Twenty-four hours.

That could mean almost anything, not just poisoning. Maybe he's going to try again, throw a bomb or set a fire, who knows?"

"The police are taking precautions for that," Nissen responded.

"I think Henry may be right," Blackwell stopped for a moment to relight his pipe, and then continued. "At least we have to assume that he's right until someone else proves otherwise. Do we know what he wants?"

"All we know is what's on that sheet." Nissen pointed to the blue slip lying on his desk. "It might be money, but that doesn't seem likely, not using the Secretary as a target. I expect we'll find out at 4:00."

"I repeat, how do you know that he's not going to try again?" Stecker persisted.

"I don't, but I think he would have used a gun in the first place," Nissen said.

"Not if he wanted to be reasonably sure of getting away. If Kramer hadn't been near our hospital, his method might well have worked, cutting the radial artery. You said yourself that Kramer lost over a pint of blood—"

"But what about the note?" Dressner interrupted. "The weapon wasn't an ordinary sharp blade . . . not with that tearing wound it made . . . I think the attacker didn't intend that wound to be fatal . . . he was up to something else . . . some kind of blackmail, it would seem, from the note, but *what* . . . ? What does he want? . . ."

"All right, then, I assume we're all in agreement." Nissen looked around the room, noting that Stecker didn't object this time. "I think we should get to work immediately, before the damage, *whatever* it is, becomes irreversible. I've already ordered a hypnotic screen and heavy metals."

"I doubt those'll be helpful." Stecker spoke out again. "If your assumption's correct, that this guy's not a conventional assassin, then I suspect he's also too sophisticated to use barbiturates, opiates, tranquilizers, or anything else like metals that can be easily detected."

"Suppose it's something we don't even have a test for. Or even a cure?" Blackwell's words momentarily numbed them into silence.

"He's offering a trade. How much is Kramer's life worth? . . . Well, surely if he has the cure, so do we," Nissen briskly added and turned to Dressner. "Where do we start?"

"That's not easy, but there are a few clues. Those twenty-four hours, if they're not some kind of smoke screen, help eliminate some of the poisons that might take weeks to do their damage. Similarly, others that work immediately like strychnine and curare. We wouldn't have anything to talk about if he'd used either one of them. Botulism is a possibility that comes right to mind—it's right around that second day that its victims start gasping for air."

"Can you test for it?" Nissen asked.

"There's an experimental blood test but I doubt anyone at this medical center has any experience with it. Fortunately we do have the antiserum."

"What about snake venom or one of the marine toxins? They're just as likely," Stecker added, getting caught up in things finally.

"Possible."

"Or some of the heart medications. He could have easily gotten digoxin or quinidine," Stecker went on, beginning to visualize a whole inventory of possibles from his pharmacopeia.

"Also possible, but—"

"What about viruses?" Blackwell broke in. "I don't want to be the gloom-and-doom man again, but it could just as easy be rabies or encephalitis . . . Remember the Monkenberg virus that killed two doctors and every technician that came near them until they could destroy it."

"Or bacteria? Like tularemia or the plague, something our government's *still* got stockpiles of for germ warfare, as the papers tell us." Stecker, a long-time pacifist, shook his head vigorously in disgust as he said it, and then proposed the "Andromeda Strain" as well—his irony falling rather flat on the others.

"Okay, okay, before we go through the entire alphabet of poisons I think we're going to need some direction," Nissen interrupted, upset by the growing list of possibilities. Turning to the pathologist Dressner again, he said, "Suppose you and Harold list all the possible poisons you can come up with and then make a flow sheet. I'll get the labs downstairs to put off everything except highest priority tests. Bob, can you get an emergency cart equipped and placed outside the Secretary's room, and get someone to watch that cardiac monitor from now on?"

Blackwell nodded, but added that he wanted to see the wound first. Stecker and Dressner agreed. With that the meeting broke up and the group quickly walked toward the elevators.

Downtown, it seemed half Chicago's police force was concentrated within the two-block area. In the past hour and fifty minutes no useful clues had been found. Marshall Field's had been combed from the remotest corners of the budget basement to the credit offices on the top floor and back down again. A check of the bathrooms yielded up a shoplifter hiding stockings in her blouse and an old man masturbating. Every sales clerk, janitor and customer was questioned; none had seen the actual assault or anyone running away. At the same time another team of officers searched the Washington Street subway station; their findings were essentially the same.

State Street remained closed to traffic, creating a tremendous snarl on several ancillary streets, Buses were rerouted to Michigan Avenue and then back onto Lake Street to the north and Jackson Street to the south. Hundreds of people were milling about. Many had been requested by the police to remain, but others stayed, feeling sure they had some important information to add. Descriptions of the assailant ran the gamut.

The sky was gray, threatening rain again, and there was a chilling breeze. All four lanes were littered with wet confetti, dozens of torn banners and smeared posters. Police cars with their blue lights and shrill sirens came and went, occasionally splashing the oily contents of long puddles over the high cement sidewalks and into the crowd; most Chicagoans were accustomed to splattered trouser legs or hose.

The WGN cameras were set up on the opposite side of State Street over a block away from the site of the attack. Although police had taken statements from each member of the crew, their prime interest was getting a copy of the videotape being processed at the main studio.

When questioned, Roger Thornton's description of the assailant was vague. Trying to be honest, he couldn't be sure of the man's clothes, age or even race—too much was happening too far away all at once and most of his attention was directed to Kramer. In contrast to most of the witnesses, however, he now felt certain that the subway had been the escape route, although originally he had assumed the assailant had gone into Marshall Field's department store.

Thornton was a relatively new resident of Chicago, living in a bachelor apartment in the Marina Towers. He'd joined WGN ten months before as a news writer, but when the anchor man left for a position with a nationally affiliated station he was given the eleven o'clock news spot. At the time he was the station's youngest reporter, only twenty-nine, but his delivery was smooth and yet happily free of that apparent indifference to human suffering so many reporters felt obligated to affect. Years of swimming and tennis had kept him trim and muscular; he was six-one with sandy brown hair and azure blue eyes that rarely escaped comment. Still single, he'd been engaged twice. Originally he came from Urbana, where his father was a history professor at the University of Illinois. Through high school and college his grades were a fraction shy of an A average. He studied acting and after graduation left for New York City with a hundred dollars in his pocket and the presumption that he would succeed with ease. Instead he found himself parking cars and waiting on tables during the first year. He tried writing, worked behind the scenes as a prop man and took acting lessons, but at the end of four disappointing years managed to land only a small part in two Broadway shows, one of which folded, and a minor role in a TV detective series. The combination of an old friend with a job offer and his own disillusionment placed him on an FM radio station in Baltimore. From there he went on to an ABC affiliate station doing five-minute daytime news spots, during which he found that he enjoyed reporting the news and didn't mind the long hours involved. Propitious timing gave him a story of national prominence, exposing gross mismanagement of federal poverty funds. Two weeks later WGN asked him to join their news staff.

Until now he had stayed with the WGN van, but after the police left he took the opportunity to fill out his story and joined several other reporters who were already questioning witnesses. He took along a pocket tape recorder and began wandering through the crowd.

The first man he came across was an executive type, near sixty, and annoyed with the police officer questioning him. Thornton turned the recorder on.

"Here's my card. I'm with the Board of Trade. If you have any more questions come by my office." He pulled an engraved business card from his vest pocket, but the officer didn't seem interested.

"I'm sorry, sir, but you'll have to stay. That black man you saw running into the subway. Can you describe him?"

"You don't seem to understand. I was merely passing by here. I have a lot of important business to attend to. I did *not* come to see Secretary Kramer nor did I see that young man do him any harm."

"He was young? Would you say between twenty and thirty?"

"I only saw his *back* for an instant."

"Can you describe what he was wearing?"

The man threw up his arms in disgust. "A gray jacket and dark pants."

Thornton next found two housewives, both carrying Carson-Pirie-Scott shopping bags. One described a suspicious looking long-haired "freak," who disappeared right after the assault, while the other claimed that the boy was never near the front and couldn't have done it. Her assailant was a "sort of" old man in a dark trench coat, who used a small handgun with a *silencer*. Thornton smiled a little. Afterward he found an elderly lady with a strong European accent who felt certain that an Arab was responsible. A dude standing behind her, wearing purple pants with a vest to match, a white shirt with black polka dots and high black boots, interrupted to argue that a honky with a crew cut was the assailant.

Toward the end of his tape Thornton came across a young art student by the name of Trudy Myers who tended to corroborate the first man's story. She was between classes when she stopped to watch from under an awning outside Field's. Although she was not enthusiastic enough to get wet, much to her dismay the Secretary was standing exactly in front of her when he was attacked. She described seeing him shaking hands, some screaming as he fell backward and then several people pushing through the crowds, among whom was a black male wearing a blue Windbreaker. A moment later she was knocked to the ground and almost trampled. She said that the black man was approximately thirty years old with pock marks on his face and short hair. As she recalled he came from her left and might not have been near enough to the Secretary at the time.

Thornton's tape ran out with fifteen descriptions recorded, including several hippies, two more or less old men, and a very strong identification of a black assailant. Unknown to him at the time, three other people had also described a black man in a Windbreaker. Altogether twenty-one witnesses were finally taken to the Twelfth Street precinct to study mug shots.

At 2:30 Raymond Pritchard, an FBI investigator, boarded a 747 jet at John Foster Dulles Airport outside Washington, D.C. With him were two military physicians, Colonel Lawrence Fitzgerald, a cardiologist from Walter Reed Hospital, and Major Lewis Ryan, a well-known toxicologist working for the National Institute of Health at Bethesda, Maryland. Pritchard's assignment was to take charge of the investigation. He had been given dossiers on ten potential assassins known to be living in the Chicago area and five rolls of movie film covering the last twelve trips that the Secretary had made around the country.

At approximately the same time, the President boarded a special Air Force jet near Bonn, Germany. It was evening there, and he had to be called away from a champagne dinner in his honor.

After the WGN film was processed a copy was rushed back to Presbyterian, where a makeshift command post was being set up. Under normal conditions the hospital maintained a small security force, five officers at the most per shift, communicating with pocket walkie-talkies and working out of an office in the basement. Now their ranks were swollen with dozens of Chicago policemen, Secret Service men and detectives from homicide. The man usually in charge was Neil Schaeffer, a timid administrator whose problems to date had rarely exceeded petty theft, lost and found, graffiti and, occasionally, a violent patient who needed restraints. Now he was glad to share his office with Lieutenant Woodsley and Captain Walter Rondowski, the latter a short-tempered, rather pompous man who had been with the Chicago police force for over thirty years. They stationed men on every floor and on the roof, and doubled the force outside Kramer's Executive Suite. When the tape arrived they borrowed a projector and special television set from the University. The young man who accompanied the equipment was also a projectionist, and as he loaded the cartridge the three officers huddled around a twenty-one inch screen.

The beginning shots were warm-ups, first scanning Chicago's ragged skyline, then quickly along the parade route focusing on a distant billboard for the CTA, the Chicago Transport Authority, and barely touching any of the crowd, next climbing up the John Hancock Center until the top floors disappeared into dark clouds, switching back to the equally huge Sears building, down to the elevated subway and a passing train at the south end of the Loop, and finally settling on two smiling faces across the street. After a few dark frames Roger Thornton's voice could be heard as his cameras were aimed straight north at the approaching motorcade. The mayor came in sight, and then Kramer was stepping from his limousine. As he walked to the east side, part of the crowd came into view, but the scene looked more like a barrage of hands attached to mangled, faceless bodies buried under a cloak of umbrellas. Thirty seconds later the Secretary was grabbing his hand and falling backward. As the camera followed him, a heavily coated man with his back to the camera jumped from the crowd and disappeared off the screen. The rest of the film showed Kramer being helped to the car and the car racing off.

Captain Rondowski had the technician rewind the film several times, but nobody could see the assailant's face—if he was the assailant—or his weapon.

"I can't see a goddamn thing, not a damn thing," the stocky captain hollered at the projectionist, as if it were his fault. "That damn film isn't worth a thing . . . that black dude in his purple jumpsuit got right in the way! What we need is stills. Can you at least do that?" he continued, projecting his frustrations.

"Yes, I—"

"How long?"

"A couple of hours, sir."

"I want everything you can get from just before and just after the Secretary is attacked, and anything else that shows the crowd on that side."

"I'll try."

"Don't try, boy, just do it, and don't waste any time at it."

Chapter IV

At 3:00 Dr. Nissen was introducing his three colleagues to Kramer as a special duty nurse was checking his vital signs. His temperature had risen another two-tenths of a degree, but his pulse and blood pressure remained the same. In addition to the low-grade fever, however, he was complaining of worsening pain and a feeling of numbness along the tips of his fingers. His only relief was the return of his anguished campaign manager Thomison to the Palmer House.

Nissen used scissors to cut away the large gauze bandage as Blackwell and Dressner watched from close by. Stecker, being a pharmacologist, seemed not quite so interested and took a place behind Dressner. Blood always seemed to bother Stecker.

The edges of the wound were jagged with a tiny flap of loose skin at one end. The area immediately surrounding the wound was markedly inflamed, and swelling had spread across his wrist and down the creases of his palm. Using the back of his own hand, Nissen compared the temperatures of each forearm, noting that the right side was much warmer than the left. When he went to inspect the other side of his wrist, Kramer reflexively pulled his hand back.

"That wound looks like it might be infected," Nissen said, and Blackwell agreed. "It's probably best if we take some of those stitches out and give it room to drain."

Nissen stepped to the door, opened it halfway, and asked the

46

nurse who was watching the oscilloscope to bring him a surgical tray, size seven, sterile gloves, and a culture tube with two glass slides for staining purposes.

"I think the major question's going to be what antibiotics to use," Nissen said.

"First see if there's any fluid for your gram stain. Hopefully, that will give us some idea," Blackwell said as he leaned closer to look at the injury.

When the nurse returned she laid out the sterile tray on the bedstand while Nissen washed his hands in the bathroom. After putting on his gloves he used fine-pointed scissors to snip the sutures at the skin line just below each knot. The Secretary didn't react until Nissen started pulling each individual stitch out with forceps. Because there was little tissue resistance, the procedure took barely a few seconds. Then, using his thumb and index finger, the spread the wound apart. This time Kramer let out a yelp. Nissen quickly collected three drops of a clear, yellowish fluid and let go. Part of the minute specimen was put directly into the culture tube while the remainder was spread across the glass slides and allowed to air-dry. After Nissen carefully rebandaged the open wound the four men left for the bacteriology laboratory. On the way they stopped by Toxicology and discovered what Stecker had already predicted. The hypnotic screen was negative, and some of the preliminary readings on the heavy metals were failing to show anything.

By this time the entire city and most of the nation were aware the Secretary of Defense had been attacked. Telephone calls began overloading the hospital circuits, limiting many of the more legitimate callers. Although most of the people were merely curious, intermittently there was a crank call threatening to repeat the attack. As a consequence, Rondowski had each worrisome call tape-recorded and stationed a policewoman at the switchboard,

47

posing as the supervisor. Her job was to keep the caller on the line, if possible, until the message could be traced. She also asked for a description of the note. Although no one was able to repeat it, one loquacious suspect managed to get himself arrested.

By 3:30, one half hour before the deadline in the threatening note, another television station had set up its cameras. Both *Newsweek* and *Time* were on hand and were soon joined by menbers of the foreign press.

Two security officers had to be assigned to keep newsmen out of the emergency room and business offices. Dr. Wheelin found himself imprisoned, unable to go to the washroom without getting his picture taken. Many of the hospital's routine activities were paralyzed by the overwhelming number of reporters with their determined curiosity.

Bacteriology, or Bac-T as it was usually called, was located on the second floor, next to Hematology. It was a new temperature-controlled laboratory, lined on one side with glass-front incubators, some of which were specifically labeled for blood, urine and stool. Technicians worked on the opposite side of the room at separate work benches. Each person had his own microscope, Bunsen burner, and stack of sterile Petri dishes. The standard procedure was to place a drop of the sample, such as urine from a patient with a kidney infection, on a thin wire loop and streak it across the surface of agar, a gelatinous material filling the bottom of each Petri dish. After forty-eight hours in the approximate incubator set at thirty-seven degrees centigrade, the bacterial colonies would be stained and identified. It took another twenty-four hours to determine antibiotic sensitivities —this was sometimes too late for the patient.

When the small group of doctors arrived, the shift was changing and there was a long line standing next to the time clock. Nissen handed Kramer's culture to one of the new girls, who fired her loop in a blue flame, waited for it to cool and then gingerly streaked the yellow fluid across three different types of agar. Meanwhile Nissen took his slides to a sink at the far end of the laboratory and balanced them on a wire stand. One side of each had dried to a fine opaque film, which he proceeded to flood with a purple stain. After waiting thirty seconds he washed both slides with tap water, dried them and counterstained them with iodine. While the other three doctors silently watched, he cleared the excess stain with acetone and restained with safranin, leaving an orange hue. Finally he set the slides out to air-dry again.

"Well, I hope something's there," Nissen said as he took some tissue paper from a drawer and began wiping the lens of a nearby microscope.

"I suspect it's far too early to see any bacteria," Dressner said.

"Maybe, but this is all we have right now."

"It could be a reaction to the presence of a foreign body or any number of poisons." Dressner moved his chair closer.

"It might also," Blackwell added, "be a secondary infection from a dirty knife and have nothing to do with poisoning."

Stecker remained unusually quiet.

As soon as the stains were dry, Nissen picked up the closer slide and, holding it carefully at one corner, placed it on the viewing stand. He set the microscope for low power and, after adjusting the eye pieces, began slowly scanning from one end to the other. The stand made a gritty sound as it moved horizontally across his viewing field. Intermittently he would stop and wipe the lens, or refocus, but he was unable to find any evidence of bacteria. When he switched to high power, however, he discovered a small clump of darkly stained material which, after adding the oil immersion lens, disappointingly turned out to be a couple of white cells and amorphous debris from the wound.

"Nothing but junk," Nissen said as he moved to the side to let Blackwell take a look.

Blackwell, a practicing internist for years before achieving his exalted position, took his time studying the same areas, but after a few minutes his conclusions were the same. Dressner was third, and his approach was different. As a pathologist the microscope was his tool of trade, and being a perfectionist he changed the light refraction and repositioned the slide. Once things were exactly right, he nervously jumped from area to area. Without saying a word he changed slides and went through the same motions on the second specimen. About halfway across the slide he suddenly stopped and began fiddling with the fine adjustment. A second later he blurted out, "Crystals. There are crystals on both slides!"

"Where? What kind of crystals?" Nissen, surprised, returned to take another look.

"There are only a few and you'll have to dim the light. Otherwise the glare burns right through," Dressner said as he moved aside. "I don't know what they are, but I know that they shouldn't be there."

Each man took his turn again, including Stecker, who was less accustomed to using microscopes. They all agreed that some type of crystalline material was present, but no one could identify it. Dressner added that its presence did not rule out an infection, but did make it seem like a chemical or drug reaction. As Nissen telephoned Schaeffer's office to tell them of the new finding, the other three men returned to the Executive Suite to collect as much fluid as possible from the festering wound.

State Street had been reopened to traffic, and the milling spectators had been replaced by an early Friday afternoon rush hour. Like swarming bees, the people hurried from every doorway, pushing into waiting buses and down the subway stairwells. Everyone appeared to be killing themselves to get home to relax. A second's delay seemed intolerable.

Only a few squad cars remained parked outside the huge bulk of Marshall Field's department store, while most of the other police had returned to their regular duties. The spot marking the attack was still roped off as two criminal experts made last minute measurements. Altogether there had been three major investigatory agencies: the FBI, the Secret Service, and the Chicago Police Department. Duplication, particularly in the questioning and re-questioning of witnesses, plus the multiplicity of conflicting stories plagued each group.

The WGN van returned to the studio, but Thornton convinced that there was more to be learned, remained behind. Deciding to do some investigative work on his own, he entered Field's, made it through the revolving doors, and then changed his mind. Instead, he decided to follow the crowds into the subway station outside. Staring at the dark entrance, it was easy to visualize the attacker quickly disappearing down there.

As he descended the cold concrete steps he could hear the roar of distant trains. The first few stairs were covered with soggy ticker tape, while the second half had the usual complement of dirty gum wrappers and cigarette butts. At the bottom people were scurrying in every direction across a dimly lit platform, which extended the entire width of State Street above and was lined with turnstiles on both sides. In the middle of each metal army were small change booths and behind them, stairs going down to the north- and southbound trains. Thornton stopped to study the area. Directly across from where he was standing were another two sets of stairs going up to the west side of State Street, either of which the assailant could have climbed and subsequently watched the investigation in relative comfort and safety. In addition there was a small entrance to his left that led into Field's budget basement. Had he gone into the department store, he still could have taken a circuitous route and made it to the subway without being noticed. The station was like an enormous rat maze, filled with people instead of rodents, with six easily accessible escape routes—with nothing to indicate to Thornton which might be the more promising to follow.

Long lines had already formed in front of the booths, making it impossible for him to question either of the change makers. It

51

didn't seem likely the assailant would have stopped for change, but the girls might have seen someone running past them . . . nonetheless, for now he'd forgo the questioning.

He proceeded to a small newsstand at the opposite end of the subway station. Lost in an eye-catching display of girlie magazines, comic books, racing forms and newspapers was a very small old man in baggy brown slacks held up with elastic suspenders, a wrinkled red flannel shirt and scuffed work boots. At the time he was busily setting out the latest edition of the *Chicago Tribune*. Taking up half the front page were the words "KRAMER ATTACKED BY MYSTERIOUS ASSAILANT" and below was a picture of the cabinet member falling back into the arms of one of the Secret Service men.

"Paper?" The old man looked up as Thornton approached.

"I think I will." He found the money in his pocket and set it on the narrow counter top next to an empty cigar box and a row of Lifesavers. "That must have really been something . . . Hey, were you there, by any chance . . .?"

"Not me." His sale made, the old man abruptly went back to laying out the rest of his papers.

The stand had a perfect view of the entire subway station. It was unlikely that anyone could pass through without being seen. As Thornton spent a few minutes reading the lead article, most of which was pure speculation, he realized that he was being watched.

"You want anything else?" The old man tucked a corner of his shirt back into his pants and squeezed behind his counter.

"No . . . I was just reading about Kramer. It was right up there, wasn't it?" Thornton pointed toward the stairs that he had just come down.

"You a cop?"

A man stopped and bought a paper.

"No, a reporter."

"I already told 'em that I didn't see nothing."

"No one running through here? Like a black guy in a blue jacket?" Thornton folded the newspaper under his arm.

The old man started laughing, showing a mouthful of silver and gold fillings. "Sure, I saw someone running through here. I see people running through here every day like their lives depended on it. Everybody's in a hurry. Not me. People don't know how to relax—"

"At noon they're not rushing through here."

"Any time of the day!"

"What about a black guy wearing a blue Windbreaker?"

"It doesn't matter, black or blue. Everybody's in a hurry!"

It was becoming apparent that the old man was either too senile or too hipped on his one-note philosophy to help. Thornton thanked him and joined a long line of commuters waiting for change to get in to board the southbound trains.

The line moved slowly and by the time he reached the front, some ten people were waiting behind him. A young girl mechanically gave him change without looking up and released the turnstile to let him through. From there he walked past an ugly row of battered telephone booths and rode down a crowded escalator. Near the bottom the irksome sound of its metal teeth scraping against broken glass gave him chills.

Despite the welcome warmth two levels below ground the air was unpleasantly stale. He found himself on another platform that stretched over a hundred yards to another set of stairs that led to the Madison Street subway station and another likely escape route. Along the length of one side, commuters were packed two and three thick, jockeying for some strategic position as if they alone knew exactly where the magical doors would open. Thornton walked along the back of the crowd, then, to his dismay, found another down-going stairwell. This one had signs for change-over to the Dearborn Street subway. He was tempted to quit. The number of possibilities had become overwhelming, and he could now understand better why the police were having so much trouble

53

tracking the assailant. As he descended the third set of stairs he barely escaped the deafening sound of another train. This time he found himself at the beginning of a long brightly lit tunnel. From his vantage point the exit, a block away, appeared to be the size of a half dollar. Within the narrow passageway people were rushing in both directions, intermittently crashing into one another and knocking an occasional parcel or shopping bag to the ground. It was against the rules to stop or to offer an apology.

In the distance, a man appeared to be lying on the ground, ignored by everyone who passed. As Thornton got closer he made him out as an old beggar sitting on a torn army blanket and playing an accordion. He was wearing a blind man's glasses, an old navy pea jacket and dark trousers, one leg of which was folded under his stump. Lying asleep next to him was a dog whose top half resembled a German shepherd, but whose legs surely must have descended from a dachshund. On the other side was a can of sharpened pencils and a fisherman's cap with a few small coins. Although his song was slightly off key, it was discernibly "America the Beautiful."

Thornton stopped a few feet away and quietly listened. He had the distinct feeling that the old man could see and the dark glasses were a part of the scene. The moment he moved closer the music came to an abrupt halt and the beggar's coins quickly found their way into a side pocket. He resumed with "Easter Parade." His head never moved.

Not wanting to frighten him Thornton continued his slow approach and when he reached the edge of his blanket, bent down and began petting the dog. With "you'll find yourself in the Sunday review," the mutt rolled onto his back and in a spread-eagle position begged for more ardent attention. Thornton obliged with a good scratching until the song ended, then finally tried conversation.

"Been here long?"

Silence for a moment. "You a cop?"

"No, just a reporter."

"Oh."

"You been here all day?"

"Yeah." There was an annoyed tone to the beggar's short answers.

"Did you hear about the attack on Secretary Kramer?"

"Yeah." The old man remained motionless, as if he were concentrating on a point on the opposite wall.

"Did you happen to see anyone running through here, about noon?"

"I can't see."

Thornton proceeded to take a five dollar bill from his wallet and laid it on the blanket. The money disappeared.

"Did you see anyone?"

"Two people."

"Two people?" That didn't make sense and he had the feeling that he was being taken. "What did they look like?"

"Couldn't see them too well."

With some reluctance Thornton pulled another five from his billfold, but this time held onto it. As he moved the green into plain view, the dog got up and began humping on his pants leg. Each time he tried to push the mutt away, the animal returned more excited. Holding him at arm's length, he repeated the question. "What'd they look like?"

"Honest, it's hard for me to see, but there was two men for sure. One was black. The other was shorter, older. He was white."

"What were they wearing?"

"The big guy had a dark jacket . . ."

"Like a Windbreaker?" Thornton was getting more interested, though he did note the second five had disappeared.

"Yeah. And the other guy had a long coat."

"Anything more?"

"Just that they caught the train going south, probably the one that goes out the Eisenhower."

55

"How do you know that?"

"I feel the vibrations from the train in my foot first when they go south and last when they go north."

Unaware that a threatening note had been received, Thornton didn't realize the significance of the train's direction, which would have a stop at Presbyterian-St. Luke's Hospital. He gladly left the beggar and his dog and headed in the same direction that the two men just described to him had gone. He climbed two flights of stairs to a platform that was indistinguishable from Washington Street, noted the huge crowds and continued his exit.

Outside it was beginning to rain, but he welcomed the fresh air. From the entrance he could see Picasso's enigmatic sculpture in front of the Civic Center and immediately thought of the beggar's dog.

It was almost 4:00 and the prospect of being caught in the rush hour traffic worried him. As he hurried toward Michigan Avenue and his car the downpour worsened, and after a block he was forced to take refuge in Field's. Inside the first set of revolving doors he spotted two of the investigating officers and told them about the beggar's story. They said they found it hard to believe that there were two assailants, one black and one white, both rushing through the Dearborn tunnel, but they promised to look into it. They had a point, Thornton had to admit.

As long as Thornton had to wait out the storm, he decided to do some browsing. Field's, one of Chicago's oldest and probably finest department stores, had nine floors containing practically every brand of every conceivable consumer product marketed. His favorite browsing at most times was in bookstores, and in Chicago he especially favored Kroch's and Brentano's and the book department at Field's.

Wandering past one of the cosmetic counters on the way to the book department, he took immediate note of an attractive blonde salesgirl wearing a brown miniskirt and a pink sweater. She was waiting on an elderly woman at the opposite counter and as she bent over to get a bottle of perfume he watched her short skirt slide up the back of her thighs and rest against the edge of her panties. The view deserved respectful attention. He stopped, not so suavely pretending an interest in a few nearby perfume samples, even spraying one on his wrist. His eyes remained on the girl's long tan legs, unaware of a counter-top mirror revealing his reflection.

The next time she stooped she turned to the side and looked his way. An embarrassed smile crossed his face as he clumsily tried to spray his wrist again. Her eyes were a soft green, and there was a subtle spattering of freckles across her cheeks. Thornton now took to fumbling with some packages of bubble bath as the girl completed her sale and approached him. She seemed to get even more attractive with each step closer, and beneath her cashmere sweater she appeared delightfully well endowed.

"Can I help you?" Her businesslike tone disrupted his fantasies.

"I'm just browsing . . . have to buy a few presents —"

"Wife, girlfriend or mother?" It sounded more like "Coffee, tea or milk?"

"I'm not married, but—"

"I don't mean to be corny," she interrupted, "but you do look familiar."

It was always a good feeling to be recognized. "That's sort of a switch," he said, and smiled, feeling like Walter Cronkite.

"You really do look familiar, but that's silly—"

"Well, I do the eleven o'clock news on WGN—"

"Of course. . . . Did you hear . . . oh of course you did . . . that's probably why you're here, right?"

"Kramer?" Thornton set the bubble bath back on the counter and began straightening his damp coat. "Have you heard anything new about his condition? I haven't been able to get away from the scene since it happened."

"Not really. I was out there in the crowd for a while but my

57

lunch hour ran out before he came by. It was awful, anyway. People pushing to get up front. Some old guy hit me right here with his cast.'' She pointed to a spot just below her left breast. ''It felt like a lead pipe and almost knocked the wind out of me. You should have seen the look he gave me when I hit him back.''

Thornton couldn't help smiling, then asked, ''You didn't happen to see anyone running past here, did you?''

''Only police. They've been swarming over this place all afternoon. Anyway, what about your present? Or is there really a present?''

''Of course . . . for my secretary. It's her birthday tomorrow.''

''How about Estée Lauder?''

''I suppose . . . look, why don't I go straight? I'm here because I saw you and liked what I saw. Are you by any chance free tonight?''

''Well, that's at least refreshingly honest if a little abrupt.''

''I suppose I get impulsive sometimes. How about it?''

''You don't even know my first name: Pat.''

''All right, Pat. Now, how about dinner tonight? Besides, I really would like to talk about this thing with somebody besides the police and the station people. What time do you get off?''

She looked at him closely, then, ''Six-thirty, but I can't be ready, not straight from work.''

Thornton smiled and started to leave. ''You look just fine. I'll have my car parked right outside the State Street entrance.''

She allowed a smile and nodded. Thornton walked happily through the revolving doors and out into the pouring rain. It wan't going to be such a bad day after all.

Chapter V

By 4:00 the entire fifth floor except the Executive Suite was vacated, forcing some of the more well-to-do patients into charity wards. The Secretary appeared a little worse. His face was peaked and the prescribed analgesics were not controlling his pain. His entire right hand was swollen and the inflammation had spread halfway up his arm. The vital sign sheet hanging at the foot of his bed indicated that his temperature had risen to 99.6 degrees while his pulse and blood pressure remained normal. Although his working pace had slackened somewhat, he continued reviewing an upcoming arms budget.

A few minutes earlier, Dr. Blackwell had managed to squeeze a few extra drops of serum from the seemingly infected wound. Immediately afterward Dressner and Stecker gingerly divided the material and hurried off to their respective laboratories. Before Blackwell left he ordered three additional blood tests for further toxicology screening, blood cultures and a repeat CBC. He also assigned two special duty nurses to Kramer, one to sit by his bedside and the other for running errands and to keep an eye on the cardiac monitor. In addition Dr. Wheelin was taken from the emergency room and reassigned to the fifth floor.

Lieutenant Woodsley and Captain Rondowski were downstairs in the telephone office anxiously waiting for the 4:00 call, but the switchboards were relatively quiet. The tape recorder was ready and a representative from Illinois Bell was waiting on another line to start the trace. By 4:15 they began to worry that something had gone wrong, possibly the first message was misinterpreted.

At the Twelfth Street Precinct, witnesses were beginning to study the thousands of mug shots on file. The crippled beggar was not among the group. By the time the two investigating officers made it to the Dearborn tunnel, he was in a liquor store on South State Street, spending part of his new-found fortune on a bottle of muscatel.

Trudy Meyers continued to be one of the most promising witnesses. She was a pretty girl with long black hair that fell below her shoulders, large gold hoop earrings in her pierced ears, and dark brown eyes. Underneath her heavy coat she wore a loose-fitting halter top with a revealing side view. She had quickly become an attraction in her own right in the police station.

Another witness was Herbert C. Britte, which according to him was "spelled with two T's" because he was "twice as bright." He was the owner of Petfair, a grooming shop in Oak Park, and had cancelled two poodle shampoos and an Airedale trim just to see Kramer. He had been a long-time admirer of Kramer—a "*forceful* man," he'd often told friends—campaigning door to door in his own neighborhood and attending every rally possible. When he arrived at the station his chubby small face was red with anger, quite unlike him, and he seemed to race through the mug shots with a personal vengeance. He had also described seeing the same black assailant wearing a dark Windbreaker.

The executive from the Board of Trade was also among the group, but his enthusiasm was considerably less than the others'. He maintained that he had not seen the man's face and after a short while he was released.

"Glass. Goddamn glass!" Stecker threw his notebook down on the workbench just as Nissen walked into his laboratory. "I can't dissolve them in anything!"

"What's glass?" Nissen appeared confused.

"Those crystals Dressner found." Stecker walked to the end of the room and returned with two small flasks. "This one's hydrochloric acid and the other's sodium hydroxide."

"Are you sure?"

"Of course I'm sure. They're glass all right." Stecker angrily set the two flasks next to his notebook, almost spilling the acid on the bench.

"That doesn't make sense. Why would Kramer have glass in his wound? It didn't come from us." Nissen held the flask of alkali up to the light.

"You can't see them that way, but under the microscope they're still there, I assure you."

Stecker mounted a drop of fluid on a fresh slide, pushed it under the microscope and after a moment of focusing, moved aside. "Just look at this field. It's been like that ever since I got the crystals. I tried distilled water first, then saline. Nothing works. If you examine them closely, you'll see that every one's irregular. The *only* thing I know that will do that is glass."

Nissen did not appear as disturbed as his younger colleague. "That may be important in itself."

"What do you mean?"

"If we didn't put it there cleaning the wound, which is remotely possible, I guess, but not likely, then it must have come from the assailant's weapon."

"A glass weapon?"

"Why not? . . . Say, a glass syringe. It would work a lot faster than those plastic throw-aways that we use around here, but under abrupt pressure it might have chipped."

Stecker hesitated a moment, intrigued with Nissen's suggestion, then countered with, "It could be from some poison that was *kept* in a glass vial?"

"Also possible, but either way we still have an unknown poison and no real clues to its identity."

Stecker moved the two flasks to a more secure part of his desk and then the two men proceeded to Dressner's laboratory, where they discovered that the pathologist was also having considerable trouble. . . .

By 4:30, Captain Rondowski was convinced that a mistake had been made. Worried that something was overlooked, he left the telephone office to find Dr. Nissen. Meanwhile, Woodsley stayed behind and as the door closed behind the captain, a call lit up the corner of the switchboard. The operator gave Woodsley a signal. He, in turn, hesitating only for a second to set his cigarette in a nearby ashtray, flipped on the tape recorder and then contacted the telephone company. There was a raspy male voice on the other end asking for Secretary Kramer.

"Who's calling, please?" The operator tried to remain calm. They needed at least thirty seconds to get an area trace and close to a minute to be exact.

"My call is expected."

"I'm sorry, sir, but I'm not permitted to let any call through."

The clock overhead showed ten seconds. Woodsley relit another cigarette, unaware that the first one was still burning in the ceramic dish.

"This call is extremely important and I can only tell you that I'm expected."

"I'm sorry, but I will have to transfer you to my supervisor."

The policewoman delayed another five seconds before answering. Woodsley stood nervously behind her, watching the second hand move slowly along the smaller numbers.

"This is the supervisor. Can I help you?"

"I have to speak to Secretary Kramer. There isn't much time and this is extremely important."

"Can you give me some type of identification?"

"That's impossible. I demand that you place this call!"

"Please hold on, sir. I'll check with the Secretary's staff upstairs."

She placed him on hold and took a deep sigh. As the clock

62

passed the thirty second mark, she was afraid to leave him any longer and got back on the line. "I'm sorry, but I can't reach his secretary. Could you give me your name or repeat your earlier message?"

"No! Tell him to read today's classifieds!"

"I'm sorry, what—"

Click.

Woodsley quickly got on the phone to Illinois Bell. The call had lasted forty-one seconds. They were able to pinpoint it to Chicago's near North Side, somewhere between Broadway and the Lake, south of Belmont Avenue and north of the Loop, but it was too large an area to send a man out to cover.

Woodsley had the operator put out an emergency page for Rondowski and Nissen to meet him in Schaeffer's office and then headed for the hospital gift shop, which was located on the other side of the noisy lobby. Several reporters tried to stop him, but like a bulldog he pushed through the crowd, scooped up the *Sun-Times* left over from the morning delivery, announcing the Secretary's arrival in town, and two *Tribune*s with their story of the attack.

There was a short line at the cash register and after waiting a few annoyed seconds for an elderly woman to find the right change in her overflowing purse, he stepped to her side and impatiently tossed a dollar bill on the counter top. Before the clerk had realized that he had paid, Woodsley was hurrying back across the lobby again. The two reporters who had followed him into the shop were close behind, but the detective still wouldn't stop to answer questions. He went straight to the telephone office, slamming the door behind him, and with one big push cleared the desk and began skimming through the *Sun-Times*. He was slightly out of breath by then, but lit up another cigarette anyway. Nerves.

Within a short while both Nissen and Rondowski were downstairs, pushing through the other reporters. When they entered the office they found Woodsley buried in a cloud of smoke, and surrounded by newspapers.

Rondowski spoke first. "What the hell are you doing?"

"The man says that there's a message in the paper—the classifieds." Woodsley looked up for a moment and then signaled the female officer to rerun the recording.

While the two men listened, in the background Woodsley continued his frantic scanning of the classified columns. At the end he explained why they couldn't pinpoint the caller, and then added, "Well, dig in."

Each man took a different newspaper, initially discarded the front sections, and then closely scrutinizing every advertisement, not sure what to look for but suspecting that the message might be in the personal columns. Rondowski suggested that they circle anything that seemed even remotely relevant; within a few minutes the small group had thirteen ads marked off in red. Rondowski then proceeded to cut out each one, carefully following the printed lines, and after tossing the remainder of the papers onto the floor, spread the small squares across the top of the metal desk as if he were playing a game of solitaire. One, addressed to an Aunt Dotie, caught Nissen's eye, but because it didn't make any sense at all he left it unmarked. None of the other thirteen squares lying in front of him, however, seemed to make all that much more sense. Nowhere could the Secretary's name be found and only one two-liner resembled a threat:

> Time is important and your life may
> depend on it. Meet me as before.

The first part was all right, but the meeting place was an enigma. Woodsley suggested that they send a man to wait outside Marshall Field's but Rondowski argued that neither the officer nor the assailant would know who the other was. Before Woodsley could respond, however, Nissen said that they couldn't overlook the possibility and Rondowski agreed, stopping for a moment to call his office.

They focused their attention on another ad:

> PR: I need money before it's too late.
> Contact me at the station.

Woodsley was quick to emphasize the money motive, but again Rondowski's argument applied equally well to the second notice and this time he didn't stop to send a man out.

The room was quiet for a while as the three men read and reread the cryptic messages, trying to make mountains out of mole hills, sense out of nonsense . . .

Secretary Kramer's son was on board a United 747, sitting toward the back, deep in thought and ignoring most of the activities around him. He could have demanded a special Air Force flight to Chicago but the time lost was minimal and anyway he was beginning to blame the U.S. Government for his father's life and had vehemently argued against his running for Vice-President. He even blamed the heart attack on the overwhelming stresses of political life and felt that he could see the strain taking its toll on his father's usual good health. In a way it was as if he had predicted that the attack would happen, only lacking the details of how, when and where.

As per usual two Secret Service men were sitting close by. They'd followed from his apartment to the airport and, unprepared for the unannounced trip, were forced to buy tickets to Chicago themselves. The son resented their watchful eyes. He rarely gave advance notice of any change, and in previous months seemingly spent more time trying to lose them than concentrating on his own studies. The boy shunned public appearances, was seen only on very special occasions, never campaigned and rarely permitted interviews. Nonetheless the Secret Service was always there, keeping tabs, living in an apartment situated one floor below him, eating in most of the same restaurants, following him on dates and on occasion even using the next stall in a public washroom. The Service had dossiers on all of his friends and acquaintances, teachers and neighbors. On holidays, however, it often turned into a game of cat and mouse. Once he managed to lose five Secret Service men on a Greek island south of Athens and was finally found a week later disembarking from a ferry boat in southern Italy when Customs required him to present his passport. Over the past few months, he'd become a master at disguise and an amateur escape artist, taking pleasure in his successes. Now that was all over. There were too many deaths in his past, too vivid once again with this attack on Kramer. He was adopted, true, but the Secretary was his only relative, and truly his best friend.

"We're missing something!" Nissen broke the silence, running his hands across his scalp and leaning back in his chair to stretch. "None of these ads say anything about poison or ransom . . . they're mostly about going back to God or some husband trying to get out of his wife's debts . . ." His eyes lit up as he turned and began rummaging through the pile of discarded newspapers. A moment later he ripped out a fourteenth ad and laid it in front of his two colleagues, pointing his finger at the three-liner:

Aunt Dotie: Lawson, Giovanni, Millitz,
Akubar, Madison, and Weisberg are going
on a trip in the A.M.

"Aunt Dotie . . . aunt dotie . . . auntdotie . . . could be . . . *antidote.*" Nissen shouted the word. "An antidote . . . for those names . . . maybe some kind of a trade—"

Both Rondowski and Woodsley were silent as they reread the ad, not too sure of Nissen's interpretation, however plausible.

"It must be," Nissen maintained. "It certainly fits, it makes *sense* . . ."

"Then who the hell are Lawson, Giovanni, Millitz, Akubar, Madison and Weisberg?" Woodsley said. "They *don't* make sense, and what trip are they going on in the A.M.—"

"Wait a second," Rondowski interrupted. "Lawson and Madison . . . I know those names . . . they go with a couple of guys in prison right now for murder, right here in Illinois."

"Antidote for murderers?" Woodsley said.

"If the doctor's right, that's what it looks like," Rondowski said. "None of the other ads fit at all. Cons? What kind of trip would *they* be going on unless it's a jail break. But why announce a jail break in advance? . . . I'll check out these other names with the FBI."

While Rondowski placed a call to Washington, Nissen returned to the second floor to check on any new lab results. When he arrived he found the repeat CBC, this time without a threatening note. Judging by the rising white count with an increase in neutrophils and band cells, he concluded that Kramer's condition was getting worse and an infection seemed to be setting in, although the unchanged hemoglobin and hematocrit indicated that his slight anemia was stable.

Hematology Laboratory
CBC
Time Drawn: 16:00

Test	Result	Normal Values
Hemoglobin	13.0	14-18 gm/100 ml
Hematocrit	39%	42-52 ml/100 ml
Red Cell Count	4.15 million	4.6-6.2 million/cu mm
White Cell Count	11,300	5-10,000/cu mm
neutrophils	73%	54-62%
bands	3%	0-5%
lymphocytes	19%	25-33%
monocytes	3%	3-7%
eosinophils	2%	1-3%
basophils	0%	0-1%
metamyelocytes	0%	0%
promyelocytes	0%	0%
MCV	92	82-92
MCH	31	27-31
MCHC	34	32-36
Platelets	272,000	2-300,000/cu mm
Sedimentation Rate	25	less than 15 mm/hr

Red cell morphology: unchanged
Atypical lymphocytes: none

Chapter VI

At 5:00, the Secretary looked even worse. His latest temperature was recorded at 100.4 degrees and his pulse had increased to one hundred beats per minute. It was becoming apparent to everyone who was caring for him that the obscure poison or whatever was starting to show its effects. Nissen proceeded to lower his official condition from good to fair and then cancelled the dinner at the Palmer House, despite repeated objections from Thomison, who had made three nervous trips back and forth in the last few hours.

When Kramer was informed of the newest message and its possible interpretation, his quiet mood changed to outrage. He refused to be blackmailed, if they were right that he was the victim of outrageous blackmail—convicts for an antidote?—and reconfirmed his confidence in the medical staff at Presbyterian. As Wheelin listened he wanted to disagree but before he could say anything a page for "Dr. Blue" came squawking over the intercom.

"Dr. Blue, third floor! Dr. Blue, third floor! Dr. Blue, third floor!"

It was the code for a cardiac arrest to which every physician in the hospital was expected to respond. Wheelin hurried from the suite and ran down the stairwell, almost falling as he skipped several steps in an effort to get to the third floor. Time was always critical—once the patient stopped breathing, his brain had four minutes to live.

As Wheelin passed through the fire door he spotted two nurses dragging an emergency cart into a distant room. When he arrived he saw an elderly lady lying motionless in bed, her face blue, and not breathing. An attendant was just climbing onto the bed and beginning cardiac massage, rhythmically pushing the palm of his hand into the center of her chest. The sound of her fragile ribs could be heard cracking.

Wheelin hollered for the nurses to start her breathing with the plastic football-shaped bag with an attached piece that fitted over her mouth and nose as he slid his hand into her groin and felt for a femoral pulse. He could feel the rush of blood every time the attendant smashed down on her chest, but otherwise her heart did not appear to have an intrinsic rhythm of its own. As the intern called for the electrocardiograph machine, Nissen and several other physicians arrived, one of whom was her own private physician. He said that the lady had been admitted two hours earlier for observation, having had several episodes of dizziness and he had not yet had time to evaluate her fully. When the ECG was finally hooked up, her tracing was a straight line. Another physician called for intracardiac adrenaline and then stabbed a three-inch needle through her chest wall and injected the medication directly into her heart. Everyone stepped back to watch, but the straight line continued. Another stab missed the heart. The third, however, found its way into the heart cavity but again was without any effect.

Wheelin looked toward the private physician, essentially asking if they could stop. The older man stepped to the end of the bed and, using a pen light, saw that her eyes were fully dilated and unresponsive to light. He nodded his consent and the nurses began cleaning up as everyone else stepped outside.

Meanwhile downstairs in the lobby, Harrison, with Kramer's approval, was distributing copies of the first threatening note to the press but refused to speculate on its meaning. The phone call and "Aunt Dotie" classified ad were still being kept a secret. They felt that the public needed an explanation for Kramer's continued hospitalization and yet the police also needed an unimpeded head start.

Nissen slowly returned to his office. Even before the last communication the evidence suggested that Kramer's wound represented more than just a bad laceration. Now that it was almost certain that he had been poisoned, Nissen began to worry even more. Poisoning was completely out of his expertise and Presbyterian, despite its gigantic size and large academic staff, had never handled an emergency of this sort. He was afraid that it might not be adequately equipped to research every possibility. His first thought was to transfer Kramer back to Walter Reed Hospital, but that idea was quickly rejected. If anything went wrong on the trip, little could be done en route. Bringing in experts to the Secretary, however, could be managed. Nissen immediately picked up a phone at the nurse's desk and called Dr. Lawrence Mellow, the Chief of Toxicology, for advice. A moment later Mellow's secretary informed him that her boss was away on vacation in the Yucatan Peninsula and could not be reached —which Nissen already knew, having seen Mellow at a meeting the day before he left, but in the confusion had forgotten.

Nissen quickly placed another call, this time long distance, to an old friend, Dr. Eric Larson, a toxicologist at Stanford. Dr. Larson was reported to have suffered a serious heart attack during the previous night and although his condition was listed as fair, he'd been isolated in the University's intensive care unit and was unable to receive any telephone calls.

Nissen appeared stunned. Death and dying were commonplace for the medical profession, but this seemed a little too close. Determined to find help somewhere, his call went to Dr. Louis Waxman, a man he didn't know personally but whose credentials were internationally known and whose research work was highly respected. Waxman was primarily an epidemiologist, but was board-certified in both internal medicine and infectious disease. He was a graduate of Harvard Medical School in the early days of its

70

glory, with specialty training at Johns Hopkins and a master's degree in Public Health from Columbia University, where he was presently a full professor on staff.

Because it was past working hours for most people, Nissen had to go through the long distance operator for information and Waxman's home phone number. While he waited, he began to feel increasingly confident that Waxman would be the right man and if he weren't available to help he would certainly know who would be. Finally, after a few anxious minutes, a phone was ringing and an elderly lady's voice answered.

"Is Dr. Waxman at home, please?" Nissen's voice reflected the urgency of the situation, but the frail voice at the other end seemed unresponsive to it, though perfectly cordial.

"No, I'm sorry. Dr. Waxman's away. Can I help you? This is Mrs. Waxman."

It didn't seem possible that his third call would fail. He decided he had to try to track down the professor. "This is Dr. Nissen from Presbyterian-St. Luke's Hospital in Chicago. It's very important that I speak to your husband. Is there some way that he can be reached?"

Nissen's hands began to fidget with a pile of newly sharpened pencils lying on the desk in front of him.

"He's on a lecture tour, you know. He'll be back early next week, I'm sure. I can have him call you then, if you don't mind leaving me your number—"

"I need him now!" Nissen's voice was emphatic. "Where can I reach him?"

"Let me check his schedule." The next thing Nissen heard was the receiver bouncing on a table top, then silence. As he waited, he could hear the sound of his own breathing.

Once she'd returned, Nissen could hear the rattle of paper in the background before she spoke. "He was lecturing at Notre Dame today and he goes to Northwestern tonight. That's in Evanston . . ."

This news was music indeed in Nissen's ear. Evanston was a

northern suburb of Chicago. He quickly thanked Mrs. Waxman and hurriedly confirmed that Waxman was a scheduled lecturer. He further determined that the professor would be staying at the Evanston Hotel and had reservations for 9:00 that evening. Nissen's last call was to leave a message with the hotel's switchboard.

It took about twenty minutes for Rondowski's answer to come about the names in the classified ad. The call was transferred to Nissen's office, where he had arranged for the surgeon's secretary to type the reports over the phone. By 5:45 he was on his way back to Schaeffer's office, where Woodsley, Nissen, Blackwell, Stecker and Schaeffer were waiting.

"Here's your trading cards." There was a disgusted look on the captain's face as he tossed the six reports on Schaeffer's desk. "Real beauts. Not one of them worth the cost of a long distance call to Washington."

Rondowski went back upstairs and arranged for two of his men to check on the source of the advertisement as the others took up the dossiers and began to devour them.

As Rondowski had said, they were, indeed, "real beauts." . . .

PROFILE ON ERNEST PHILLIP LAWSON
#241782
Date of birth: September 21, 1955
Place of birth: Chicago, Illinois
Race: Negro
Religion: Baptist

Convicted on eight counts of first degree murder on October 16, 1973, in the Cook County Courthouse, Judge John Kinley presiding. Victims were Mary Thurmond, age 15, Joanne Fiest, age 14, Rhonda Gelman, age 13, Margaret Browley, age 11, Elizabeth Robbins, age 12, Christine MacCrae, age 10, Kathleen Sykes, age 14, and Susan Bennett, age 16. Pleaded guilty to all counts. Sentenced to life imprisonment. Now serving at Joliet State Prison.

Previous arrest record: None

Social Service Report:

Mr. Lawson is the fifth of six children and has lived in Chicago his entire life. He grew up on the South Side and dropped out of high school after the ninth grade. He has never been in trouble with the law before. [Not even an ironic exclamation point here.]

His father, John Lawson, is a known alcoholic (is said to drink over a pint of whiskey each day). Ernie Lawson is the product of John Lawson's second marriage. His first wife was killed in a car accident in 1949 when, apparently under the influence of alcohol, he skidded on an icy pavement into a telephone pole. Because of his drinking and having failed numerous rehabilitation programs, he has been unable to hold a permanent job. At the time of this report he is hospitalized at Cook County Hospital with cirrhosis and bleeding ulcers. The family has been maintained on welfare.

Mrs. Lawson, Ernie's mother, was eighteen when she married John. Apparently she was unaware of his drinking problem at the time. She comes from a poorly educated but very religious family. Her father was a sharecropper in Georgia who moved to the North in hopes of a better life. She seems to be the head of the household, a strong disciplinarian who forces all six children to attend church every Sunday. She also conducts a Bible reading session every night. The idea of divorce is untenable.

Elizabeth, the youngest child at eighteen, has not yet been permitted to date. Her curfew is eight o'clock. Ernie was under the same rules, but has been known to disappear for days.

Maggie Lawson, the second oldest, has a long record of drug abuse and prostitution and has tried to commit suicide twice. Her older sister, Edith, was raped at the age of thirteen and now lives alone a few blocks from the family. At twenty-nine she has never married. John Jr. has followed in his father's footsteps and has had serious problems with drinking.

William is studying for the clergy.

It's a bizarre family situation, to say the least. Only one of the children, besides the defendant, still lives at home. They share a small apartment in the Mother Cabrini project.

As stated earlier, Ernie managed to complete only the ninth grade. He was a poor student who failed two times in the past, but managed to have an almost perfect attendance record. His last teacher says that he had a limited attention span and the reading ability of a fifth grader. Ernie has had difficulty keeping jobs, which have included two car washes, a grocery store and a gas station in the last six months. His major concern in life seems to be spreading the gospel.

He has spent most of his time at home, alone behind locked doors, listening to religious music. He has never shown an interest in hobbies and does not seem to have any friends. There is no indication that he has ever had a date.

Neighbors describe him as shy and polite, but he also is known to lose his temper when criticized. On one occasion when Maggie came home from prison he dragged her into his room, beat her until she was bloody, ripped most of her clothes off and threw her out into the hall bloody and dazed.

He says that the girls he killed were just like his sister. He followed them for days and sat outside their houses at night. Voices from heaven directed him, and he is convinced that these girls deserved to die. Each girl was strangled to death and left with a cross beside her body. He was apprehended standing over the body of Susan Bennett and subsequently confessed to the other killings.

(Signed) Harvey Raskin,
Social Worker

MEDICAL EVALUATION:

Medical History:
    Childhood Diseases: None
    Immunizations: Polio, diphtheria, tetanus
    Hospitalizations: None
    Injuries: None
    Habits: Does not smoke or drink alcohol
    Drugs: None
    Family illnesses: Father and brother alcoholics

Physical Examination:
    Height: 6 ft. 4 in. Weight 245
    General Appearance: Husky, well-developed
    Vital Signs: BP 120/72, HR 60, Temperature 98.6

Integument: Shaves pubic hair. No scars, tattoos, sores.
HEENT: Vision 20/20. Hearing normal.
Neck: No abnormalities
Chest: Lungs clear. Normal heart sounds.
Abdomen: Negative
Genitourinary: Not circumcised
Musculoskeletal: Negative
Neurological: Reflexes normal
Impression: Normal physical examination

(Signed) C. Field, M.D.

Psychiatric Evaluation:

Mr. Lawson is a somewhat withdrawn individual, soft spoken and seemingly shy. Outwardly he is passive, with few emotional expressions; during the first half hour of my interview most of his answers were "yes" and "no." His affect was flat. He brought along a Bible and constantly read to himself.

He considers his mother an angel, but would not speak about his father. When I mentioned his sister's name, he returned to his Bible.

He described his life as happy, with no objective evidence for that claim. He says he enjoys being alone, as well as beating his head against his pillow while listening to religious music. God, he says, communicates with him daily and through him to man and the rest of the world.

When we touched on his feelings toward women his anger became difficult to control. He denied any interest in females, considering them evil, and would not talk about masturbation. There was a suggestion that his sister fondled his genitals when he was going through puberty and probably earlier.

He proudly admits each killing and readily describes datails. He is not contrite and I am sure that he would repeat his crime if given the opportunity. Nonetheless he is aware of the law and says he knew that he could be punished.

He is schizophrenic with paranoid tendencies and auditory hallucinations. He is extremely dangerous and should be confined for the rest of his life.

(Signed) G. Kleema, M.D.

PROFILE ON LOUIS ANTHONY GIOVANNI
#/241101
Date of Birth: March 6, 1907
Place of Birth: New York City, New York
Race: Caucasian
Religion: Catholic

Convicted of smuggling heroin on September 5, 1972, in the downtown court house, New York City, New York, Judge H. Greenberg presiding. Sentenced to twenty years at Attica State Prison.

Previous arrest record:
January 18, 1929: Armed robbery, served ten years
May 3, 1940: Charged with murder, found innocent
March 25, 1941: Charged with jury tampering, found innocent
October 6, 1950: Charged with income tax evasion, fined $5000
July 21, 1961: Charged with smuggling drugs, found innocent

Social Service Report:
Mr. Giovanni refused to be interviewed. He is a well-known syndicate figure who was connected to the 1939 Giardello murder that ended in a hung jury. He has been suspected of drug smuggling for years, but evidence was circumstantial. The conviction now results from six months of intensive effort involving wiretapping and two underground agents. He has been married twice and has three sons, one of whom is suspected of working with the syndicate.

PROFILE ON CAREY MILLITZ
#241002
Date of Birth: July 3, 1931
Place of Birth: Oklahoma City, Oklahoma
Race: Caucasian
Religion: Catholic

Convicted of kidnapping and first degree murder of Ronald J. Heller, age 7, on August 5, 1972, at Santa Barbara County Court House, Santa Barbara, California, Judge William A. Fendley presiding. Now serving a life sentence at San Quentin.

Previous arrest record:

November 5, 1953: Convicted of armed robbery. Sentenced to ten years at Soledad Prison.

March 17, 1962: Convicted of child molesting and drunkenness. Sentenced to eight years at San Quentin.

Social Service Report (filed July 30, 1973):

Mr. Millitz is a forty-two-year-old male who has spent most of his adult life in prison. Born in Oklahoma, mother moved with him to California when he was a year old. He is an illegitimate child and has never known his father.

His mother was seventeen years old at the time of his birth. This was her second pregnancy, the first terminating with an illegal abortion. When they arrived in Los Angeles she managed to acquire false identification cards and began working as a barmaid, then became a prostitute. Carey says he remembers seeing her "friends" in bed with her. By the time he was nine she had overdosed twice and slashed her wrists. At ten he was made a ward of the court. Six months later his mother jumped in front of a train.

Carey was placed in a county orphanage and later tried in several foster homes where he was described as an uncontrollable, hyperactive child. At fourteen he was arrested by the juvenile authorities for shoplifting. His story was that another boy had forced him at gunpoint to steal and then had disappeared when the store detective caught up with him.

His education: too many schools and too many behavior problems. He finally quit school in the tenth grade. Several teachers, however, commented that he was bright but would never try. At eighteen he left the orphanage.

Socially retarded: He did not begin dating until he was nineteen, with a thirty-six-year-old divorcee, Marjorie Neilsen, mother of two children by a previous marriage, who tended to treat him as her third child and seemed to fulfill his needs. He managed to keep two reasonable jobs, each for more than a year.

The relationship lasted almost three years. It ended when she discovered him undressing her ten-year-old daughter. Thereafter he was fired from several different jobs and began drinking. He managed to buy a gun but was easily apprehended when he tried to hold up a gas station.

According to his prison record he was regarded as an ideal prisoner and consequently was released on probation two years before full term of his sentence. The structured situation of prison seemed to give him welcome support. While incarcerated he became interested in medicine and within a short period of time became knowledgeable about minor medical problems. He read constantly, reviewing all of the medical texts that the prison library had on hand. He worked in the dispensary and volunteered for every research project. During the same period he earned his high school diploma and enrolled in a variety of college courses.

After his release he began work as a hospital orderly but soon quit, apparently feeling that the position was beneath his qualifications. He tried work as an x-ray technician but was soon fired as unreliable. He then began wandering the city of Los Angeles, started drinking again and got into numerous fights. On one occasion after a weekend binge he followed a ten-year-old boy home from school, took him behind a store and was apprehended while molesting the boy when a passerby happened to hear the boy's cries.

Carey spent the next eight years in San Quentin, working in the dispensary. When he was discovered stealing drugs, he was moved into the kitchen. During his second year he was placed in solitary confinement for fighting. His claim was that another prisoner had tried to rape him.

His interests shifted from medicine to law, he became fanatical in his study of law textbooks, and became known as a "prison lawyer" by the inmates and even offered advice to some of their lawyers. He now contends that the warden kept him in prison not because of his negative behavior but because he was too intelligent to be let out.

After serving his second sentence, he moved to the Bakersfield area and worked on a lettuce farm. He travelled about the San Joaquin Valley following crops as they ripened. He then disappeared for two months. Having learned in his travels about the Heller farm and the family's wealth, he kidnapped their seven-year-old son and demanded $250,000. The ransom was paid, but the boy was found smothered to death in a tool shack. Carey was captured four weeks later loitering outside a girls' school.

My impression of Mr. Millitz is that he is a sociopathic personality, unable to function in society. He's highly intelligent and very articulate but without any concept of the standard right and wrong. It is doubtful that he could ever be rehabilitated.

(Signed) L. Fugamen
Social Worker

MEDICAL EVALUATION

Medical History:
   Childhood Diseases: Measles, mumps and chicken pox
   Immunizations: Diphtheria, pertussis, tetanus
   Hospitalizations: None
   Habits: Smokes three packs of cigarettes per day, drinks heavily
   Drugs: Placed on phenothiazines at San Quentin
   Family Illnesses: Unknown, mother committed suicide.

Physical Examination:
   Height 6 ft. 2 in. Weight 169
   General Appearance: Thin, pale
   Vital Signs: BP 132/82 HR 64 Temp 98.8
   Integument: Two tattoos—one of a man's face circumscribing the
          anus, representing the figure's mouth; the other, on his
          left shoulder, of a heart with "Mother" in the center.
   HEENT: Full length beard
          Poor dental hygiene
          Vision and hearing normal
   Neck: No abnormalities
   Chest: Lungs clear
          Short systolic murmur at the apex
   Abdomen: Slightly enlarged liver
   Musculoskeletal: Negative
   Genitourinary: Indirect hernia on left side.
   Neurological: Reflexes normal
          Personality disorder
Impression: Normal physical examination
          Psychiatric problem, probably schizophrenia

(Signed) J. Caren, M.D.

Psychiatric Interview, August 1, 1972:

Mr. Millitz is a highly rigid individual, hypersensitive and hyperalert. He appears to be in constant readiness for any situation, as if it might be an emergency, and does not seem to trust anyone. Everything he does is thoroughly designed and calculated in advance, down to the minutest detail. He is incapable of yielding to logical argument and projects many of his own feelings of paranoia onto others around him.

Knowledge to him is a form of power, a way to manipulate his environment and to express his feelings of superiority. Within this form of defense he seems to be a very insecure person, such insecurity deriving from his illegitimacy and lack of parental love. This insecurity also drove him to study medicine at one time and most recently law—he needs to control others and, by knowing more, feel able partially to fulfill his drives and relieve his deep sense of vulnerability.

Unresolved sexual conflicts, partly because of early parental separation, play a major role. He has trouble establishing a sexual identity and cannot maintain a mature relationship. For a period of two or three years he lived with a woman twice his age, a mother-son relationship. Because of his sexual needs and inability to express them in an acceptable manner, he seeks out children. Talk of homosexuality seems to upset him, though he does acknowledge several male contacts in prison.

He is blatantly paranoid, very guarded in most of his responses and watching intently every move I make. He has classic delusions of grandeur. Most of the interview was spent in competition with me rather than any effort to cooperate.

Mr. Millitz is aware of his crime and demonstrates no feelings of guilt. According to him, the "family deserved what it got."

Impression: Schizophrenia with delusions of grandeur.
    Paranoia
    Homosexuality

        (Signed) R. Talbot, M.D.

PROFILE ON MUHAMMED AKUBAR
#241802
Date of Birth: Unknown
Place of Birth: Palestine
Race: Caucasian
Religion: Moslem

Convicted of the second degree murders of Henry Washington and Robert Smith on November 6, 1973, at the Alameda County Courthouse, Oakland, California, Judge R. Lang presiding. Sentenced to life. Now serving at Soledad Prison.

Previous arrest record: None
Social Service Interview: None
Medical Evaluation: None
Psychiatric Interview: None

Muhammed Akubar, a member of the Black September Guerrilla Organization, was captured with an Ethiopian passport in Oakland, California, on October 1, 1973. He was responsible for the sabotage of a munitions plant and the killing of two night watchmen. He is suspected of being one of the Arab hijackers who escaped after forcing a BOAC jet to fly to Libya. He is also wanted by Israeli police in connection with the bombing of a school bus that killed three youngsters and injured seven others.

PROFILE ON GEORGE ANDREW MADISON
#241411
Date of Birth: August 30, 1938
Place of Birth: Dill, Mississippi
Race: Negro
Religion: Baptist

Convicted of hijacking and the second degree murder of Patrolman Michael Salinski on April 23, 1975, at Cook County Court House, Chicago, Illinois, Judge A. V. Walden presiding. Now serving a life sentence at Joliet State Prison.

Previous arrest record:
   September 5, 1952: Curfew violation
   September 29, 1952: Curfew violation
   February 7, 1953: Shoplifting
   April 7, 1953: Disturbing the peace
   June 20, 1953: Vandalism
   October 3, 1953: Gang fight
   February 13, 1954: Gang fight
   March 30, 1954: Drag racing
   May 11, 1954: Car theft, served six months in the county jail
   December 27, 1954: Drunken driving
   January 18, 1955: Suspected rape, case dismissed
   March 16, 1955: Suspected armed robbery, case dismissed
   May 24, 1955: Assault, charges dropped
   October 12, 1955: Armed robbery, served ten years at Joliet
   June 2, 1969: Concealed weapon, served two years on county farm

Social Service Report (April 15, 1975):
   Mr. Madison lived in Chicago since age seven, when his parents and eight siblings moved from Mississippi. Both parents were uneducated and arrived in Chicago with thirty dollars. Soon after, his father found work in the stockyards, cleaning the slaughterhouses at night. The salary was small but it kept the family fed and sheltered. He remained at this job for over ten years, until he was injured by a falling crate and confined to bed for eight months. The meat packing house refused to pay his medical bill, which exceeded five thousand dollars. During the time of his confinement, the oldest daughter, seventeen at the time, did domestic work while her brother, a year older, got a job parking cars downtown. Subsequently the father tried working again but the pain was unbearable.
   Their apartment has three small rooms. Five of the children remaining at home sleep on two mattresses. Money for rent and food comes primarily from welfare, and from two of the older children, who are now out working. One of the girls has sickle cell disease and has been hospitalized six times for crises. The youngest boy almost died from a rat bite last year.
   As a youth the defendant's life was deprived, including wearing

82

hand-me-down clothes from the older children and a local church charity. He never failed in school, but quit in the ninth grade. For self-protection he was forced to join a neighborhood gang when he was only thirteen. Later he joined the Egyptian Cobras, a conspicuous group of dropouts who wore green turbans and terrorized a large segment of the ghetto. He was arrested several times for gang warfare, and two of his friends nicknamed Wolfman and Attila were convicted of murdering a white high school youth who was waiting for the elevated subway on the South Side. When the youth refused to give them his wallet, they stabbed him several times in the chest.

George left home at the age of sixteen after an argument with his father and managed to support himself with petty crimes and drug peddling. Most of his stealing was directed against whites. Later, he was charged with the rape of a white school teacher; charges were dropped two days before his trial.

In 1955 he was convicted of armed robbery on three counts and served the full sentence of ten years. He would have been eligible for probation after seven years but he was considered a troublemaker and responsible for one of the prison riots. The warden labeled him as recalcitrant and dangerous. Toward the end of his prison term he became fanatic about black power and after his release joined the Black Panthers.

For the next three years he participated in and promoted marches, strikes and demonstrations. He disappeared from the country for six months at one time, and was thought to have been in Algiers. After returning, money was a problem and in an attempted liquor store robbery he shot and killed Patrolman Salinski. He was arrested, escaped two days later and managed to hijack a plane bound for Geneva from Kennedy Airport. He forced the pilot to fly to Cuba instead, but when the plane stopped to fuel in Miami he was apprehended by FBI agents.

He says that no American prison can hold him.

(Signed) R. Raskin
Social Worker

Medical Evaluation: None

Psychiatric Interview: None

PROFILE ON DR. GERALD WEISBERG
#241503
Date of birth: December 25, 1927
Place of birth: Miami Beach, Florida
Race: Caucasian
Religion: Jewish

Convicted of the first degree murder of his wife Joyce Weisberg on May 21, 1973 at Dade County Court House, Miami, Florida, Judge Robert Yellin presiding. New serving a life sentence at Florida State Penitentiary.

Previous Arrest Record: None

Social Service Report (May 1, 1974):

Dr. Weisberg is a 46-year old, well-known, wealthy psychiatrist who has never had problems with the law before. Indeed, he has never had a moving violation and has only received one parking ticket in the past ten years.

His parents, Mr. and Mrs. Harold Weisberg, are presently living in an expensive condominium in Fort Lauderdale. Mr. Weisberg is semi-retired but still owns a six-store chain of men's clothing. His assets are estimated at over four million dollars. Dr. Gerald Weisberg is also independently wealthy with assets of his own of over a half million dollars.

According to a friend of the family, Dr. Weisberg was a quiet child, well behaved and polite. He was able to read before he started school. Throughout elementary and high school his grades were consistently superior; he graduated valedictorian of his class. All along he had taken interest in science and was known to spend many hours alone in his own laboratory in the basement of his home. He was very secretive about the experiments he was conducting, but several pets from the neighborhood disappeared mysteriously. Throughout high school he avoided extracurricular activities and made few if any efforts to make friends.

In June of 1952 he graduated from the University of Miami Medical School second in his class of 100, took a rotating internship at Jackson Memorial Hospital and then served two years in the U.S. Army. After discharge he did a psychiatry residency at Jackson Memorial.

In reviewing his Army records I am unable to ascertain anything out of the ordinary. In fact, his record is strikingly routine. He spent both service years in Munich, Germany, as a general medical officer. His commanding officer says that he was hardly aware of him.

His wife, the former Joyce Anderman, was a girl whom he met in college. Within two weeks of his return from the Army, he proposed. Her family was also well-to-do and provided a five hundred guest reception at the Americana Hotel in New York City. A fellow psychiatrist at Jackson, Dr. James Whiley, was the best man.

The marriage was barren. The wife turned out to be a domineering individual who apparently could never be satisfied and made the doctor's life miserable. She was not well liked; one neighbor commented that "she deserved what she got." Our records indicate that the maid discovered her body in the bathtub, and an autopsy revealed that she had been poisoned. Dr. Weisberg maintains that he is innocent.

(Signed) T. House
Social Worker

MEDICAL EVALUATION

Medical History:
Childhood Diseases: Mumps, measles, non-paralytic polio
Immunizations: DPT, boosters x2
Hospitalizations: Tonsillectomy, age 7
Appendectomy, age 11
Asthma, age 13 and 15
Habits: Does not smoke or drink.
Drugs: Tranquilizers and sleeping pills
Family Illnesses: Mother has diabetes
Father had heart attack 1969

Physical Examination:
Height 5 ft. 8 in. Weight 150
General Appearance: Thin, but healthy
Integument: Psoriasis

HEENT: Wears glasses for reading
       Hearing normal
Neck: No abnormalities
Chest: Scattered wheezes
       Heart sounds normal
Abdomen: Slight tenderness over the epigastric region
Musculoskeletal: Negative
Genitourinary: Circumcised
Neurological: Reflexes normal
Impression: Asthma
            Possible ulcer disease
            Psoriasis
                                        (Signed) M. Bartlow, M.D.

Psychiatric Evaluation:

It is difficult to interview a colleague with comparable training and experience, and so I cannot be altogether confident in my assessment. However, Dr. Weisberg does appear to be genuinely distraught over his wife's death and quite adamant about his own innocence. There are a few abnormal personality traits but nothing to justify a diagnosis as psychotic or legally insane.

The patient appears to be a timid man, somewhat passive-aggressive. He is also a meticulous individual, well-organized and known for his punctuality. I suspect that behind this quiet veneer he is an angry man who has learned to keep his rage inside.

He says he loved his wife and blames himself for the lack of children. This seems to have been a significant problem in their marriage, but the most striking is her persistent "riding me," according to Dr. Weisberg. I do not get the impression that he wanted to kill her, but must add that being a psychiatrist he would know how to conceal that feeling.

                                        (Signed) W. Lourvette, M.D.

"Real beauts," indeed, as Rondowski had said.

Chapter VII

Between 5:00 and 5:30, two separate limousines arrived at the front entrance to Presbyterian-St. Luke's Hospital. The first had been sent to the airport to pick up Kramer's son, whose concerns did not lie with the who or why but only with his father's condition. When he finally made it upstairs through the reporters he found the Secretary talking on the telephone. It was obvious that his father didn't feel well, he could see it in his face when he embraced him; he also was shocked to see he could only lift one arm.

"Am I glad to see you, boy, but you didn't have to leave school for this," Kramer said, forgetting about the receiver he'd left sitting on the bedstand.

"It's not every day a guy's father gets shot at or something." Robert glanced down at the bandaged arm. "Bad aim, I guess."

"Not bad enough, from my point of view." Kramer began with the earlier motorcade. While he was relating the progression of events, sparing a few of the more gory details and rather tired of repeating the story in any case, the second limousine arrived downstairs. Inside was his older sister, frantic with worry and determined to see him as quickly as possible. Unlike the boy she had heard of the first threat on the car radio. When she entered the lobby there were two security officers with her but none of the reporters inside recognized her and only a few, noticing the police escort, came over to ask her questions.

Once she'd made it to her brother's suite she found the boy

sitting at his father's side with tears in his eyes. The last time that she had seen him cry was at his mother's funeral. The telephone receiver was still lying on its side, ignored by Kramer; it was Thomison and the campaign manager had already hung up.

She quickly embraced the two of them, offering her brother a quick kiss on the forehead and immediately demanding to know what was going on. Kramer started his story once again from the beginning. When he'd finished, they simply couldn't believe what they'd heard. The prospect of his being poisoned didn't seem possible; the fact that they couldn't do anything but sit and wait was impossibly frightening.

Nissen was the first to finish reading all six profiles Rondowski had gotten from Washington, and immediately asked, "Do we know what Dr. Weisberg used to poison his wife? It's probably foolish to think that he'd order the use of the same thing. . . but who knows."

"Strychnine," the captain answered, leaning against the edge of the conference table.

"Too bad." Nissen set the profile down in front of him. "That's not what we have here, but poison does appear to be his method. Could be he's the mastermind behind this thing?"

"He's both too obvious and too unlikely, to my mind," Blackwell countered. "He doesn't strike me as someone who would want to kill Kramer—only a nagging wife. If you assume that only one man is responsible—and you must since they're all in different parts of the country and couldn't possibly have gotten together —then some of these names were purposefully added to throw us off. Why else would anyone want *all* these men released?"

"If your assumption is correct," Woodsley said, continuing Blackwell's thought, "then it has to be someone with a fair number of contacts."

"Or one good one," Stecker interrupted.

"But no one randomly picks a group of six murderers," Woodsley went on. "No, there must be *something* in common. Giovanni being part of the mob might just be that something. Even though his sentence is the only one not for life, it might as well be, at his age."

"I think Dr. Blackwell's got a good idea," Rondowski argued. "I also think we can eliminate Lawson . . . I don't see any religious angle to this thing, unless some private God told him to do it—"

"What about the Arab?" Schaeffer asked. *"There's* a political motive, if I've ever seen one . . . the Secretary of Defense . . . I'm sure he's got enough contacts on the outside—"

Stecker disagreed. "Madison's more likely . . . he says he wants revenge and I believe him. You don't need that many contacts, just one or two who are crazy enough to try. I know some of the Arabs are fanatic enough, but this thing's just too well-calculated for hotheads. They like to die in the act . . . hero stuff, kamikaze, you know? And as for Giovanni, I've read the syndicate doesn't want him back—"

"His son might," Rondowski argued.

"What about Millitz? Calculating, medically informed?" Blackwell asked. "Except what in the world would he have to do with Kramer? . . ."

"All right, so I guess we know who they are, at least," Rondowski began again. "And it's clear any one of them or any combination is probably behind this, but why Kramer . . . and what 'trip'?"

There was a sinking feeling around the room. It was becoming apparent that little had been accomplished in the past six hours while Kramer's condition had steadily worsened —and the exact *cause,* still unknown.

While they were still arguing, more negative laboratory results were coming back. The special chemistry results were all at normal serum concentrations. Only lead of the heavy metal screen was elevated, but its concentration was essentially negligible. It was too early to expect any bacterial growth in the wound culture.

Special Chemistry
Time Drawn: 16:45

Test	Result	Normal Value
Calcium	9.8 mg	9-11 mg/100 ml
Phosphorus	3.7 mg	3-4.5mg/100 ml
Amylase	65 units	6-80 units
Magnesium	2.8 mg	2-3 mg/100 ml
Copper	100 ug	100-128 ug/100 ml
Zinc	120 ug	100-140 ug/100 ml
Cholesterol	230 mg	160-230 mg/100 ml
Fatty acids	460 mg	380-465 mg/100 ml
Acetone	1.2 mg	0.3-2.0 mg/100ml
Thyroid studies		
PBI	5.0 ug	4-8 ug/100 ml
T3	23%	25-35%
T4	5.9	3-7

Toxicology

Heavy metal screen
Time drawn: 13:10

Lead	5 micrograms	less than 20
Arsenic	0	0
Mercury	0	0
Antimony	0	0

Bacteriology
Wound culture
Time taken: 15:00

Result: no evidence of any bacterial growth at three hours.

At 6:00 Kramer refused a specially prepared dinner and was complaining of nausea, muscle aches and a persistent headache. His temperature had continued its slow, unrelenting climb, now at 100.8 degrees, and his pulse remained around 100 beats per minute. When Dr. Blackwell went to change the bandages he noted that the wound was a bright red color and exquisitely tender, much more so than he would have expected from earlier manipulation. The pain was so severe that it even hurt when he accidentally bumped the bed. Blackwell rewrote the analgesic order, switching from the oral tablets ordered by Nissen to a stronger intramuscular injection, and resumed his watch on the patient.

Outside the room the cardiac monitoring system continued to noisily blip at a rapid rate. Dr. Wheelin, who had taken ten minutes to shove down an unappetizing hospital tray, took up a position across the hall where he could hear every beat on the monitor, too nervous to sleep and too restless to read or watch television. He thought of the cardiac he'd lost, and wondered if he might be repeating the same brutal resuscitation on Secretary Kramer later that night.

At the Twelfth Street Station dinner was brought in from a nearby McDonald's. Fifteen of the twenty-one witnesses had already been sent home, unable to pick out a familiar face from their mug files. Trudy Myers, the art student who was seemingly the closest, was still among the remaining group but it was her second time through the thick volumes. Sitting next to her was Mr. Britte, the dog groomer, who in contrast to the others, managed to pick out several possibilities. Unfortunately each one was serving a prison sentence or was listed as dead. The black witness who had labeled the attacker as a young honky turned out to be an ex-convict by the name of Lucas Marion and was dismissed when he became more obstructive than helpful.

A mound of Big Macs and eight soggy bags of French fries were laid out across an unused desk, while the cups of coffee were kept in a thin paper carton. Mr. Britte refused the free meal, saying that the grease would upset his gall bladder and probably give him gas. The other witnesses were not so particular, including Trudy, who eagerly reached across her desk for one of the hamburgers, and as she did so her loose halter top swung downward, uncovering a striking gap between her breasts, which Mr. Britte easily ignored.

91

At 6:15 Inspector Pritchard's 747 jet touched down at O'Hare Field. It was raining again; dark clouds overhead. Since it was a Friday, the beginning of a weekend, the terminal was packed with travelers waiting for planes that were running behind schedule. Outside every parking facility was filled to capacity and roads in and out of the world's busiest airport were jammed.

Pritchard was a husky, robust man with a short blond crewcut, in his middle forties. He was a military man, recently resigned, who had earned his commission through ROTC at the University of Pennsylvania, had been promoted to captain during the Korean War and earned a colonel's wings in Army Intelligence during the war in Vietnam. He sustained two shrapnel wounds in his back during that Korean conflict and received the Congressional Medal of Honor as well as a Purple Heart. During 1967 and 1968 he worked with the CIA in its surveillance of antiwar activists and was partially responsible for planning the police counterattack that Mayor Daley used on demonstrators outside the Democratic Party convention. Later he was involved in the investigation of the Kent State tragedy. When he reached the twenty-year mark in his Army career he was offered a relatively high level position with the FBI, internal security division.

He was proper going on prim, conservative, always serious, collected and extremely bright. Every morning he rose at 6:00 A.M., did thirty minutes of calisthenics, made his own breakfast and was at his desk by 7:00, an hour before anyone else. At night he would run through another set of exercises. He often said—and never doubted—that a healthy body made a healthy mind. Emotion of any sort rarely surfaced in his life. He was well known and respected for his diligence, especially as an investigator.

As Pritchard disembarked he was closely followed by the two uniformed physicians. An FBI agent waiting at the gate hurried the group through the half-mile-long corridor of large crowds to a waiting limousine double-parked outside American Airlines.

Once the huge car was out in traffic the agent began briefing the three men. Pritchard was familiar with the names of Akubar and Lawson. He listened quietly, recording detail, oblivious to the traffic snarl outside.

The four doctors were reassembling in Nissen's office. No one any longer seriously doubted they were dealing with a poison, but so far the best they could produce was a few tiny crystals of glass. To save time Nissen arranged to have the hospital kitchen send four dinner trays, and he had already called his wife to tell her that he would be home late. All of the books and papers from his desk were piled in a nearby corner to make room for the trays. After glancing at the so-called fricasseed chicken, Stecker decided to eat a tuna sandwich left over from lunch.

"I know what you're going to ask us to do and I'm willing to try," Blackwell told Stecker as he fumbled with the edges of a small milk carton. "I don't think it's possible, though."

"I know, this hospital isn't equipped for something like this—" Nissen began.

"Who is?" Stecker interrupted.

Nissen took a deep breath, sighed. "That's a good question. We've already eliminated many of the common poisons"—he used a knife to shave a few slivers of meat from a drumstick—"but we have to try. If Kramer definitely refuses to trade the antidote for the convicts, and in a way I suppose he feels he almost has to refuse at this point—after all, we haven't told him there's no alternative—it puts a tremendous burden on us. I don't think that the police are any closer than we are. Fortunately Dr. Ryan will be here any moment and as some of you know Dr. Waxman is due in town this evening. I've left a message for him to call me. They should be able to help . . . There are a few more routine studies pending and I expect the results within an hour, but judging by everything else so far I suspect that they'll be negative too."

"If we only had some indication from his *symptoms*," Blackwell said. "I suggest we get some other baseline studies, like a clotting screen and pulmonary function. An early change in either one might at least head us in the right direction. . . . This isn't like a ten-year-old boy with a snake bite or a heroin addict coming in with pinpoint pupils and labored breathing. There's no history, no pill vial, no rusty nail, no tainted meat or recent travel to some tropical locale. I don't wish Kramer any harm, but until he gets sicker I can't even *guess* what this is."

"Can you imagine some foreign agent dropping this whatever-the-hell it is in the water?" Stecker said as he poured himself a cup of coffee. "Suppose it wasn't Kramer but thousands of people complaining of headaches and nausea, who we were sure were poisoned, but couldn't prove it . . . that's if we had enough hospital beds to keep them. They'd probably all die before we could do anything—"

"Harold, I think you're being a little melodramatic," Dressner said as he joined the pharmacologist at the coffeepot. "Anyone else want coffee?"

Both Blackwell and Nissen said they did, and as Dressner brought the filled cups back to the desk he continued, "I don't see foreign agents in the woodpile here, but no doubt we've got ourselves a crisis and a frustrating mystery added in. I can't blame anybody for being pessimistic. I made a list of every common poison I could find plus some of the more esoteric toxins that I doubt our man would have access to . . . At least that I hope he doesn't. . . . Well, I'll go through the list, you'll see that some of them can be eliminated fairly easily. And some of them can't be eliminated at all."

Dressner took a small packet of stapled sheets from his coat pocket. "First, insecticides. You could include every ant, roach, and moth poison, foremost of which are malthien and chlordane. There are over twenty types, any one of which could have been used. It's good news, bad news. There's a test, but we don't have the equipment—"

94

"We'll get it," Nissen said.

Dressner nodded his head, then continued. "Under flammable poison, particularly those that anyone could find around the house, we have methyl alcohol, several aldehydes, methenamine, kerosene, methyl bromide, and carbon tetrachloride, which is common in dozens of cleaning solutions. But just taking cleaning solutions without it we can add solvent distillate, lye, ammonia, bleach in the form of hypochlorite, oxalic acid, drain cleaners such as sodium acid sulfate, rug cleaners such as chlorinated hydrocarbons, wallpaper cleaner and aniline.

"Almost every medicine we use here in the hospital can be classified as a poison if given in high enough dosage, which in many cases might be a very small volume. Even aspirin or dramamine. Most of the tranquilizers were eliminated with the hypnotic screen, but there are a few left that can't be tested for. As Harold can attest, the list of potential poisons in the pharmacy is over two hundred long, but here's a few: all reducing pills, all antihistamines, some cathartics, Neosynephrine, belladona, digitalis, Quinidine, Veratrum, boric acid, chloride and chlorine, iodides, camphor, atropine, every cancer drug, cocaine, phenacetin, curare, almost every antibiotic except penicillin and every form of insulin."

Dressner stopped to take a sip from his coffee cup. "Suppose our man just went to the drug store, he could get silver salts, potassium bromate or aniline from many of the cosmetics. Or the hobby shop for selenium. Or the camera shop for toluene or any one of the twenty-five photography chemicals. No one really knows how to treat some of these.

"Take the storeroom behind the house for a little paint thinner, lacquer, shellac or wood bleach—don't laugh, people have tried to use these things for suicide. This guy doesn't have to be a scientist. All he has to do is grow up in something that resembles civilization. Even moth balls could be used as a poison. Just grind 'em up.

"I've left off most of the things that would kill him immediately. Suppose he's a botanist or a horticulturist, he could extract toxins from the foxglove, the thorn apple, any one of ten poisonous mushrooms, the oleander, the monkshood, poison ivy or even the benign cherry pit that has cyanide within its structure. . . ."

Dressner stopped for another gulp of coffee, then continued, sounding a little out of breath. "Also, try mistletoe, rhododendron, bittersweet, buttercups and holly berries. Any of the poisons could be extracted, and there are another ten plants for each one I've named. Any one of them could have been used on Kramer. Suppose, though, it was a bacterial product. We could be dealing, for instance, with botulism. Unfortunately there are five types—by morning Kramer could be paralyzed and we might not know which one it is. It might also be anthrax, in which case he'll suffocate to death, or the toxin from diphtheria, which would take care of his heart in short order. Other possibilities are cholera, typhoid, plague, tularemia, leptospirosis, and paratyphoid. Those are just *some* of the agents, and God knows what the army has cooked up at Pine Bluff.

"If it's bacteria, then antibiotics or antitoxin might help in some cases, but there's a whole battery of different viruses that could be stolen from a research center. . . . I doubt that it's encephalitis but I can't be certain of that either . . . We can watch for seizures tonight. It could also be rabies, polio, lymphocytic choromeningitis . . . Had enough?"

Nissen looked annoyed. "Just go on, please."

"All right. We move on to snake venoms, which I think might be a pretty good possibility. There are four poisonous snakes in the continental United States—the cottonmouth, the copperhead, the rattler and the coral snake. Their venoms could be gotten relatively easily and the antitoxin could be the antidote that he's talking about. I think the police should check with the army about any recent thefts, and we should call some of the snake farms, like, for example, the one near Dr. Weisberg's home in South Miami. . . . Anyway, to continue, there are any number of insects like the black widow, the pruning spider, the funnel web and the tarantula.

They each have a poison that can kill a man. So do scorpions, bees, wasps, hornets, caterpillars and certain ticks. Back to Florida, there's another thousand possibilities from the sea, including stingrays, jellyfish, Portuguese man-of-war, scorpion fish and sea snakes, the worst of them all—"

"Dr. Weisberg's territory again," Stecker put in.

"What? Oh, right," Dressner said. "And I remember the report said he has family there too. Somebody could have gotten one of these under Weisberg's direction . . ."

"What possible motive, though?" Nissen said. "From a nagging wife to a secretary of defense? That's a long way for suppressed rage to travel. Well, we must tell the police in any case . . . though it's pretty flimsy grounds for suspicion, I'd think . . . Is that it, doctor?"

"The last thing I reviewed was marine biology and I found out that there's research going on at several universities on the poisons from sea anemones, coral, shellfish and Moray eels. The most interesting one, and possibly the most worrisome here, is ciguatera, which is gotten from a tiny marine snail that fish eat. If a man happened to eat the fish that's eaten the snail he would become paralyzed. I believe the toxin has been isolated but I don't know who has it—"

"Find out!" Blackwell interrupted in an uncharacteristic outburst. The tension was beginning to get to all of them.

"I intend to try, doctor. . . . Well that's my *abbreviated* list. A fair night's work ahead, wouldn't you say?" Dressner finished.

"More like a month of Sundays." Stecker sounded as depressed as he felt.

"Where do you suggest we start?" Nissen asked.

"I'm not really sure. Except keep watching him for any change," Dressner said. "The poison should attack one of the systems, his kidneys or his liver, and then maybe we can throw out at least part of this list, refine it down. Meanwhile I'd begin stocking the hospital for any eventuality. If we ever do make a diagnosis we should have everything we need on hand. Unfortu-

97

nately we might not get our answer until the autopsy. I do think we can rule out several of the bacterial infections tonight. There's a complicated test for snake venom, and the hospital at the moment doesn't have the equipment to assay for many of the drugs, but we'll get it. Right now one of us might be able to test for the insecticides, perhaps with Dr. Ryan's help. At the same time we can start analyzing the serum for any foreign component, and if we find one, isolate it and then try to identify it. Quite frankly, even with all the expertise in the world, unless we're lucky, or the police catch our man and make him talk, we might be in for trouble.''

"Or Mr. Kramer may be, unless he decides to make the trade —and even then, of course, there's no guarantee, I suppose, that we'd get the antidote turned over, assuming the theory is correct about this whole business . . . the antidote, the convicts . . . Well, damn it, the man is sick. It's most likely he's been poisoned. It's up to us to find out *that* culprit and not depend on Aunt Dotie or anything else. . . .'' Blackwell was really worked up now. "What about a biopsy of the wound?''

"Right away, I agree, and send part of the specimen over for the electron microscope. Maybe they'll detect something besides glass. We'll also need a pint of his blood and a large urine specimen,'' Dressner added, and turned to Nissen. "Is Bac-T set up for viral cultures? Not that they'll be ready by noon tomorrow—our deadline—but for our own information later, if we can still use it—''

"I'm sure it can be arranged,'' Nissen said, and proceeded to assign Dressner to the toxicology laboratory, Blackwell to Bacteriology and the insecticides and drug assays to Stecker. He planned to do the tissue biopsy himself.

The classified ad section of the *Chicago Tribune* was shut down for the night by the time the two detectives sent to investigate the Aunt Dotie advertisement arrived. After showing their identification to a night watchman at a side entrance, they climbed four flights to the night news service. Behind a plain unmarked door, the officers found a noisy room with more than a dozen haggard-looking newsmen lost in a haze of smoke, their voices drowned in the cacophony of typewriters.

Extra editions with headlines of the assassination attempt were strewn about on every desk. They stopped at the first desk.

"We need some information about classified ads."

A youngish-looking reporter was finishing off a story. He looked up, annoyed. "Wrong section, too late. Try Monday morning." He started to go back to his typing. One of the detectives took out his badge and held it in front of the typewriter.

"Police?"

"Homicide."

"You going to advertise for a killer?"

"Not exactly."

"Very mysterious stuff . . . This by any chance have anything to do with Kramer?"

"This has something to do with classified ads. Period."

"Well, I told you, they're closed at night. You'll probably have to get security to let you in. Being an obliging type, I'll take you there myself."

He led them to the main security office and from there a guard took the three of them to the dark classified offices and left them in a cavernous room filled with filing cabinets. It quickly became apparent that the job before them would be impossible without help. The eager-beaver reporter wanted to join in, but neither detective would tell him what they were looking for. After a few minutes of fruitless effort, they telephoned Mr. Blackman, the supervisor of the section. He was at home eating his dinner when the call came, but promised to be there in thirty minutes.

Chapter VIII

At 6:29, Thornton was waiting outside Field's in his Karmann Ghia, an off-white, glorified Volkswagen with a somewhat aging black convertible top that had needed replacing twice in the past four years. He was forced to park at the end of a bus stop, squeezing up against a green Chevrolet and hoping that by putting a "Press" sign in his window the police would pass him by. He kept the windshield wipers going so he could watch the entrance to the department store—his back window was hopelessly fogged.

State Street was back to normal, at least for this time of day. Rush hour traffic was still in force but beginning to clear. Despite the new downpour, policemen, wearing plastic raincoats, were directing traffic at every intersection. Each time the light changed color, they accompanied it with their whistles. An endless line of people could be seen pushing into the subway station as hundreds of others waited, huddled, at each corner for the proper bus. At 6:30 the street lights came on.

As Thornton listened to the rain pounding incessantly on the canvas top, he kept his eyes on the revolving doors a few yards away. A gray-uniformed guard waited at the doorway, unlocking it for each employee as he or she left. He waited with mixed feelings, excited about the new girl and worried she might not show. No sweat. Within a few minutes Pat was visible at the doorway. She said something to the guard, glanced at the parked cars and, as she stepped outside, opened an umbrella. Thornton immediately began leaning on his horn. Once he'd caught her attention he rolled down the window on the opposite side and called out her name. She smiled and scampered inside the door he'd just opened.

"A wonderful day in sunny southern Chicago," she said. Her smile persisted as she pushed the wet umbrella into the small back seat. "Do you mind if we go to my place first?"

"Just point the way," Thornton said as he pulled the Ghia out into the snail-pace traffic, then stopped abruptly at the first traffic signal.

"Head toward Rush Street. I'll tell you from there."

"Tough day?" Thornton asked, starting up again as the light changed.

"Not really. Except for Secretary Kramer and that mess, it was pretty much a day like most other days." She hesitated for a moment and in an obvious good mood began to laugh. "But you were there. As a matter of fact, that's who you remind me of. The eminent Walter Cronkite."

"He's taken, I'm not," Thornton said—suavely, he hoped—as he proceeded north on State Street.

She nodded. "Well, that sounds promising . . . By the way, how's he doing—Kramer . . . ?"

"I haven't had a chance to get back to the station, but according to the radio, not too good. They say that he's got a fever and his hand is worse. Also, there was some kind of threatening note saying that he'd be contacted at 4:00—"

"But that was over two hours ago."

"I know, but apparently there hasn't been any word yet." Thornton hit the brakes to avoid a yellow cab changing lanes.

"Why would anybody want to contact him?"

"I'm not sure. The word is he's been poisoned, maybe something to do with that. Who knows . . ."

"You're kidding." Her smile was gone.

"Afraid not." He stopped at another red light.

"I sure hope they catch that guy." Pat used an old Kleenex to wipe the steam from her window as Thornton drove across the Chicago River and past the *Tribune* offices. Two blocks later a small accident forced him to detour to Michigan Avenue. He took advantage of the time to ask her about herself, and she seemed pleased enough to tell him.

Her full name was Patricia Kaye Norman and this was her third month in Chicago. Hometown was Terre Haute, Indiana, where her father was an old-fashioned general practitioner. She was the middle child of five, the only girl and always protected. Both sets of grandparents came from Norway and all of the children had cotton-white hair when they were born. At seventeen she was Terre Haute's hopeful in the Miss Indiana contest, settled for second after going blank for at least five horrible seconds in her pantomime. She felt she'd survived without undue trauma.

At the University of Indiana her major was psychology, although she never did figure out her beauty-queen blackout. After graduation she was too impatient to stay for a master's, was anxious to get out in the big city on her own. She came to Chicago, took the sales job at Field's until she could save some money and get something else.

She was a strikingly attractive girl, had had three proposals —two from college, the third from a photographer she'd met on Oak Street Beach. His ploy was a modeling career. When he asked her to pose nude she told him to get lost. She wasn't that corn-fed. Since then there had been lots of dates, nothing remotely serious.

Thornton liked everything he heard, and even more what he saw. He turned north now on Michigan Avenue, where traffic was thinning, drove past the famous Chicago Firehouse that looked more like a Spanish dungeon, and turned left once again near the Hancock Center with its hundred stories melting into a gigantic oil derrick. From there Pat directed to an old red brick apartment building. She lived on the edge of the gold coast, once the richest part of the city. Because several beaches and the nightlife on Rush Street were within walking distance, rents remained three times what they should have been. Most of the residents were single or divorced and, with few exceptions, under thirty. Many of the older buildings had at one time been luxurious mansions, but the upkeep for any single family had now become too expensive and they had to be partitioned.

The closest parking place Thornton could find was over two blocks away, and the wind flipped her umbrella inside-out as they ran. By the time they reached her porch they were both drenched but laughing happily, even while they were further drenched by a leaky storm drain above the doorway. Pat pushed through the front door, Thornton right behind. The wooden steps creaked beneath a musty green carpet as they climbed to the third floor where there were four apartments—hers was the one in the back; small but quaint, two and a half rooms, the half a clothes closet converted into a tiny kitchen. Her furniture consisted of a faded, tattered chesterfield, a big cedar chest with a desk lamp, and two crates of unpacked books. There was also Gestalt, a white alley cat with gray face, paws and tail. He was napping on the couch when they entered, glanced up under heavy eyelids, stretched one leg with a yawn, and went back to sleep.

"Where for dinner?" Pat asked as Thornton helped her out of her coat.

"Anywhere you like," Thornton grandly offered.

"How about the Continental Plaza roof?" she answered casually and bent down to pet her lazy friend.

Thornton was acutely aware of the restaurant's high prices. "Sure . . . great."

"Well, maybe not," she said. "How about Jack In The Box instead?" and began hanging Thornton's coat in the bathroom.

"The hell with this," Thornton said. "Look, do you like Italian food? How about Gino's?"

"I thought you'd never ask . . . Now just give me a few minutes to change. There's beer in the fridge."

The bedroom door shut.

It was almost 7:00 when Mr. Blackman finally made it to the *Tribune* building. A nervous man, the presence of police tended to make him ramble and repeat himself. There were, however, few questions for him. Their only interest seemed to be an ad in the personal column, or rather, identifying the person who placed it. The reporter stuck close by.

Mr. Blackman proceeded to one of the front desks, nervously put on his bifocals and began skimming through a thick ledger. While the detectives watched, the reporter got a glimpse of the circled ad and started a barrage of questions. "Who's Aunt Dotie? Who are those names? C'mon, this must have something to do with Kramer, right?"

"Look, knock off the front page routine, okay? We were just told to come here and get some information," one of the detectives told him, trying to rid himself and his partner of further questions.

"Here it is"—Blackman had located the reference number, and a moment later retrieved a folded receipt from a nearby cabinet—"But I'm afraid it's not much help. It came by mail—that is, the money order came through the mail. Probably won't help you at all. Ah, last week. There's two dollars and fifty-four cents change, you can have it if you want—"

"Thanks a lot. Do you have a record where it came from?"

"Yes, it says 'Manhattan Post Office.' That's all."

Noticeably disappointed, the two detectives left with this meager bit of information. In contrast, their shadow was excited. He quickly clipped the small advertisement from another copy of the newspaper and rushed upstairs. To his dismay, however, he wasn't able to decipher the short paragraph and after a while forlornly began taking it around to other reporters, who paid him something less than fascinated attention.

Pritchard's limousine arrived at the hospital at 7:00. He and the two service doctors with him were immediately taken to

104

Schaeffer's office and further briefed. Afterward, while Pritchard and Dr. Fitzgerald went to confer with Kramer, Dr. Ryan was escorted to the toxicology laboratory. Both were informed of Waxman's expected participation, and both seemed pleased at the news.

A new set of vital signs had already been recorded. Kramer's temperature was 101 degrees, with a pulse of 104 beats per minute. His blood pressure was still around 120 over 80. Although the injections were controlling the pain in his arm, his headache had made him extremely uncomfortable and very irritable. Both his son and sister were sitting in the room watching his every movement, but it had become increasingly difficult to carry on a conversation with him. Intermittently he would become more argumentative, almost to an irrational point, and had twice snapped at the special duty nurses. His son had never seen him act like this before, his worry was beginning to change to alarm.

Kramer immediately recognized Dr. Fitzgerald as he entered the room and offered his left hand in a clumsy handshake. "They didn't have to fly you out here, I've just got the damn flu or something—"

"No way that they could have stopped me," Fitzgerald told him, a smile fixed on his face. Turning now to his side, he introduced Inspector Pritchard, who was studying the layout of the room.

The FBI investigator nodded in his customary deadpan fashion and then abruptly said, "Do you mind if I have a few minutes with the Secretary before you begin your examination?"

"Well, sure . . ." Fitzgerald gestured with his hand and stepped aside, somewhat startled. He was a soft-spoken man who had known Kramer socially as well as professionally for many years. Although he came from a sophisticated medical center, he seemed more like a country doctor, a good listener who usually had sound advice at the end. Pritchard's style was to the point, exacting and deliberate. Indeed, the questioning sounded more like an interrogation, and it was clear that Kramer was becoming annoyed.

Nonetheless he repeated his story, trying to disregard some of the Inspector's interruptions, and emphasized the unusually tight hand grip that immediately preceded the shooting pain. He added, with renewed annoyance, that he hadn't actually seen the assailant or even his weapon.

Ten minutes later Pritchard was on his way back to Schaeffer's office, stopping first at the nursing station for directions. He planned to review the WGN film next. As he left the room, Fitzgerald was opening his black bag and asking the family to step outside for a few minutes.

Dr. Ryan, a short chubby man with a curly black and gray streak of beard, already knew Dressner but had to be introduced to Nissen.

"This is what we've got so far," Dressner told him, handing over the list of negative results. "Glad you're here, we're going to need help."

Ryan began to read over their results while Nissen and Dressner stood by uneasily, almost as though they were on trial and the toxicology laboratory was their courtroom. Actually, the lab was a well-lit, immaculately clean, modern and air-conditioned facility that offered its services twenty-four hours a day, seven days a week. There were no windows, only long white empty walls with a small bulletin board at one end. Two formica-topped work benches flanked the room, cluttered with an array of expensive electronic equipment such as the atomic absorption spectrophotometer, flasks and test tubes in a dozen different sizes and hundreds of reagent bottles, many of which already held poisons. At each end of the long room were stainless steel sinks with floor pedals for technicians with their hands full. A sprinkler system crisscrossed the high ceiling. In one corner there was an emergency shower in case of a serious lab accident, plus a fire blanket and two kinds of extinguishers.

The chief technician for the night shift was a graduate student who by day was working on his Ph.D. in biochemistry at the University of Chicago. Two of his assistants were junior medical students. Altogether there were eight technicians on duty that night, five of whom had volunteered to stay over from the day shift.

Kramer's blood had been drawn a half hour before Ryan's arrival. The pint was then carried to the blood bank, where the red cells were separated out by centrifugation, which took about fifteen minutes. Afterward the serum was given to Dressner, the cells were preserved in a refrigerator.

When Ryan had finished reviewing the list, Dressner gave him a quick tour of the laboratory. One technician was standing on a metal stool, carefully pouring a small aliquot of the yellow serum into a hundred centimeter Sephadex column, a long transparent cylinder filled with a special sugar that could sort out chemicals by their molecular weights. As the sample slowly drifted down, diffusing through and disappearing into the small beads, an assembly line of test tubes passed beneath. Each tube collected exactly twenty drops and then automatically moved to the spectrophotometer, where another technician analyzed the new specimens for light refraction. Subsequently, the results were graphed and compared with other human sera known to be normal. A technician was also setting up a laboratory dialysis machine in which small amounts of serum were placed in porous cellophane bags and floated in specially prepared salt solutions. The material that diffused through the bags was then collected and analyzed. One space over was gas chromatography, reeking of benzene, with another technician using ultraviolet light to analyze the small paper strips,

Nissen joined Ryan and Dressner as they moved to Bacteriology, which was on the same floor and where they found Dr. Blackwell busy helping some of the technicians. Blackwell conducted another tour, which included the animal cages in a specially isolated room. Four of eight guinea pigs had been injected with minute amounts of Kramer's blood, but so far they appeared healthy. Experiments with the bigger rhesus monkeys would begin shortly.

Blackwell's staff was smaller than Dressner's—altogether there were only four people working—but most of the procedures in Bac-T did not require the same time-consuming, intricate procedures or constant monitoring. One member, though basically perfectly competent, tended to provide comic relief—a pudgy, very tense medical student by the name of Mickey Kirkland from the University of Illinois; he was twenty-four but looked more like seventeen, with straggly orange-reddish hair, remarkably thick glasses and a red polka dot bow tie. As the group passed his station he was washing Petri dishes and, startled by the group's attentions, moved abruptly and splashed suds on Dr. Ryan's coat and vest. Going for a towel, he then knocked over a container of stool. Dressner quickly led Ryan to the door, murder in his heart for one Mickey Kirkland. He also gave Blackwell a pained, inquiring look.

Stecker's lab was the last stop. For the past hour the pharmacologist, working alone, had been trying to assay for insecticides. Despite the use of a cookbook toxicology manual, his experiments were all frustrating failures. Ryan, after reviewing the procedure, offered a few suggestions he felt might improve the sensitivity of the test. Stecker, grim-faced, said thanks, he'd try them.

When Ryan and Dressner left to return to Toxicology, Ryan asked if by chance anyone had checked Kramer for radioactivity. In fact, that possibility had not been considered but . . . The two doctors immediately changed directions.

Chapter IX

Gino's was located just off Michigan Avenue about a half mile from Pat's apartment. With the rain stopped, they decided to walk it. Thornton had three hours before he had to be back in the studio. Wisps of steam formed whenever they spoke. The air had a damp chill, and there were puddles everywhere, glistening with the reflections of street lights. The neighborhood was quiet, and in between the sound of their own footsteps they could hear the distant splashes of passing cars. For once the old buildings had a clean look, the lantern lights making them sparkle.

It was unusual for this part of Chicago to be so peaceful, and as they approached Rush Street life did change dramatically. It was Friday night, singles' night, and hundreds with false I.D.'s flooded the area. As one band would take a break, everyone would rush for the exit and head for another discotheque with live music. Throughout the night there was an endless parade up and down both sides of this particular neon jungle—paupers dressed like kings in mod, bankers dressed up—or down—to look like debtors. People sat by the hour looking on from sidewalk cafés at the moving exhibitions, while those in the parade found delight in staring back at the starers. Pickpockets, dope peddlers, prostitutes and drunks mingled easily with the crowd.

Males outnumbered females by some five to one, many, of course, looking for pick-ups, but even more standing around the edge of the dance floor, watching, juking by themselves. For the frustrated and horny there were the strip houses—the one that attracted the most attention, even created traffic jams, projected the dancers' silhouette in the front windows. Most of the girls who came down Rush Street seemed to fall into three categories: the plain but faithful regulars who traveled long distances only to stand around night after night; the snobs, who never could find anyone good enough; and the "tourists," the one-shots who ventured out to look and see—their clothes were conservative, their dancing styles about a year behind and they never, well hardly ever, had more than one drink a night.

Division Street, running perpendicular to Rush, belonged to stewardesses, pilots and determinedly swinging young executives. They had their own games. Their cellar bars featured cool jazz and occasionally one of the clubs booked country music. Interspersed were some of the best restaurants in town and a couple of avant-garde movie theaters. Togetherness was a keynote—even those who had to do their own wash could shoot pool in the same laundromat. . . .

The evening's crowds had not yet quite formed as Pat and Thornton made their way down Rush. Near the end of the short slanted street they cut over to Michigan Avenue and made their way to the restaurant past a row of expensive boutiques and jewelry shops. Gino's was already busy, but they were still able to find a quiet, candle-lit booth near the back.

The good life, for some, went on.

At 7:45, the President's jet set down at Andrews Air Force Base. During the transatlantic flight he had used the special communications center on board to keep in contact with Kramer and had called Dr. Nissen twice in the last hour, but the information which he had received thus far was disappointing and confusing. The only fact that clearly stood out was that the vice-presidential candidate's condition had definitely begun to deteriorate.

Even so, no one at this point expected Kramer to die—at least no one admitted as much in public. Nonetheless, a select group of top Washington officials was secretly preparing for the eventuality, just in case. A list of alternative candidates had already been formulated and was waiting for the Chief Executive to choose from, while some were actually debating the propriety of burial at Arlington Cemetery with full military honors. Some of the big metropolitan newspapers and the TV networks were already pulling their obit files and preparing backgrounders for the morning, just in case. At the Justice Department prosecuting attorneys were being selected, and the procedures set forth for a prompt trial of the individual or individuals responsible, when and if caught. . . .

Leaders from both political parties and three Cabinet members were waiting in the cold night air as the plane taxied across a long runway and finally stopped next to the military V.I.P. terminal.

The President appeared to be tired as he descended the boarding ramp, recognizing the anguish on familiar faces and the absence of the usual exuberant entourage, military band with color guard and noisy Washington residents who always seemed to know when he would be arriving. The time lag from Europe had placed his body mechanics six hours ahead of everyone else's but there were too many problems to allow much time for sleep.

The President was a very short, almost frail man, the second shortest President in history at five foot five; in his middle sixties, his hair was a wavy gray. Thick glasses perched on coarse features–altogether a far cry from the Kennedy charisma of the sixties. He had been in politics for over thirty years, having served two terms as Governor of Pennsylvania and three years as Secretary of Health, Education and Welfare. This was the first time that he had ever paid more than passing attention to a threatening note. In the past they were considered a fact of political life and readily found their way to the circular files. He almost considered Kramer as part of his personal family and debated continuing the air flight to Chicago, which his advisors finally talked him out of.

111

An Air Force helicopter was waiting nearby and after a few routinely cordial greetings, the Presidential party climbed on board and headed back toward the White House. En route the President's advisors attempted to distract him with jokes, talk of the misfortunes of the opposition and the building position of his own campaign. He heard none of it, unable to keep his thoughts from Kramer, the apparent poisoning, and the bizarre trade seemingly demanded by "Aunt Dotie." Kramer had told him not to worry —that the doctors would dope it all out. Dr. Nissen had sounded less reassuring. . . .

At Presbyterian, Homicide Captain Rondowski was completing his calls to the wardens at the five state penitentiaries. Each was aware of the State Street assault and subsequent twenty-four hour threat, but none had heard anything about a proposed trade for prisoners. That part came as a surprise, and each warden immediately promised to help. Plans were formulated to isolate the men for interrogation, through the night if necessary, to confiscate all personal belongings and to forward a list of all visitors in the last six months for FBI checks.

Both Lawson, the religious killer, and Madison, the black militant, were in their separate cells at Joliet prison when the call came. Lawson had been an ideal prisoner, excluding several attempts to proselytize the guards and numerous prisoners in his cell block. He was always cooperative and pleasant, and no one on meeting him would have guessed that he was capable of nine brutal murders. In the previous six-month period there had only been two recorded visits, both by his mother.

Madison, on the other hand, had seen several different visitors in the short time of his incarceration, and several could not be traced. He was considered a troublemaker, trying to promote prison revolt and constantly arguing with prison personnel. He had boasted to several inmates that he would not be in prison long.

When the two were confronted by the warden, both appeared confused by his accusations—a fishing expedition, actually—and denied having anything to do with the Kramer assault. . . .

When Captain Rondowski's call went to Attica, Warden McCabe was still working in his office. A few minutes later Giovanni, the ex-mobster, was pulled from the prison movie and taken directly to solitary confinement for questioning. He also denied any knowledge of the attack, but was pleased to hear that he might be released in the morning. During his interrogation he seemed conspicuously calm. In his cell they found several old letters from his son, two paperback detective novels and a recent issue of *Playboy*. His list of visitors was extensive and included several known syndicate members. . . .

Millitz, the kidnapper, was in the prison library at San Quentin when summoned, deep in medical texts, all opened to the toxicology section. He said that he had heard about the attack on Kramer and the speculation about poisoning over the radio and was researching the possibilities. When he was told about the proposed trade, he too seemed surprised. His prison record was clean, no problems and no visitors. His only friend was a Frank Meanor, another schizophrenic, who had been released two months before and was on probation. . . .

Dr. Weisberg was working in the infirmary when Warden Jacovitz called for him. Although the State of Florida had revoked his license, the prison took advantage of his training. When confronted with his possible involvement, he broke into near-uncontrollable laughter. Except for a recent letter from his lawyer and a Herman Wouk novel—*City Boy*—his cell was empty. In the infirmary, however, they did find two toxicology manuals and a handbook on poisoning. Weisberg said that they were routine medical texts and, to his knowledge, had never been used —certainly not by him. His list of visitors was small. His lawyer had come twice and Dr. Whiley, his best man at his wedding, once. When Warden Jacovitz tried calling Whiley, an answering

113

service reported that the doctor was on a weekend fishing trip in the Florida Keys. . . .

Akubar was the only prisoner who openly enjoyed the news and, like Giovanni, was ready to start packing. He denied any knowledge of the plot, but hinted that the perpetrators might be friends. He even requested that when the time came that he be taken to Yemen. There were no visitors, but the guards at Soledad Prison did find two letters in Arabic. Translators were immediately called for—a scarce item on a Friday evening in Oakland, California, its scholarly environs, or, for that matter, anywhere else in the country.

Finding a usable Geiger counter did not turn out to be as easy as Dressner had hoped once Ryan raised the question of testing Kramer for radioactivity. Despite the fact that radioactive accidents were beginning to be reported across the country and nuclear war had loomed as a threat for almost three decades, the cigar box-shaped detector was not carried as a standard piece of emergency equipment. In the end they found it necessary to borrow a special key from the security office and search the nuclear medicine department, which was always locked in the evenings. Once they located a new counter, they had to check its sensitivity and calibration against several different medical isotopes that were stored in a large lead-lined cabinet. Finally, satisfied with its performance, they quickly proceeded upstairs.

When they entered Kramer's room, the Secretary appeared to be somewhat confused, thinking that he was back in his own bedroom. A nurse was standing next to him and taking his 8:00 vitals as his personal physician, Fitzgerald, sat in a nearby chair, quietly watching. Without saying a word Ryan switched on the counter and began scanning Kramer's body, concentrating first on the bandaged wound site. There was a small detectable flicker, but it barely exceeded background activity and could not be considered abnormal. The same pattern persisted throughout. What had seemed a good idea turned out to be a dismal failure, and Ryan and Dressner left to return the borrowed equipment. As they did so, Kramer rather grandly thanked them for coming and asked them to check in with him in the morning . . . a comment that struck everyone as rather peculiar. Until now they had continued to think of Kramer as essentially lucid and oriented, but unmistakably bizarre behavior such as had troubled his son, together with disoriented remarks such as he had just made, strongly indicated that the poison was causing systemic effects. The nurse reported that his temperature had risen another two tenths of a degree and that his pulse was ranging around 108 beats per minute, neither of which was that severe, but his change in sensorium was troubling. When Fitzgerald got up to recheck him, he noticed that the arm had become so swollen that his ring would now have to be cut off and that the edge of the wound was changing to a dark brown color, as if it might be dying. The military physician arranged for another CBC to be drawn and ordered aspirin for the climbing fever. At 8:15 Kramer was moved to an operating room for Nissen's biopsy of the wound. He couldn't understand why they were taking him from his "bedroom" and appeared almost drunk.

Meanwhile the room directly across the hall from his suite was converted into an emergency supply room, stocked for every possible medical problem that the staff could conceive of. The usual complement of two beds was moved to the basement. In its place were several complicated machines, including an old iron lung with its huge metal capsule and tiny headrest at one end. Next to it was a new MA–I respirator. This was a much smaller apparatus, but equally effective if connected to a tube in his trachea. Across the panel were twelve dials to control the concentration of oxygen, its flow rate, the flow pressure, the volume, the respiratory rate and the number of sighs per minute. There were also several built-in alarms if any of the parameters were exceeded. The three large oxygen tanks were lined up against one wall.

In addition to the respirators was a dialysis machine, in case his kidneys began to fail. Its use was not expected but the precaution had to be taken. Cardiology had furnished three types of pacemakers—one of which was for emergency installation through the chest wall; the other two, more complicated, needed insertion through an arm vein under fluoroscopy. A staff cardiologist would be on call all night in case one of the pacemakers was needed.

Other precautions included a defibrillator, which was plugged in and ready to shock him if his heart began fluttering, and an electric cooling mattress for uncontrollably high fevers. The two closets were used to house several sterile surgical trays, chest tube equipment, endotracheal tubes, cut down trays, tracheotomy trays, spinal tap trays, Foley catheters and diagnostic equipment for liver and lung biopsies. There was a CVP line to monitor the right side of his heart and a Swan-Gans for the left side.

A crash cart of medications was also set up, including Lidocaine and Pronestyl for irregular heart rhythms, Digoxin for heart failures or certain rapid heart rates, atropine for life-threatening slow rates and possible insecticide poisoning, Isuprel and Levophed for low blood pressure, Apresoline and Arfonad for high pressures, adrenaline if his heart stopped completely, bronchodilators, clotting factors, albumin, plasma, thyroid extract, steroids for shock, antispasmodics and belladonna for stomach problems, narcotics for severe pain, thiosulfate for cyanide poisoning, Compazine for nausea and vomiting, and several types of intravenous electrolyte solutions for containing glucose, potassium, sodium and chloride for intravenous maintenance in case the patient couldn't eat.

An entire shelf of the refrigerator at the nursing station was needed to store the antibiotics. Occupying a second shelf were four types of antivenin, antitetanus serum, botulism antitoxin and diphtheria antitoxin, plus five units of whole blood. On a tray near the doorway were several labeled syringes, already loaded with emergency medications and some of the stronger analgesics. All seemed at the ready for . . . precisely *what*, of course, they still didn't know.

Pritchard sat through the videotape three times and then compared it with the still shots that had just arrived. At the time of the mysterious handshake, only the sleeve of the assailant's coat could be seen. It appeared to be dark gray and possibly wool. Unfortunately, when the Secretary began to fall he blocked part of the camera's view and only one of the photographs was worthwhile. Using a magnifying glass, Pritchard thought that he could make out the edge of the attacker's wrist. If it was skin that he was seeing, it definitely wasn't black. Frustrated, he began pacing the room, holding the photos in one hand and slapping them against the other. Woodsley, who was sitting behind Schaeffer's desk, lit another cigarette.

"It doesn't make sense," Pritchard began. "There's no way for this guy to know where the Secretary would get out of his car. It could have easily been the other side or up the street a block. It's almost as if Kramer had prearranged to meet him—"

"I can tell you *that* wasn't the case," Woodsley said, tossing his match to the floor. "You know, he might have been lucky, just happened to be in the right spot at the right time . . . there weren't specific plans for him to get out of the limousine at that time. . . . But what if there were several men waiting? Say, on each side and on every block. No matter where he stepped out, one of them would have gotten him—"

"I suppose that's possible, but there's another way . . . like the attempt on Wallace. Suppose this guy's been tracking him, waiting in every city as the Secretary traveled through and ready to move whenever and wherever the opportunity presented itself. . . . Yes, he'd be lucky, if you want to put it that way, but if he hadn't succeeded this time, it might well have been the next trip. . . ."

Woodsley wasn't ready to accept Pritchard's theory. "I still think the possibility of more than one person is good. That could also explain why the witnesses downtown can't agree."

"Perhaps. Meanwhile, I've brought film covering several of his last trips."

While Woodsley loaded the projector, Pritchard called Rondowski and Schaeffer. A few minutes later all four men were watching a panorama shot of Wilshire Boulevard in Los Angeles. It was a sunny day in September. As the Secretary stepped from his car, there were numerous outstretched hands. There were, however, no discernible attempts on his life or suspicious spectators.

They ran the film twice in slow motion before changing to the New York City clip. This time it was Fifth Avenue and the scene was pretty much the same. They studied every face possible; none seemed familiar or suspicious.

The third film clip was from a Boston appearance, and while the film was rolling Pritchard thought he finally had an idea that felt right. "What if there are ads in those papers?"

"What do you mean?" Rondowski said.

"If our man is in that crowd, then there ought to be ads in the local papers. Just like here. He'd have no way of knowing in advance when he would attack. . . . How late is the public library open?"

Rondowski quickly called to check. "Nine. We can get there in five minutes."

The two men left the room, leaving Woodsley and Schaeffer to review the remaining strips. Using the siren and red lights of a squad car, they sped out onto the Eisenhower Expressway.

More test results were coming in. Toxicology results were all negative, and there was no evidence of a coagulation or clotting problem. The new white count, however, indicated that an infection was brewing somewhere while the hemoglobin and hematocrit had fallen a few more points.

Hematology Laboratory
CBC
Time Drawn: 20:00

Test	Result	Normal Values
Hemoglobin	12.0	14-18 gm/100 ml
Hematocrit	36%	42-52 ml/100 ml
Red Cell Count	3.92 million	4.6-6.2 million/cu mm
White Cell Count	14,300	5-10,000/cu mm
neutrophils	79%	54-62%
bands	5%	0-5%
lymphocytes	16%	25-33%
monocytes	0%	3-7%
eosinophils	0%	1-3%
basophils	0%	0-1%
metamyelocytes	0%	0%
promyelocytes	0%	0%
MCV	92	82-92
MCH	30	27-31
MCHC	33	32-36
Platelets	250,000	2-300,000/cu mm
Sedimentation Rate	57	less than 15 mm/hr

Red cell morphology: some fragmented cells
Atypical lymphocytes: rare

Toxicology Laboratory
Screening
Time Drawn: 18:30

Cyanide	None detected
Nicotine	None detected
Aniline	Negative
Bromides	None detected
Typhoid	0
Brucella titer	0

Hematology Laboratory
Clotting Screen
Time Drawn: 18:30

Prothrombin time	100% of control
Partial thrombolplastin time	99% of control
Thrombin time	100% of control
Clot retraction	normal
Fibrinogen	normal titer

When Pritchard and Rondowski pulled up in front of the library, two elderly guards were asking patrons to leave and systematically turning off the lights. The librarian, a skinny gray-haired woman frightened by the siren, was frozen in her seat as the two men hurried inside. Her fantasies instantly conjured up a crime most heinous. Doubtless in the stacks.

Pritchard was first through the door. "Where do you keep your out of town newspapers?"

"Our newspapers?" Her fear changed to confusion.

"Yes, papers, where are they, please?" Rondowski showed his badge.

The librarian pointed to a dark room on her left, and as they began walking quickly away she asked, "Which paper? We don't keep all of them, you know."

Returning to her desk, Pritchard said, "Boston, New York, Los Angeles."

"Only the *New York Times*, besides our own local papers, of course. Unless you need something from the last few days, it would be on microfilm."

Pritchard took a small notebook from his pocket, thumbed through the first few pages. "Can you get us the *New York Times* for August 18th and 19th?"

It took her several minutes to locate the films, and while she was looking, the guards closed up the library. Both dates were recorded on the same strip and Rondowski and Pritchard immediately crowded in front of the small viewing box . . . scanning the classifieds. Finally . . . on August 19th . . . there was the ad for Aunt Dotie and her six friends.

Precisely as it had read in the *Chicago Tribune*.

Chapter X

At 9:00 the Secretary's temperature was measured at 101.4, up nearly half a degree despite the aspirin; his pulse and blood pressure remained unchanged. He was becoming increasingly annoyed with the hourly checks, but Fitzgerald refused to change the standing orders. The biopsy was done by Nissen under local anesthesia and had required about twenty minutes. Afterward the specimens were sent to the pathology laboratory for frozen and permanent sections, to the electron microscope laboratory, and to bacteriology for further cultures.

At approximately the same time, the story about the proposed trade broke over the national wire services. Reporters at the *Chicago Tribune* claimed they'd managed to decipher the cryptic advertisement . . . apparently the eager-beaver reporter had finally convinced his colleagues he was really on to something.

At exactly 9:03, the hospital's page operator announced that there was an outside telephone call for Dr. Nissen. The surgeon had just left an operating suite, where one of his junior residents had requested his assistance on a motorcycle-accident victim. The teen-ager had ripped open his abdominal cavity on the handle bars and had arrived in shock, his intestines hanging on the stretcher, blood coming from his mouth, nose, ears and the back of his head.

Nissen returned to the dressing room and dialed the operator, who, in turn, made the appropriate connection.

"Dr. Nissen? This is Dr. Waxman. I got your message . . ." The voice on the other end sounded weary.

"Dr. Waxman, thank you for getting back so quickly. . . . I assume you've heard about Secretary Kramer—"

"Yes, of course . . ."

"I'm sure you must be tired from your lecture tour but we really could use your expert help. Dr. Mellow's in Central America and Larson's just had a heart attack . . . I really don't know who else to call—"

"I don't quite understand . . . I thought it was only a small laceration. Surely you don't need me for that?"

"No . . . but we're quite certain the Secretary wasn't just stabbed—more likely he was clumsily injected with some poison . . . I realize this may sound farfetched . . . it's in the paper already. It appears we're being offered an antidote in exchange for the release of six criminals—all murderers. . . ."

"My God. . . . No, I hadn't heard that. . . . I guess I've been either in a plane or a lecture room . . . I'm not sure I can help you, I can barely keep my eyes open as it is. . . . How is the Secretary's condition?"

"Until an hour ago he seemed all right except for a low grade fever and pain, but now he's also becoming confused . . . It's very strange. . . . You know Lewis Ryan, I'm sure. Well, he's here now. It appears we only have until tomorrow morning to find the antidote ourselves. . . . Look, Dr. Waxman, I understand your being tired, but I can have someone come out and pick you up—"

"That won't be necessary . . . just give me a few minutes to freshen up. I'll take a taxi there."

At the Twelfth Street Precinct, Trudy Myers found a mug shot that resembled the man who knocked her over. When Mr. Britte was shown the same photograph he readily concurred, but two other witnesses were not as certain. The man's name was Woodrow Lee Thomas, and when his record was pulled they discovered that he had known George Madison in the fifties. Both men were revolutionaries, and both had once belonged to a South Side Chicago street gang known as the Egyptian Cobras. Since then, Thomas had served several short sentences for burglary and one for assault. Thomas' home address was Ashland Avenue, not from from Presbyterian-St. Luke's Hospital. Three squad cars were immediately dispatched to his house, while four other teams were put on back-up. It obviously was critical that he be taken alive.

As police cars drove south on Ashland Avenue, Pritchard was returning from the library, pleased with the new-found proof of previous advertisements. He felt that it gave him a better perspective on the case, confirming his notion that one man—not several—had been tracking Kramer and finally had found conditions right for making his move against him. When he arrived at the hospital there was a message from the warden at San Quentin informing him that Frank Meanor, the scholarly Millitz's friend, had jumped probation and was reported to be hiding out in the Chicago area. An immediate APB was put out with his description.

Gino's restaurant was known for thick pizza, more like a pie with an open top, altogether too clumsy to eat without a fork. As Thornton was cutting into the last piece and listening to Pat's account of early innocent parochial school days back in Indiana, an ancient two story boarding house on Ashland Avenue was quietly being surrounded: two blue and white squad cars parked a block

123

away from Lee Thomas' building. A third turned off its headlights and slowly cruised to a halt in the back alley amidst several overflowing dented garbage cans and pieces of broken furniture. They in turn waited for back-up teams to get into position. No one knew if Thomas was home, but most of the rooms were lit and a blue light from a television set on the first floor could be seen from the street. There was only one other car parked in the alley; its closed, steamed windows obscured the presence of police to the lovers inside. Otherwise, the street was quiet. . . .

Thomas was in his room, flat on his back, snoring, very drunk. He was fully clothed, and wearing a Windbreaker; a half-empty bottle of whiskey lay at his fingertips, about to topple over. Just below his window two police officers were stepping onto the building's wooden porch. . . .

The waiter brought two cups of espresso, momentarily interrupting Pat's ongoing story of her life and times in Chicago. Things had been fairly rough since she'd arrived—as she suspected they were for most girls not so different from herself. First there was finding a place to live, even knowing which neighborhood to look in. She'd hoped to find a small apartment that would be close enough to the mainstream of Chicago life and still quiet enough for privacy—a sort of decompression chamber between small town and big city. For a while she used a girls' dormitory as home base—almost immediately most of her best clothes and jewelry were stolen. When she did manage to find a place near Old Towne and had signed a lease, she promptly discovered that the plumbing was in chronic breakdown, the walls were apparently made of paper, and the swingers on the other side possessed a stamina as difficult to believe as its noisy accompaniment was to tune out. The lease was for two years, and it took nearly that much of her savings to hire a lawyer to get her out of it. After her second move, the old Ford she'd used all through college decided to stop running, and she couldn't possibly afford the cost of repairs. Since then, while using the subway, she'd twice encountered exhibitionists—one male, one female—a kind of equality she would have been pleased to have pass her by. . . .

One police officer knocked on the front door while another stood to the side, his hand hovering near his revolver. A near-toothless man, faintly jaundiced from years of drinking, answered the door. He said yes, Thomas lived there but no, he didn't know if Thomas was in his room or not. He pointed in the direction of the stairwell. As the two officers started climbing the creaky wooden steps, several boarders suddenly appeared at the front entrance and moved across the street, putting distance between themselves and trouble; it seemed an almost routine drill for them.

One of the officers knocked on Thomas' door. There was no response. After trying a second time, he announced that they were the police and demanded Thomas open up.

Again, silence. The officer tried turning the door knob. It was locked. Using the heel of his boot, he kicked the door open and the two men swung into the tiny room with their guns drawn. Thomas looked up for a moment, muttered something unintelligible and immediately fell back to sleep. . . .

Once Thornton had paid the check at the table, he and Pat began to walk back toward his car. It was important that he be at the studio by 9:30 to review the late news and practice timing for film cut-ins and station breaks. He invited Pat to come along and she seemed pleased to accept. Moments later they were hurrying through long lines outside several discotheques and in and out of traffic jams made worse by latecomers and tourists all hunting for nonexistent parking places. The sky was still cloudy and there was a fluffy haze around the moon. . . .

At about this same time a yellow taxicab squeezed through a different crowd outside Presbyterian Hospital and came to a halt next to a small gap between two large television vans. Sitting quietly in the corner of the back seat was Dr. Louis Waxman, fifty-seven, silver gray hair combed far to one side, piercing blue eyes staring at the security force surrounding the hospital. The guards had already been told he would be coming and were instructed to accompany him to Dr. Nissen's office as soon as he arrived.

The nervous clamor inside the lobby diminished slightly as Waxman was led to the elevators, but once the doors closed the noise returned with a new note of curiosity about the identity of the latest VIP. Although not a political figure, Waxman was soon identified and word spread via UPI and AP wire services that a Dr. Louis Waxman had been called in on the case. No one was exactly sure why, but knowledgeable theories quickly began making their way around the room. One of the reporters whose specialty was the medicine-and-science beat was aware he'd recently won the Ernest Heinemann Award in ecology for demonstrating how certain species of bacteria could be used to destroy a variety of industrial poisons in polluted waterways. None of the "backgrounders" included the information that he had been called in on previous government cases requiring medical detective work.

Nissen was sitting in his office when Waxman came in, and it was easy to see that the surgeon was pleased to see him. The strains of the day were momentarily erased from Nissen's face as he helped the professor with his trench coat and then offered him a cup of coffee. Waxman politely declined and quietly sat down in a chair opposite the desk. Nissen quickly poured himself a cup and began updating the professor. As he spoke he seemed to become more nervous, his speech more hurried. Waxman listened attentively, without interruption. Once certain Nissen had finished, he began his questions as though from notes. His tone was soft, his mannerisms mild. He did not seem perturbed that Nissen couldn't give answers to all his questions.

Occasionally Waxman would stop for a few moments, squint his left eye appraisingly and then switch to a completely different point, not allowing himself to be rushed and thereby extracting considerably more information than Nissen had imagined relevant. His questions were mostly medical in nature but tccasionally he would digress to the police activities and whatever additional information they could offer. A thorough man, Nissen thought. His thoroughness and total absence of any appearance of panic or alarm such as Nissen himself was beginning to feel helped put Nissen at ease; the surgeon was soon convinced he'd made a good choice in calling on Waxman's help.

Nissen now handed him the complicated flow sheet, pointing out the poisons that had already been eliminated and others presently being worked on. Again Waxman was calm as he scrutinized the large chart that appeared more like a maze of twisted arrows, rectangular boxes and lists of exotic names.

Waxman examined each step, agreeing for the most part, but shaking his head negatively on several occasions and twice putting large check marks in the margin. Nissen sat back in his chair with the coffee cup in his hands, watching every movement, anxiously waiting for Waxman's opinion. At the end, Waxman did not seem too pleased and told Nissen outright that he felt they might be wasting precious time on tests that would take too long and at best offer ambiguous results. Large groups of toxins could easily be eliminated, he said, with a variety of fairly simple laboratory tests, and if any group was positive they would only have to concentrate on that one particular area.

Chemistry hardly being his specialty, Nissen felt ill at ease trying to explain or defend a protocol designed by others more knowledgeable in the field than he. He interrupted Waxman and suggested that he introduce him to Dressner and Ryan, who he said were better qualified than he to discuss the details. Realizing that

127

he apparently had put Nissen on the defensive, Waxman quickly apologized and agreed that Nissen's suggestion was a good one. Before going to the laboratory, however, he wanted to see Kramer. When they arrived on the fourth floor it was just past 10:00 and the night nurses were recording Kramer's newest vital signs. His temperature had climbed to 101.6, his pulse was racing at 110 beats per minute and his blood pressure was 134 over 88. The graph measuring all three parameters, each in a different color, was beginning to show a worrisome upward slant. In addition, one of the nurses reported that Kramer's behaviour was irrational, that he'd been shouting at them every time they came in the room.

The preliminary report on the frozen section was lying face down on the nursing desk, waiting to be added to Kramer's burgeoning chart. The typewritten note on the opposite side was brief and offered little more than they already knew:

> Specimen taken from wrist wound had a large amount of inflammatory tissue, mostly polymorphonuclear cells and a few mononuclear cells. The area at the edge of the wound appears to be dying. There are some unidentified crystals within the subcutaneous tissue, but I believe that they are probably glass. The biopsy can only be interpreted as consistent with a marked inflammatory reaction. Further delineation must await permanent sections.

Before the two men entered the Secretary's room, Waxman insisted on examining the emergency equipment stockpiled in the room next door. While Nissen stood outside the doorway talking with one of the nurses, the professor spent several minutes checking each instrument, making sure that each was functional and rummaging through the various drugs that had been set aside. He seemed to pay particular attention to a group of preloaded syringes and when he came out he commented on the danger of leaving medications about in the open.

When they finally entered Kramer's suite they found the Secretary in an extremely irritable mood and arguing with Dr. Fitzgerald, who was trying to calm him down. His headache had worsened and the blurred vision that it caused was making him nauseated. Nissen's enthusiastic introduction of Waxman met with bare acknowledgement and the conversation quickly reverted to Kramer's complaints. He was now demanding relief from his pain, and when Nissen tried explaining that the use of narcotics might obscure other symptoms and thereby hamper their research for the actual cause of the trouble, he didn't seem to understand. Nissen promised to use stronger analgesics later, but Kramer began hollering, accusing both Fitzgerald and him of quackery and gross incompetence.

Nissen inwardly bridled at his outburst—after all, they were doing everything possible—but he quickly reminded himself that the Secretary could not be held responsible for what he was saying. Once Kramer had quieted again Nissen stepped aside to give Waxman a chance to examine the wound. The professor hesitated, saying that he was afraid he might set off another tirade. Nissen shrugged his shoulders, as if to say there was nothing they could do about that, but when Waxman came closer and began asking a few simple questions the Secretary actually began screaming. As Waxman gingerly started to unravel the bandages Kramer swung his good arm across and knocked the professor back and away from his bed.

At 10:10 Pritchard received an answer from one of the night editors of the *New York Times*. Although he was aware of the proposed trade his paper hadn't yet gone to press and he tried using the request to get further information to embellish the *Times* story. After some meaningless responses to his fishing, the reporter told Pritchard that the Aunt Dotie advertisement had run a full three days in their personal columns. He also added that the exact amount was paid anonymously by mail via a money order drawn at a Fifth Avenue currency exchange. Since this was the second money order from Manhattan, Pritchard now suspected that New York City might be the assailant's home base. This also supported his thesis that the Chicago attack followed several previous attempts in other cities—ones that had failed to provide the opportunity for the confrontation and assault that the Chicago appearance on State Street had.

Dressner and Ryan were busy working at one of the larger workbenches when Nissen brought Waxman into the toxicology laboratory. Ryan was the first to see them approaching and after pouring the contents of a test tube into a small flask he extended a friendly hand to a familiar face, and before Nissen could make any formal introductions Ryan proceeded to introduce the professor to Dressner as if he and Waxman were old friends.

Ryan's and Waxman's acquaintance dated back almost three decades, having begun at an army base in San Antonio in the early 1940's, but—with the exception of those six weeks of special indoctrination for M.D.'s and occasional games of chess—they were not what one would call close friends. In fact, there had been disagreements over the years when they had shared podiums at international seminars. Each was familiar with the other's research work, and both had published conflicting articles on similar topics.

As Ryan started reminiscing with the other doctors about old army days during World War II, Waxman's own thoughts went back to the same period, except his impressions were somewhat more mixed, and in particular were focused on an incident in Germany evoked by the present doctor's dilemma with Kramer. As a recent graduate of Harvard Medical School and a newcomer to the combat zone, he had belonged to a mobile medical team a few miles behind the lines, generally just far enough back to be out of gunfire range but close enough to receive the wounded within minutes of the time they were hit.

130

Altogether there were five physicians in his team, four of whom were surgeons eager to practice their trade. Waxman didn't share their enthusiam. He was the only GMO (General Medical Officer) assigned to everything and anything that didn't require a sharp blade or catgut suture. His typical cases were foot infections, flu and combat fatigue. Nonetheless, when things got rough and the wounded backed up, he was called on to assist in surgery, a chore he had no stomach for, not to mention the strong back required of a surgeon—his being congenitally weak.

As his battalion moved acrosss southern France and into Germany, the fighting became fiercer and Waxman began finding himself in the operating room with increasing frequency. His medical team tried working in shifts, but the enemy's time clock rarely cooperated. Even during a lull there was a booby trap victim with a torn and shredded leg or a sniper's bullet drilled into some teen-ager's skull. . . . Thirty hours without sleep became commonplace. The only chance for rest seemed to come when the team broke camp and started traveling, but invariably the emergencies would start lining up before the tents could be unfolded again. Whenever possible, they made use of captured villages, piling dead and dying soldiers on the tops of wooden tables in deserted restaurants or along benches in bombed-out train stations.

Waxman's previous life had been a fairly protected one, and his brief medical experience had been pretty much of the "white smock" variety. No clean whites now, nor, in many instances, minimal sterile techniques. The bleeding had to be stopped, even if it took a dirty hand thrust into a gushing abdominal injury, or major chest surgery on the grass outside of the operating tent when the only tables inside happened to be occupied.

During the first few months Waxman existed in pretty much a constant state of dismay and dread—suffering more than was practical or medically acceptable at the sight of still another teenager wounded or dead. On some days stretchers with crying bodies arrived by the truckload, and during the relative quiet of the night, he could still hear their crying, their screaming.

Two months before Germany surrendered and the fighting began to slacken, he saw how suffering was hardly the exclusive condition of the soldiers in uniform. An occasional civilian casualty straggling into camp for help or an orphan stealing from the garbage or begging for food had been customary, but now he saw the homeless by the thousands and the massive starvation that followed the war. The horrors were compounded when the battalion commander called his team up front to help clean up a concentration camp. The mutilated and cachectic bodies were all that—more than—his stomach could handle.

It was a few days after the concentration camp duty that Waxman had his first opportunity to make use of his special aptitude and training. During the previous night a corporal had been brought into camp complaining of blurred vision and was found to have a low-grade fever also. One of the surgeons still awake happened to see the case and readily diagnosed his symptoms as the flu, sending him back to his outfit. Eight hours later the corporal was found dead in his tent and two of his buddies began complaining of similar symptoms.

This time Waxman was called in for an opinion; he decided to keep the two men under observation. As the day progressed their symptoms worsened, and by evening one of them couldn't swallow water, regurgitating most of it back up through his nose and almost choking to death. Waxman had both soldiers transferred to a military hospital and set out on some detective work of his own—without, of course, the luxury of texts for reference, but nonetheless with a compelling suspicion.

He borrowed a jeep and drove to the front lines, where he immediately began checking the food supplies. After four hours of intense searching he'd come up with nothing and was beginning to have serious doubts about his presumptive diagnosis of botulism. Meanwhile, sporadic skirmish fighting had broken out, and as he started to leave, one of the officers informed him that a fourth man had become ill. After a quick examination Waxman began questioning the soldier, almost as if he were a prosecuting attorney. It didn't take long to discover that the men had stolen some jarred fruits from a German cellar. Waxman quickly proceeded to gather up whatever jars remained and send them back to headquarters for testing. Two days later, a report confirmed that the jars were contaminated with botulism spores—

Waxman's thoughts returned abruptly to the present when Nissen interrupted Ryan's vocal reminiscing to remind him of the work at hand. Waxman added his agreement, then asked to review Kramer's flow sheet. As Nissen proceeded to leave, he suggested that somebody ought to introduce the professor to Blackwell and Stecker.

The Florida police were having trouble locating Weisberg's friend, Dr. Whiley. As it turned out, the motel he was supposed to be staying in had never heard of him; also, none of their new guests fitted his description. At about the same time, Chicago police were having no better luck finding Millitz's friend, Frank Meanor, although nearly every bar and halfway house in the city had been checked. . . .

Chapter XI

When Nissen arrived on the fifth floor, Fitzgerald was preparing to do a spinal tap on the Secretary. The persistent headache and accompanying bizarre behavior had him worried and he wanted to be certain that they weren't dealing with some type of meningitis or encephalitis. While one of the night nurses proceeded to set up the sterile lumbar puncture tray, a commercial product that came set up with all the necessary equipment, and two male aides were being paged to assist, Nissen pulled Fitzgerald outside and tried convincing his colleague that they should start broad spectrum antibiotics regardless of the spinal results.

"Up to two days' coverage is practically harmless," Nissen maintained, "and if we delay waiting for proof of necessity we might find ourselves treating him too late."

"There's no evidence that he needs antibiotics yet. Besides, I suspect that we're dealing with something that will not be sensitive," Fitzgerald said, accustomed to the surgical tendency to use antibiotics more freely than an internist would. "To use any of them without conclusive proof, in my mind, would not be advisable."

"But can we take the chance?" Nissen countered.

"I don't know . . ." Fitzgerald hesitated. "I just don't know."

"I don't either, but I think it's a necessary risk in this case . . ." Nissen, not wanting to initiate the step alone, hoped that Fitzgerald would agree.

"Which would you use? I wouldn't go to any that might be toxic to his kidneys, like gentamicin, not yet anyway . . ." Fitzgerald seemed to be changing his mind, worried that he might be wrong. "The old standbys, pen and strep, ought to suffice for now." Fitzgerald reluctantly agreed; for a moment he considered a different combination, but treating something wholly unknown gave him little grounds to argue on. He shrugged his shoulders and re-entered Kramer's room.

Nissen went directly to the nurse's desk and began writing up the new orders on Kramer's chart—one million units of penicillin every six hours by intravenous infusion, one gram of streptomycin every twelve hours intramuscularly . . . .

"How about it, doc?" Thomison, the campaign manager, had come up to him unnoticed.

"As well as can be expected," Nissen said, startled and giving the rather banal response without thinking. He then returned to the chart.

"When are you people going to find out what it is? He's been here almost nine hours and he looks a lot worse to me—"

"This has been a very difficult problem—"

"It can't be all that difficult. This hospital with all the doctors here and all of the blood you've been taking . . . How can it be that difficult? If he'd gone to Walter Reed—"

"This isn't Walter Reed, but I assure you, Walter Reed wouldn't be any further along than we are—"

"I wonder."

Nissen slammed the chart closed, glared at the campaign manager and quickly left the floor.

On the other side of the door Fitzgerald was instructing two husky aides on how to hold the Secretary for the spinal tap. He wanted him rolled up into a ball and kept still as possible to avoid breaking the needle or injuring part of his spine. Both men were accustomed to holding uncooperative children, but Kramer was considerably larger and undoubtedly stronger.

It took the three of them to roll the Secretary to his left side, amidst loud objections. Then one aide forced Kramer's head and neck downward while the other took a firm grip behind his knees and pulled them tightly up against his chest. Now they both leaned across his body with all of their weight, pinning him against the mattress.

Kramer threatened to kill everyone in the room once he got loose. His screams carried outside into the hallway, where his family and Thomison were waiting. They couldn't believe what they were hearing.

After putting on sterile gloves, Fitzgerald cleansed a large area over Kramer's lower spine with a red antiseptic solution, injected a local anesthetic that felt like a bee sting and at which the Secretary bitterly complained, and then, taking a three-inch-long needle, inserted its point through the skin and into an area between two adjacent vertebral spines. At first he hit solid bone, but after working his way down a few millimeters, the needle popped into the spinal canal. A crystal clear fluid began flowing out of the other end of the hollow needle. Fitzgerald quickly connected a manometer—a calibrated vertical tube—and measured the pressure as it rose in the transparent column. Next he collected four specimens of fluid and re-measured the pressure. On gross inspection everything appeared normal, but the specimens would have to go to the appropriate laboratories downstairs for confirmation.

After Lee Thomas, the black revolutionary and friend of the convict Madison, was driven downtown for questioning, his dingy room was thoroughly searched and searched again. Both mattresses were cut open, his pillows were ripped apart, dressers and closets were checked for possible hidden compartments and all of his papers were scrutinized. The most incriminating to be found were two loaded revolvers, several crumpled up girlie magazines and an even ounce of marijuana.

When he arrived at Twelfth Street he was still too drunk to be questioned. Even with two cups of black coffee forced down him, his speech remained slurred and his eyes refused to stay open. When he was placed behind a two-way mirror, four witnesses —including Trudy Myers—positively identified him as the man they saw running away.

They were all sent home as more black coffee was brought in.

By the time Nissen returned to the toxicology laboratory Waxman had already put into effect several of his notions, thereby noticeably adding enthusiasm to a group beginning to feel the drag of frustration and tedious work. The only suggestion that met with any resistance was his plan to deemphasize viruses as a possible cause—and Ryan was the lone objector.

"I think your notion of a viral cause would just take too long to prove out," Waxman said, leaning back against a cluttered desk with his arms folded across his chest. His tie was loosened and he was now wearing a standard long white laboratory coat. "It's also pretty unlikely that a criminal would have access to any viruses, and there are very few that could be fatal within twenty-four hours. I honestly think the time could be better spent—"

"Perhaps . . . very few, but there are *some* . . . you've just said as much." Ryan had a small stirring rod in his hand and was waving it as if to emphasize his point.

"Please be specific." Waxman responded as a teacher might to his pupil.

"Encephalitis. A high dose, not even a high dose. Or the famous Monkenberg virus—"

"And do you have a cure for these? An antidote if you do prove them? I don't."

The unexpected bluntness startled Ryan. He also knew that an antidote didn't exist for the examples he'd chosen, but couldn't accept overlooking any possibility. "What if it isn't a fatal virus," he finally said, "or something we can immunize for like smallpox or rabies? At lease we should be thorough, and if it turns out to be a virus we at least might be able to do something—"

"Thorough, yes. But smallpox? I don't think that is even remotely plausible . . ." It was obvious, however, that Ryan's feelings were strong. Not wanting to antagonize him further, Waxman finally agreed, though with some reluctance and repeating his reservations and also suggesting that Ryan at least work alone rather than tie up other technicians. Once the argument seemed to be slowing, Nissen interrupted to tell them that he had started Kramer on antibiotics. Waxman turned toward the surgeon with a questioning look, but before he could comment Ryan was again talking about the research work.

"What about your computer, the one at M.I.T.?" he asked.

"That was included in my plans, but not until we get things straight here." Waxman seemed distracted as he spoke, not fully attentive, still contemplating Nissen's decision to start antibiotics. Ryan was referring to a computer the professor had once helped program to aid in cases of accidental poisonings or overdoses and which now had an infectious disease memory bank.

"The problem," Waxman continued, "is that we don't have any history, very few symptoms and relatively few informative laboratory tests. The computer would have to be programmed somewhat differently to handle this situation . . . I'm not sure—"

Waxman stopped mid-sentence and began looking about for a telephone, which he finally spotted near the doorway. After. inquiring how to get an outside line he began a long series of numbers, but after a few seconds returned, saying that the line to M.I.T. was busy and that he would try his call again in ten minutes.

Thornton showed his pass to the night guard at the side entrance to WGN and drove to a back lot that was relatively empty. Although his time was short he detoured to give Pat a quickie look through the main offices and two of the larger taping studios. Everything was quiet except the newsroom, where the teletypes could be heard from down the hall. The Associated Press wire described the newly proposed trade and gave a background on each of the six prisoners, while UPI's story gave more emphasis to the poison itself. The latter also included in-depth interviews with several well known scientists across the country and some early congressional responses.

In the adjoining room technicians were busy splicing together a long tape of the actual assault and the day's events while another reporter was waiting to dub in his voice. A third was standing by at Presbyterian Hospital for a live interview with Captain Rondowski.

Thornton directed Pat to a nearby chair and began reviewing the planned commentary, editing each sheet for smooth delivery. The number of words used was important, and copies of the final sheets had to be made so that the crew could start the news tapes as he came to the last few words of each story.

At one minute before eleven, as Thornton took his seat in front of two TV cameras, a nurse was taking Kramer's vital signs again. This time his temperature was recorded at 102 degrees. Fitzgerald immediately doubled the aspirin dosage. Results from the spinal tap and more screening tests had come back—all normal or negative. The lack of white cells and the normal sugar value in the spinal fluid ruled out meningitis.

Hematology
Spinal Tap
Time Drawn: 20:20

Test	Result	Normal Value
red cells	0	0
white cells	0	0

Special Chemistry
Spinal Tap
Time Drawn: 20:20

Test	Result	Normal Value
sugar	47 mg	45-80 mg/100 ml
protein	44 mg	15-45 mg/100 ml

Bacteriology
Spinal Tap
Time Drawn: 20:20

Gram stain on specimen negative for bacteria.

Toxicology
Screening
Time Drawn: 18:30

No evidence of snake venom
No evidence of carbon tetrachloride

At eleven o'clock the red light came on. "Vice-presidential candidate Kramer's condition continues to worsen," he began, "while police and doctors at Presbyterian-St. Luke's Hospital remain baffled. Earlier today Kramer was stabbed with a mysterious weapon and is now believed to have been poisoned . . ."

Somewhere on the near North Side a man turned on his television set and watched with an unusual amount of interest. . . .

At the same time, Waxman was connecting with the physician in charge of the laboratory at M.I.T., and arranging to have a half pint of Kramer's blood flown to Boston to be analyzed by the computer. . . .

". . . Fred Kenny is waiting in the lobby at Presbyterian with an on-the-spot report. I understand that he has Captain Rondowski of Homicide with him.''

''Yes, Roger, as you can see by the turmoil behind me . . .''

The studio cameras were turned off as a technician scampered to the podium with a cup of coffee for Thornton. The sportscaster took advantage of his off-camera time to light up an unfiltered cigarette, making use of an ashtray hidden beneath the counter . . . and on the opposite end of things, the viewer turned up the volume and moved his chair a little closer to the set. . . .

''First of all, Captain Rondowski, what is Mr. Kramer's condition now?''

''I'm told he appears to be in good spirits. A little tired from the strain, but doing as well as can be expected.''

''We understand that you have a suspect down at headquarters. Can you tell us anything about him?''

''Yes, but I should emphasize that he is *only* a suspect at this time—''

''Then you still don't know what the poison is?''

''No, but the doctors assure us that they're close. As you probably know, Dr. Ryan from the National Institute of Health and Dr. Louis Waxman from Columbia University are here now and heading up the research.''

''If that's the case, then I gather that there *won't* be any trade for the antidote?''

''I can't say at this moment—''

The viewer burst out laughing.

After five cups of black coffee Thomas finally began to come around. Richard Cantfield, a tough, aggressive FBI agent, was in charge of the interrogation. With him were two officers from Homicide.

''Okay, Thomas, we're going to try again. Where were you at noon today?'' Cantfield's face was getting red; he'd already asked the same question six times before.

141

"Oh man, what do you want with me . . . I ain't done nothin'
 . . ." Thomas' eyes were still glazed, and his responses were still
slow in coming.

"You were downtown today when Secretary Kramer was attacked. We've got witnesses who say that they saw you—"

"I ain't been anywhere near your lousy Secretary—"

"What about Madison?" one of the other officers asked.

Thomas ignored the question, pulling a crumpled cigarette from
his shirt pocket—he almost lit the filter end.

"What about Madison, George Madison?" The investigator
repeated his question.

"Who?"

"Don't give me 'Who?' We know you two guys were tight
 . . ."

As the interrogation went on, several messages were reaching
Inspector Pritchard: Giovanni's son, located in a nightclub in
Hartford, Connecticut, denied any knowledge at all about the
assault and said he was sure that somebody else was using his
father—just how, he couldn't say. The Arabic letters found in
Akubar's cell were translated—one included a promise from a
friend to help him escape. The Department of Biological Warfare
responded that none of their papers or research items were
missing. . . .

"Now, where were you at noon?" Cantfield persisted with
Thomas.

"Balling."

"What's her name?"

"Sherry."

"Sherry who?"

"I never knew her who." Thomas began laughing. "Sherry
who . . . Who's on Sherry . . . Hey, reminds me of that old
Abbott and Costello routine . . . Who's on first . . . Who's who?
You know what I mean? . . ."

"Look, Thomas, we're about to book you for attempted murder.

Murder of a United States Cabinet member, a vice-presidential candidate. . . . They'll hang you by your comedian's balls if he dies—"

"Sherry who . . . that's really great." Thomas shook his head, still laughing, as cigarette ashes fell in his lap unnoticed.

"Okay, book him." Cantfield turned to one of the officers standing near the door.

"Wait, man, just *wait* . . . Take 'er easy." Thomas' smile was finally gone. "All right, sure, I was there . . . I'd been jus' sort of browsin' through the area, diggin' the stores and the action, it's a free country, right? . . . Then I heard all the noise from this big crowd over on State Street and I just come over to see what was what . . . just like any other curious citizen. . . . Anyway, when I get there I see this crazy dude grab the man, doin' something with his arm, and then he split. Knowin' my record and not knowin' what was goin' down, I split when he did, you know what I mean? I wasn't about to be on the scene when you guys started the questions. Hey, you should have seen that dude move. I think he thought I was runnin' after him. I just wanted to get away myself, you know what I mean? Figured I was in the back and good chance nobody saw me . . ."

"You expect us to believe that?" Cantfield stood in front of Thomas and stared into his face.

"Look, I don't expect nothin', but believe it or not, I'm tellin' you . . . no way, man . . . I don't want to kill no one . . . I don't even want to shake his hand—"

Cantfield leaned in. "How do you know he shook his hand?"

"I told you, I seen him do it. Besides, I heard it on the radio all day." Thomas' eyes squinted from the light as he looked up at Cantfield.

"All right, tell us what this man looked like, what he was wearing."

"He was a honky . . . *white.*"

"What did he look like? What was he wearing?"

143

"He was oldish, long coat, I never seen the dude before. He got off the subway right by the hospital. Man, you should have seen him move." Thomas was smiling again.

"If you saw a picture, would you recognize him?"

"Who knows?" He almost smiled again.

It was at least worth a try. Cantfield told the other officers to take the suspect to the eleven volumes of mug shots.

Over half of the thirty-minute news broadcast went to the Secretary's story. Sports, weather and happy talk took another ten. Thornton barely had time to cover any of the other local happenings and had to use the last ninety seconds for an editorial on the irony of diminishing oil reserves and the American eight-cylinder way of life.

As the late movie with Pat O'Brien and Randolph Scott began, Thornton gathered his notes together and stepped from the small podium. Pat was waiting on the other side of the cameras, and as the two left the studio he got the idea of reviewing whatever old films WGN had on file that might include the six prisoners. He offered to take Pat home first. She told him she was in for the duration.

The archives were located in the basement, where only one clerk worked during the daytime. It was a long corridor-like room, poorly ventilated. The walls were lined with rows of film and videotape, each with a date and special code number. Next to the clerk's desk was a large filing cabinet with a complicated system of cross references by dates, names, events and subjects. As Thornton began quickly thumbing through the drawers, Pat recorded the code numbers he gave her.

It looked like a long night.

VITAL SIGNS

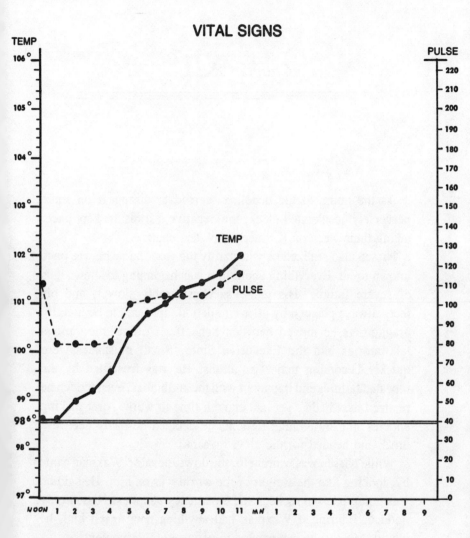

	160	136	140	140	140	136	142	120	152	152	134	130	BLOOD
	90	80	80	80	80	76	78	80	78	78	88	74	PRESSURE

PATIENT'S NAME: A. KRAMER
I. D. No.: A3-15647

145

Chapter XII

As the hours to the deadline seemed to disappear on some perversely accelerated clock, the negative test results kept pace, taking their place on Kramer's crowded chart.

Nissen also realized he was hardly the work horse he was once known to be. Everything about him was beginning to show signs of severe fatigue. His gait was considerably slower, and his feet, always plagued by poor circulation, appeared to be literally dragging as he moved between Schaeffer's office, the various laboratories and the Executive Suite. Small nuisances were quickly becoming major irritations. He was frustrated by the repeated failures and impatient with the antibiotics, even though he realized they hadn't yet had enough time to work. After making another stop by Kramer's room, he decided he badly needed a break and headed for the elevator bank.

While Nissen was waiting for the down elevator, Waxman came by, looking like the weight of the world was on him. He said he was going back to recheck the emergency supplies. Nissen only nodded, figuring if Waxman had anything new to tell him, he would. Mostly, he just wanted to get away for a moment. . . .

The elevator seemed to stop at every floor, adding to his aggravation. Once on the main floor, ignoring the lingering crowd of reporters, he proceeded directly to the coffee shop, pushed through the double glass door, got himself a pineapple Danish (left over from the morning and also showing some of the day's strain) and poured himself the largest cup of black coffee he could find.

Noticing Captain Rondowski sitting alone near the back, and realizing that Rondowski had seen him as well, he wandered over to join him.

"You look beat, doc." The captain looked up from his half-eaten roast beef sandwich and cup of coffee.

"I am." Nissen pulled a chair around to the opposite side of the table to sit facing the police chief. "How's your suspect?"

"Almost sober. Says it was someone else. Couldn't explain the peculiar coincidence of being on the scene and also a buddy of one of the convicts named for the trade—if we're all reading that damned 'Aunt Dotie' message right. He tried to explain how he happened to be there. I can't say I believe him but we've got him looking at mug shots now. He says that he got a look at the guy. Well, we'll see."

"Whether he did it or not, that's the best news I've heard all night." Nissen broke a piece off his Danish and dunked the corner into his coffee cup.

"Whoever it is, I'd like to see him end up in the chair instead of some cushy cell for a few years—"

Nissen looked closely at him. And whoever it is, I hope they find him out before this night is over, Nissen thought to himself . . . The way things were going. . . . He didn't say as much to Rondowski, who appeared more worked up about the punishment than the crime. . . .

"In fact, we ought to have public executions for this kind of thing . . . like in the old days . . ." Rondowski went on, his voice rising and attracting attention from others in the coffee shop.

Nissen was definitely beginning to regret being polite and joining the chief. "I think I could do without 'the old days,' " Nissen said, dunking another corner of his Danish and remembering the public murders of his own family by the Nazis . . . without even a semblance of a trial. . . . This was hardly turning out to be the break Nissen still badly needed. He made motions to leave, but Rondowski was just heating up.

"Well, I understand your point, but when some creep rapes an

147

innocent child and leaves her to die in the alley, or climbs through a bedroom window at night to mutilate people for a few bucks or the hell of it because of some, like the shrinks say, overwhelming urge . . . Well, I say they don't deserve to be around. They don't deserve the first meal they get in prison, not one penny of the millions to teach them how to make license plates, for Christ sakes. Rehabilitation . . . A bad joke, Dr. Nissen. . . . Our jails are full of men who were so-called rehabilitated and went out to kill again—''

''Who gave you or anybody permission to play God, to take a life?'' Nissen's tone was much softer, but he too was getting angry.

''Who gave them permission?''

''That's not the point . . . Lock them up forever, if necessary, work on the new generation. . . . I don't want those people on the street any more than you do, but you can't go around killing people like they did in 'the old days,' as you call them.''

''You're a doctor,'' Rondowski answered, as if the flat statement at once explained and refuted Nissen's feelings.

''I've also seen many of those same bodies that you have. I've probably taken out as many bullets as you've shot, probably more, and I've seen the grief in the faces of the families sitting outside the operating room, but I still could never kill someone in retaliation or pay some professional to do it behind the confines of a prison wall. That doesn't bring back the dead and it doesn't stop the killing. . . . Anyway, I don't think that we can agree on this one tonight, so maybe it's better if we just drop it, don't you think?''

''They sign their own death certificates by what they do—not us,'' Rondowski persisted.

The surgeon started to pick up his cup and leave again. ''And if you get the wrong man?''

Before Rondowski could answer, Nissen had excused himself and walked away. He'd had enough, and returned to his office upstairs.

148

At midnight, the assays for eight different drugs on Dressner's list were completed and like everything else before, they were negative. Waxman's recommended shortcuts had already eliminated all insecticides, and most of the common household poisons.

Kramer's condition continued its downward course. Although there had been a few periods that might superficially be considered lucid, his general sensorium was worsening confusion, accompanied by bouts of explosive vomiting. His temperature was up to 102.4 degrees and his pulse had an alarming rate of 120 beats per minute. His blood pressure had also risen, now measuring 142 over 92. He had also stopped complaining so much about the pain in his right hand, which Fitzgerald and Wheelin attributed to his changed mental condition. They ordered another CBC and continued the alcohol sponging, attempting to keep his temperature from rising further.

Meanwhile Rondowski and Woodsley were back in Schaeffer's office reviewing some of the films and waiting for further instructions from the assailant. No one knew how the next message would come or how to trade the prisoners, if it came to that, and everyone was hoping that Thomas would make a positive identification before the next decision had to be made.

In the animal laboratory two of the four guinea pigs were beginning to show signs of becoming ill. They refused to eat or drink water, both had fever and one was beginning to limp, unwilling to walk about the cage whenever the caretaker nudged him with a small wooden stick. The changes were reported to Waxman, who told the man to keep a close eye on them and report back in another hour.

It took Thornton and Pat almost forty-five minutes to gather all of the WGN films on the six convicts. Many were shorts buried in the stacks or lost in the midst of long unrelated newsreels whose front labels were dusty and beginning to fade. Also, many of the films were on separate reels, and by the time they'd collected those on Pat's list their hands were full and they had to struggle with the doors on their way to the viewing room. Thornton selected the films on Giovanni first, pulling some of the pretrial shots during the 1950 case of income tax evasion. . . .

At 1:00 A.M. the Secretary's temperature was still registering 102.4 degrees but he seemed to be resting. For the last half hour he'd been perfectly still, as if sound asleep, and did not respond unless someone made a deliberate point of waking him. He was still disoriented as to time, place and person, but could pretty well follow simple commands. He also seemed to be weaker, and when Fitzgerald rechecked his injury, being careful as before when unwrapping the dressing, not wanting to cause the Secretary any more pain than was absolutely necessary, Kramer didn't pull his arm away as he'd done earlier.

Fitzgerald couldn't believe that the pain had gone away so quickly and proceeded to press his fingers along the periphery of the wound and watch Kramer's face, but there was no detectable awareness. He then placed his index finger directly over the laceration and looked up. Again, no response.

"Move that arm," he ordered, but Kramer merely stared at him, face blank. "Move that arm, dammit!"

No reaction.

"Move it like this!" Fitzgerald proceeded to lift Kramer's arm straight up into the air and bend his wrist. Earlier, this maneuver might have sent the patient to the ceiling, but now Kramer only shut his eyes and went back to sleep. Fitzgerald could feel that the arm was flaccid from the shoulder down, much like a stroke victim, and when he returned to stick a pin in his arm, Kramer remained asleep. No question, Blackwell's anticipated clues were beginning to show themselves. Fitzgerald immediately telephoned Waxman to tell him of the paralysis.

Until now the family had been permitted to visit as often as they wished, even though Kramer no longer recognized them. With the discovery of the paralysis, Fitzgerald changed his mind and decided to keep them outside until things improved or . . . In any case, he didn't know what to expect next.

Kramer's son balked at the change. "You don't have the right!"

"I'm afraid I do." Fitzgerald tried to respond firmly and yet sound apologetic. "His condition is so tenuous that the slightest thing might upset the—"

"I'll be careful, please let me see him—"

"As soon as things are stable, I'll let you know how he is." Fitzgerald put his arm around the boy's shoulder.

"I don't think you're exactly telling us the whole truth, doc," the campaign manager interrupted from his chair next to Kramer's sister. "Otherwise you'd let us in . . ."

"I wish that were the case," Fitzgerald responded sincerely, but Thomison shook his head in disbelief. The whole day had been beyond his comprehension.

Meanwhile, just below him, Rondowski was back on the phone talking to the five wardens again. They were all worn out from the night's effort, and none of the prisoners had in any way broken yet. Around the same time the Florida Highway Patrol had located the motel in which Dr. Whiley, Weisberg's friend, had been staying the day before, but he had checked out long before they arrived to take him in for questioning. By contrast, the Chicago police had managed to locate Frank Meanor, Millitz's friend, in a South Side crash pad. He was immediately taken to the Twelfth Street Precinct, but when Thomas failed to pick him out of a line-up, they could only hold him for parole violation.

When the work on the new CBC was completed, the results confirmed what everyone already knew. His condition had worsened. His white count continued to climb as did the neutrophils and bands, strongly suggesting that the infection was continuing unchecked.

Hematology Laboratory
CBC
Time Drawn: 00:05

Test	Result	Normal Values
Hemoglobin	11.6	14-18 gm/100 ml
Hematocrit	35%	42-52 ml/100 ml
Red Cell Count	3.91 million	4.6-6.2 million/cu mm
White Cell Count	18,213	5-10,000/cu mm
neutrophils	80%	54-62%
bands	14%	0-5%
lymphocytes	2%	25-33%
monocytes	1%	3-7%
eosinophils	1%	1-3%
basophils	0%	0-1%
metamyelocytes	2%	0%
promyelocytes	0%	0%
MCV	89	82-92
MCH	30	27-31
MCHC	33	32-36
Platelets	240,500	2-300,000/cu mm
Sedimentation Rate	76	less than 15 mm/hr

Red cell morphology: several fragmented cells
Atypical lymphocytes: rare

Chapter XIII

At 2:00 A.M. the animal caretaker reported to Waxman that one of guinea pigs had died, seemingly paralyzed; the second guinea pig had developed a limp; and two of the rhesus monkeys were becoming unusually docile. The professor immediately began running an antibody test for botulism, but the results were equivocal at first, then definitely negative.

Upstairs the Secretary was becoming even less responsive. Dr. Fitzgerald had to shake him several times before he could get him to open his eyes. His temperature continued to rise, measuring 103 degrees despite the medical cocoon of towels drenched in alcohol. There was a hint that his left arm was also becoming paralyzed, but it was extremely difficult to get him to move any part of his body. The permanent sections from Pathology on the biopsy returned, but the pathology report was exactly the same as the interpretation of the frozen sections taken earlier, and the report sheet found itself added to the growing list of negatives in the back of the chart. Still to come were the photos from electron microscopy.

Stecker's private laboratory looked more like the aftermath of a spring sale at a downtown department store. Wadded sheets of paper were overflowing his metal wastebasket and strewn about the tiny room, his sinks were cluttered with used equipment, every cabinet door and drawer was partly open and his generally neat desktop was covered with open textbooks, laboratory manuals and drug descriptions. His frustrations were also escalating as none of his latest experiments or assays were proving out in any remotely significant way.

Meanwhile Dr. Blackwell, bothered by his arthritic hands and the lack of sleep, became the group's first major casualty. Earlier he had been making a few mistakes, ones that could easily be rectified by the technicians working with him, but as the night wore on he began dropping important pieces of equipment, miscalculating quantitive reactions and dozing at his workbench. He was wise enough to realize he shouldn't continue, and finally after apologizing to Waxman and Ryan for the mistakes of an old man, he put on his coat and hat and left for home. . . .

At WGN studios the Giovanni series was coming to an end, having taken almost an hour to survey. Thornton had managed to scribble three pages of sketchy notes, some of which would embellish the story, but there were no discernible clues to help with the State Street assault. Poisoning did not seem to be the way of organized crime, or at least Giovanni's way of doing things.

The Lawson films were next. The first strip began with his August trial, flashing back to many of the victims' parents, their homes, and several well-meaning neighbors who, for the most part, when interviewed said that the Lawson boy was a "nice boy who always went to church." They really said it. Was there ever a killer, Thornton wondered, whose neighbors spoke ill of him? . . .

At 2:30 A.M. there was a tremendous flash fire in Ryan's laboratory. The scientist had just returned from the toxicology lab. When he went to light the Bunsen burner with a wooden match, the entire surface of his workbench shot up in flames, instantly destroying most of the virus cultures and badly burning the palms of both of his hands. Ryan let out a scream that could be heard throughout the second floor, and within moments both Dressner and Waxman were running into his laboratory. As Dressner pulled a chemical fire extinguisher from a nearby wall and began covering the entire side of the room with a white foam, Waxman grabbed a handful of paper towels, drenched them under the sink spigot and quickly applied them to Ryan's hands.

"Somebody must have poured a flammable on that bench, dammit!" Ryan blurted out, tightly clasping the dripping towels between his hands and walking toward the hallway. "Damn it, damn it, damn it! It'll take hours for me to get those cultures going again. That's if I even can—"

"I think you'd better let someone else do it now," Waxman said as he examined the scientist's hands in the better light and saw that the burns were mostly first degree.

"I don't believe that was an accident . . . Somebody purposely set that up!" Ryan said angrily.

By now the security police had arrived in the laboratory, but as the dark smoke began clearing and the police scraped away the tenacious foam, neither they—nor any of the doctors—were able to detect any evidence of sabotage.

When Nissen finally arrived he immediately took Ryan downstairs to the emergency room to dress his wounds. Waxman and Dressner stayed behind to assess the damages, but it immediately was obvious that it would be hours before the room would be usable again. With little equipment that seemed salvageable, it looked clearly as though the research or viral cultures would take much too long to start over. The main gas switch to the room was shut off, the door was closed. Ryan, however, bitterly held to his suspicions. . . .

Walking back to his lab, Waxman's thoughts slipped back to another time . . . when he'd been called in as a special consultant after a laboratory accident had occurred—this time killing the head scientist and leaving two others in serious condition. . . .

He'd been at home reading in his den when the telephone rang.

155

A man's voice on the other end had abruptly introduced himself as Captain Patrick, stated that the professor's help was urgently needed and said that a military car would come by to pick him up. When Waxman had asked why, the captain merely said that the reason was classified and he didn't know any details.

Waxman, not unreasonably startled by this unusual request —actually, it sounded more like a military order—was also annoyed . . . the military still had associations for him with the suffering he'd seen close-hand during the war. He continued to question the captain, who just as persistently evaded his questions, saying only that he was told to say Waxman's help was a matter of life and death. Waxman speculated that that might mean something to do with his well-known diagnostic results in infectious diseases—a specialty that had, in a way, gotten its start with the botulism cases he'd detected during the war. With this in mind and despite his continued resentment at the manner of the summons, he finally agreed to go along. Apparently his agreement was assumed, because even before he could finish dressing, pack an overnight case and say good-bye to his sleeping wife, a green sedan had pulled up in front of his house to wait quietly under an elm at the edge of the driveway.

Captain Patrick's orders had been to deliver Professor Waxman to the rear gate at Kennedy Airport. An hour later Waxman found himself squeezed into the back seat of a jet fighter, staring at a maze of strange dials and flying above the clouds at thirty thousand feet, without any idea as to why or where. The jet finally landed at a small air force base in Arizona. Another unmarked green sedan was waiting and another silent ride took him straight into the desert. Waxman had already been given security clearance without his knowledge.

The ride was bumpy, and a cloud of dust followed the lone vehicle for over two hours as they traveled a narrow dirt road. It was just past midnight when the sedan finally pulled up in front of a two-story concrete building surrounded by a high barbed wire fence and protected by two noisy German Shepherds within the

156

metal rim. The sign at the gate read "U.S. ARMY—KEEP OUT," purposely omitting any association with the Department of Defense. A single guard was at the front door and another, stationed just inside, subsequently led Waxman down a narrow hallway and into General F.H. Russell's office, a windowless cubicle with bright fluorescent lights and sterile white walls.

Russell greeted the professor with a brief acknowledging smile, and immediately began a description of the project he needed Waxman's help on. The project lacked a specific name, he said, and could only be located in the classified files in Washington by the designation K–191–34. Until now it had been one of the most successful endeavors that the Department had managed to have secretly financed. Its research team had been able to cultivate the rabies virus found in vampire bats in the West Indies, isolate its nerve toxin and subsequently fractionate the poison into three unnamed components, Z–1, Z–2, and Z–3.

The first was a liquid and only mildly toxic to laboratory animals. The second, Z–2, turned out to be the most powerful of the three, but its properties were unstable and the poison would deteriorate within minutes of exposure to sunlight. The third component, however, was promising, easily converted to an aerosol, extremely stable under a variety of conditions and able to kill most laboratory animals within hours of exposure. In addition, as a gas it was completely odorless and colorless.

It was Z–3 that the Department wanted developed for its biological warfare arsenal, but before it would accept the toxin it insisted on having the antidote available for the protection of U.S. troops. According to Russell, the research group was very close to that goal.

The accident had occurred almost nine hours earlier when the vibration of a high speed centrifuge had quietly cracked a defective test tube that was spinning within. Seconds later Dr. Bergson, the head scientist and the only person standing close by, collapsed, unable to breathe, his hands and face turning blue from the lack of oxygen. His two colleagues, who had been working on the opposite side of the laboratory, immediately realized what had happened and flipped on an emergency switch that simultaneously set off an alarm and started a high power vacuum ventilation system specifically designed for this contingency. It took two minutes for the room to clear, and when other technicians were able to enter they found the two scientists lying on the floor, gasping for air; Dr. Bergson had already died of suffocation. Four hours later the two survivors began developing high fever and excruciating headaches.

The project horrified the professor, and his first reaction was to demand that he be returned to Connecticut. He maintained that he would not have come had he known what they were doing, and now if he found the toxin's antidote he would be making it, as the general might put it, "operational." . . .

A phone call in his laboratory abruptly shook Waxman from his reverie, and from his thoughts on its ironic parallel to this present situation. The operator was looking for Dr. Nissen. Kramer's blood pressure had taken a frightening plunge, and Fitzgerald was seeking additional help. The technician who answered referred the call to an upstairs private doctor's room, where the surgeon was still awake, lying in bed with all his clothes on except shoes and jacket. He had been too nervous to sleep.

When Nissen arrived in Kramer's room he found the nurse double checking the Secretary's pressure on the "good" arm, but both sides measured 82 over 50 while his pulse was racing at 144 beats per minute. Noting that Kramer was in near shock, Fitzgerald had opened the intravenous line to let fluids race in as fast as possible, and Wheelin had hooked up the EKG machine, worried that his heart might have suffered some additional damage; the tracing, however, was unchanged. Nissen suggested that they use plasma instead and the change was immediately made. A few minutes later Kramer's pressure was back up to 104 over 60 and soon leveled off at 120 over 70. His temperature, though, had risen to 104 degrees, and his skin felt as if he were on fire inside.

A second bottle of plasma was hung as the first emptied, and the cooling mattress was rolled in from the supply room. Outside, his rapid heart rate sounded like a muffled machine gun and terrified his sister and son as well as Thomison, all of whom were still waiting next to the nurses' station. A small tube of blood was then rushed off to the laboratory for electrolyte determinations.

Thornton's notes on Lawson were not nearly as long as those he'd made during the Giovanni series. Parts of the clips were grotesque, showing glimpses of several gory and mutilated young female bodies. Thornton rewound the spool and replaced it with a segment on Dr. Weisberg, a much shorter and less gruesome filmstrip. Pat was visibly shaken from the previous material and requested he forgo any more shots of victims.

Intermittently through the night Inspector Pritchard had been making security rounds with Schaeffer, and he was summoned from them to the Secretary's room during the crisis. He had already become dissatisfied with the work in the research laboratories, but now being told that the Secretary's condition was grave, he realized time was running out.

Cutting his rounds short, he hurried back to Schaeffer's office and dialed direct a special White House number. An aide answered, and moments later his call was transferred to the President's bedroom.

It took the President a while to wake fully—the long trip had exhausted him—and consequently to sort out not only what Pritchard was telling him but his own thoughts as well. Finally it became unmistakably clear that Pritchard was requesting that he be given stand-by authorization to make the so-called trade—make it, that is, once they were told the details of *how* it was to be made.

The President made no effort to hide his upset. Pritchard's

159

description of Kramer's condition was frightening. When first Fitzgerald and then Nissen had been spoken to, and each confirmed Pritchard's description of the gravity of Kramer's condition, the President finally gave his authorization to go ahead, unless, of course, a timely breakthrough made it unnecessary. He also reminded each of them that they and their colleagues must work even harder to discover the cause and antidote on their own. After all, there was no guarantee that the antidote would be delivered even when and if they were finally obliged to give in to this monstrous blackmail—which, he realized, they must now be prepared to do. There was not, from what they told him, any other tolerable alternative at this point.

They assured him of their complete agreement and understanding. The doctors went back to their work. Pritchard placed calls to the five wardens and told them to put matters in place and await further instructions. Meanwhile an emergency staff meeting was called for 4:00 A.M., less than a half hour away. . . .

Another telephone line was also busy downstairs in the laboratory. It was the return call from M.I.T. which everyone had been waiting for. A physician on the other end relayed that the computer's preliminary reading had indicated that a thus far unidentified virus or viral product of the RNA type was responsible. The news hit like a bombshell, particularly in the face of the recent fire in Ryan's laboratory that had given a setback to his research in this very area—Ryan almost alone had been arguing for the virus theory all night.

Waxman began a meticulous questioning of the M.I.T. scientist, logical and compelling. He quietly suggested—looking directly at Ryan—that the matter was too serious to be lost in a personality conflict or a preliminary computer readout. He then requested that they feed the data on the Secretary's newest vital signs and change in mental state into the same computer. They did so. Sixty seconds later, the machine typed out "DATA INCONSISTENT."

Waxman repeated the new information to the others around him. He then spoke into the phone again and requested that the M.I.T. people run the same sample of Kramer's blood through from the beginning once more. This time, the results would take between one and two hours. Ryan, though subdued, still disagreed with the professor's plans and returned to his old lab to try to salvage whatever work he could handle with his injured hands.

Work in the toxicology laboratory—in contrast to, and doubtless in part as a result of, the building pressure of time—began slowing down. Frustration levels, however, mounted with repeated failures, negative results, the sense of impending defeat. It seemed none of the poisons on the flow sheet offered any real promise and yet, of course, each of them had to be checked. As the morning hours approached, fatigue accidents, petty arguments and mechanical failures began piling up as well: A technician carried over from the day shift was trying to push a glass rod through a small hole in a rubber cork, and foolishly brought too much pressure to bear, cracking the fragile cylinder and sending the frayed, razor-sharp edge into the palm of her hand. It took an intern nearly an hour to pick every glass splinter from the ragged wound, which required sixteen stitches to close before she was sent home. Another technician was burned in the Bac-T laboratory when someone backed into a boiling vat and dumped hot agar into his lap. A long white coat and unusually fast reflexes kept his injuries to a minimum, but he still required hospitalization.

While they were cleaning up from that accident an anonymous call was placed to the Fullerton precinct on Chicago's North Side—a man's voice with a distinct southern drawl. After quickly giving the address of a modern high-rise building on Lake Shore Drive, the man described a noisy couple living next door who'd been arguing the whole night and now, he said, he'd just heard gunshots. When the desk officer tried to get his name, the man said only that the couple's name was Terman, and hung up.

A few minutes later a squad car pulled up in front of the

161

twenty-story apartment building. Its two officers unlatched their revolver cases as they slammed their respective car doors, startling a snoozing doorman who quickly got to his feet and nervously opened the glass doors. The Termans, he said, lived on the seventeenth floor.

As the doorman accompanied the officers inside and directed them to the appropriate elevator, the group was watched by a man waiting quietly in the shadows outside. Once the three men were out of sight, he cautiously approached the empty police car. He might have picked an apparently empty one at random, but that would have been too risky. Now he taped a sealed envelope onto the windshield. Written in large, bold print that faced the inside: FOR KRAMER ONLY.

Chapter XIV

There were tired-looking faces waiting in Schaeffer's office for Pritchard's emergency meeting at 4:00 A.M., including the flamboyant medical student Mickey Kirkland, who somehow had managed to make himself part of the core group. Most everyone had a fresh cup of coffee in hand, and the only person missing was Dr. Fitzgerald. He had been afraid to leave the Secretary's bedside.

Kramer's condition had been officially lowered to critical and his family had been informed that he might not make it through the night. His latest vital signs included a temperature of 104.2, a pulse of 150 beats per minute and a blood pressure of 96 over 40. He was now considered semicomatose and the paralysis was spreading. Just before the meeting convened, Waxman had received another call from the caretaker: The second guinea pig had died and the two remaining were lethargic and feverish. In addition, one of the monkeys was unresponsive.

Pritchard began: "As some of you already know, I've been given authorization by the President to negotiate a trade as soon as we know how. At this point, as the President himself said, we don't seem to have any other options." He turned to Dr. Ryan. "What do *you* think, Dr. Ryan? How long, if ever, do you think it will take to identify the poison and get our own antidote?"

Ryan looked distinctly uncomfortable . . . in fact, miserable. "Well, to be honest, it could take days, maybe weeks. That damn computer seems to have let us down. So has everything else. Whoever did this had to have professional knowledge . . .

know enough to be pretty sure we wouldn't get the answer in time. . . ."

As Ryan spoke a lab messenger entered the back of the room. He was carrying the results of the last blood test. Dressner was sitting closest, and when he noticed that the sugar value was abnormally low, almost life-threatening, he quickly left the meeting and telephoned Fitzgerald from a phone in the hallway. Fitzgerald found it hard to believe, but quickly injected a 50 cc solution of concentrated glucose into the intravenous tubing. A few seconds later the Secretary became more responsive and partially opened his eyes as his heart rate began to slow a little. Fitzgerald repeated the injection and Kramer's pulse leveled off at 120. His confusion and partial paralysis, however, persisted.

The meeting got started again when Dressner came back in. The lab sheet had already made it around the table and nearly everyone had a different theory about why his blood sugar should have fallen. Some, though discouraged, were less pessimistic than Ryan, including Waxman, who said he felt they were on the edge of succeeding and only needed a few more hours. . . .

A second interruption came at 4:30. This time it was Officer Cantfield, with a sealed envelope. Pritchard took it, quickly ripping the smaller end open and after scanning privately for a moment, read the message aloud:

DELIVER YOUR WELL FED GUESTS TO EDMONTON

CANADA BY JET IMMEDIATELY. PROVIDE EACH PRIS-
AND REVOLVER.
ONER WITH A PARACHUTE IF INITIATED WITHIN ONE

HOUR THE ANTIDOTE WILL ARRIVE BY NOON.

"Well," Pritchard said, "at least this note confirms our interpretation of the first, the trade of the antidote for the convicts. And that's all it does . . . We still have nothing really to connect the men . . ."

Everyone was silent for a moment except Mickey, who was

deep in his cumbersome leather briefcase, thumbing through some old lecture notes. He hesitated, then blurted out, "What about phalloidian?"

Pritchard looked up abruptly from the note. "Falloid what?"

Dr. Ryan answered. "It's the toxin from a certain poisonous mushroom—"

"It can cause hypoglycemia!" Mickey exploded, and Ryan translated the trendy illness into its unglamorous symptom—low blood sugar.

"I think he just might have a point there," Dressner added. "It could explain some of Kramer's symptoms, and there's an antidote that might work, although it's experimental and has to be administered quickly."

"Do you have it here?" Pritchard directed his question to Dressner as Mickey sat beaming and excitedly tapping his fingertips on the conference table.

"No, but I doubt that it will be a problem," the pathologist said, with some stirring of enthusiasm despite the lateness, in more ways than one, of the hour.

Waxman listened patiently, then said, almost apologetically, "I'm afraid it really doesn't fit the symptoms very well at all, at best only superficially . . . judging from the other blood tests, I'm afraid I can't believe that phalloidian is the culprit. I do agree, though, that we certainly should call for the antiserum, but I also think it would be wise to run some preliminary precipitin tests first. If we're wrong and we just give the Secretary the wrong medicine, we might make him considerably sicker than he is now."

Dressner agreed, adding a reminder of what they already were acutely aware of—that they couldn't in any case count on the assailant's antidote arriving in time, if indeed at all. And so their own efforts continued to be of life-and-death importance.

In the viewing room at WGN the films on the Weisberg trial were coming to an end. Once Thornton discovered that the physician had poisoned his wife, he paid particular attention, hoping to make some connection to the Kramer assault, but there seemed little to be learned. The strips dealt primarily with the six-week-long court battle, Weisberg's marital problems and finally a brief comment from the coroner.

Before starting the Madison clip, Thornton retrieved two cups of lukewarm coffee from the newsroom, where the teletypes were still pretty well taken over by the Kramer story. He was beginning to realize how tired he was, and noted that Pat, her head on his shoulder, could barely keep her eyes open. He decided to review a few parts of the Madison clip and then take her home. He could finish the story in the morning.

At 5:00 A.M. the hospital's other business picked up with the arrival of two private ambulances bringing in the victims of a car accident on the Kennedy Expressway. The first to reach the loading dock had a teen-age girl, barely sixteen, whose face had gone through the windshield on impact. Her long blonde hair was matted with clotted blood as were her hands as they covered her injured face. The second ambulance arrived right on the other's tail, carrying the driver of the second vehicle, a forty-two-year-old traveling salesman who had been drinking in nightclubs along Rush Street and in his drunken stupor had driven down the exit ramp just as the girl's date was coming off the expressway. He too had multiple cuts on his face and two broken ribs but was still anesthetized from alcohol as they carried the stretcher into the emergency room. The girl's date had received only minor injuries and was still at the scene of the accident.

The physician on duty happened to be the intern Wheelin's roommate and, seeing that he was short-handed, immediately called upstairs, hoping that his friend might be able to get away for a few minutes. Wheelin was doubtful and said he would have to check with Fitzgerald first. He immediately left his room and stuck his head into the Executive Suite, where he saw that Kramer was still lying on the cooling mattress and that his temperature stubbornly hovered just above 104 degrees, his pulse had started back up, registering 134 beats per minute, and his blood pressure had slipped back to 94 over 60. The night nurse also reported the paralysis had totally involved Kramer's other arm and was beginning to weaken his legs. Something could happen at any moment. Wheelin called back to tell his friend to get someone else. . . .

When the frozen antiserum for phalloidian arrived, both Stecker and Waxman took charge of the critical experiment as Mickey watched over their shoulders, excited and convinced that his idea was correct. Stecker appeared to feel the same, actually hoping more than believing that it would work, and disregarding the professor's earlier comments.

They proceeded to dilute Kramer's serum in five different test tubes with different amounts of saline, then added an equal amount of antiserum, which had melted, to each. During the next ten minutes they watched each tube and waited for a reaction—there was never a hint of precipitation. The only clear result was that the poisonous mushroom theory was wrong. They finally left the remainder of the antiserum defrosting on the side of the sink and returned to their earlier work.

A few moments later there was more bad news from the animal laboratory. The two remaining guinea pigs had died, seemingly paralyzed, and now two of the monkeys were in critical condition. Waxman sounded upset. He requested that they keep the animals in cold storage for possible autopsies later.

To add to his misery, the M.I.T. physician returned his call and reported that his computer still could not give them a definite answer. Waxman thanked the scientist for his time and told him that they probably wouldn't be needing the computer any longer.

While Waxman was apologizing to the others for the machine's inadequacies, explaining that the set-up was programmed to deal with more precise variables than, unfortunately, they had here, Mickey came racing into the laboratory with yet another of his brainstorms. This time the medical student was convinced that one section of the electrophoretic strips made from the newest blood specimens had stained much darker than it had earlier and he wanted someone more knowledgeable to confirm his observation. And this time the group was considerably less responsive. They were all exhausted and had already gone down one of Mickey's false trails in the belief that anything and everything was worth a try. Even Professor Waxman, who before had been polite and understanding, rather sarcastically asked if he might not have used too much dye. As Mickey insisted he hadn't, Stecker—less enthusiastically, to be sure, than before—once again went along. There was, he reminded them, nothing to lose by looking. They were reduced to that. . . .

The Florida Highway Patrol was still looking for Dr. Whiley when Weisberg refused to board the airliner, so that particular search was immediately called off. The other five prisoners, however, were quite eager to accept the free passage, all still denying any direct knowledge of the plot. The four planes had been rented—requisitioned was more like it—from commercial airlines at a token cost of two thousand dollars each. The last note gave them only one hour to set the operation in motion—not enough time to bring special planes to the airports involved. Each prisoner had a whole plane to himself except Madison and Lawson. After the hatch was secured, Madison demanded that the cockpit be sealed and the intercom be left off. Once the plane was in the air, he leaned back, smiled and then, shaking his head, began laughing.

The report from the electron microscope was en route from the University laboratory to Presbyterian. Included in the typed report was a brief statement that a few unidentified particles were seen that could be consistent with a virus.

168

At WGN Thornton and Pat were watching the Madison clip. The film had begun with a violent riot in Detroit's ghetto, and the sound track had immediately awakened Pat. After Thornton turned the sound off, the quiet of their viewing room was broken by a door opening behind them. A man's silhouette appeared in the hallway light; as he entered, Pat became startled and bolted from her seat. A moment later the intruder had materialized into the night security man, who quickly apologized for frightening her. That was enough, she wanted to go home. Thornton agreed, just as soon as he'd seen the rest of the film, which had only a few minutes left. . . . The next scene in the Madison film clip moved to Miami International Airport and showed two FBI agents, disguised as mechanics, moving into the tourist section of a 747 jet. A moment later they could be seen dragging Madison from the plane. The remainder of the film clip was devoted to repetitive passenger interviews. As Thornton stood up to turn on the lights, he was startled by Pat suddenly screaming out "My God . . . that's *him*! That's the guy who bumped into me on State Street . . . hit me with his cast . . . Remember the bruise I told you about? I know that's him . . . "

Thornton quickly reversed the film to the place where Madison was captured and ran the last segment in slow motion, asking Pat if she was really sure.

"That's definitely him!" Pat reconfirmed. "I'm sure that's him . . ."

The face was also somewhat familiar to Thornton, but not from State Street. The passenger they were looking at was a man in his late fifties with gray hair and an expensive tweed suit. Unlike most of the other passengers being interviewed, he appeared nervous in front of the cameras and tried to avoid questions. He did not give the reporters his name.

Thornton rewound the reel as fast as the projector would turn, grabbed Pat's hand and headed toward his car. Ten minutes later, the two were looking for a parking place outside of the Twelfth Street Precinct.

Chapter XV

The airport at Edmonton was located two and a half miles from town. Until recently its grassy fields had catered to a few dozen private planes, mostly single-engine, but now it had two separate runways that ran perpendicular to each other, the larger of which had been specifically designed to handle commercial jets. The terminal, however, was still a one-story wooden complex, dominated by a cylindrical control tower, with only two ticket booths for reservations.

Canadian authorities had already been notified by the FBI that the four planes with their five prisoners, armed and dangerous, were en route. Not surprisingly, the news was not especially well received, and at first the Canadians threatened to close their airport, demanding that the planes be diverted to some American port. They couldn't understand why they should be involved, and it finally took a last minute call from the President to Canada's Prime Minister to change their minds. Nonetheless, the notion of accepting five armed convicts was barely tolerable to the Prime Minister—even in the name of U.S.–Canadian friendship. He was reminded that this was quite literally a matter of life and death for Secretary of Defense Kramer and now vice-presidential candidate Kramer, a man who not unreasonably might be expected to become President (indeed, if they won, that was the scenario the President had in mind and told the P.M. as much). Would Canada wish to be in a position someday of having refused to help save his life? . . .

Besides, Kramer was a most popular figure in Canada—as he was elsewhere in the world among U.S. allies for his reasoned stand on a posture of strong defense in the context of détente. The Prime Minister and his advisors acknowledged all this, but they balked at the accompanying request that the convicts not be interfered with until word was passed that the trade had been safely made—and since at this point it was unclear which, if not all, of the convicts were involved, this would apply to all of them, unless and until word was passed to the contrary. Of course, whatever surveillance they put the convicts under, whatever protective escort they used at the Edmonton Airport, was up to them. But, please, nothing to frustrate the larger objective after having gone this far. Once the antidote was in hand and Kramer thereby out of danger—or if the U.S. doctors discovered it on their own in time—Canadian authorities would instantly be notified and the U.S. would join them in any way they desired in any and all efforts to hunt down and recapture these men.

Reluctantly, in the face of all the arguments, the Canadian officials went along and passed the order down to the officers at Edmonton to restrain themselves, unless and until they got word otherwise. Privately, they wondered if this would be possible. . . .

By the time that the first plane requested permission to land, the field had been cleared and surrounded by policemen, most of whom had been called from home and were still wearing their street clothes. Only two of them could qualify as sharpshooters; one of these was assigned to the small observation desk on top of the terminal and the other to the hangar next door. They and all others were told to hold their fire unless and until given orders to the contrary. All airport employees were confined to the front lobby, while the only scheduled flight was diverted to the airfield at Saskatoon. The road to the airport was closed.

The first plane coming from Illinois had Madison and Lawson aboard. The pilot, however, had radioed ahead that there had been a pressure change in the passenger compartment. The cause was uncertain, but after checking as best he could from his position, he guessed that the rear door of the plane might have been forced open. He was instructed not to attempt to communicate with the passengers or under any circumstances to leave his post and go back to check unless the plane seemed to be in jeopardy. When he reported that didn't seem to be the case, he was instructed to hold to his original orders and proceed in to Edmonton. Canadian officials also instructed the pilot to keep his crew inside the cockpit after landing until the plane had been checked out.

There was over an inch of new snow on the ground and the runway lights were still flashing as the jet liner skidded on the wet field and taxied to the far end to wait for further instructions. The sun was just beginning to light up the horizon. After the thunderous engines were turned off, the airport was silent once again. The two sharpshooters, trigger fingers itching, were focusing their telescopic sights on the emergency exits. A brown utility truck quietly scurried across the field leaving its tire tracks in the glistening snow, a small cloud of steam spewing from beneath its rear bumper. The two police officers inside wore bulletproof vests beneath heavy winter jackets. They were to be the armed "escort"—one hell of a note, they felt.

It took some thirty seconds for the van to reach the plane and stop just below an open hatch in the tail section. The two men quickly exited and swung a long metal ladder up against the silver hull. Their guns were now drawn—not to be used except under most extreme duress, was the instruction from up top—as one man held the ladder in place and the other slowly climbed up the rungs. An occasional snowflake obscured his vision as he watched for any possible movement above. Once he reached the entrance, he waited a moment for his eyes to adjust to the darkness inside. All he saw was six rows of empty seats.

At Presbyterian-St. Luke's Hospital it was nearly time for the change of shift. Although the Secretary's floor was the only ward that had remained lighted through the night, many of the patients

172

had been kept awake by the commotion outside and downstairs in the lobby. Now, with the lights coming back on again in the hospital, the rattle of food carts and stretchers could be heard everywhere.

The routine on each floor was quite similar as the often appropriately named graveyard shift hurried to complete its remaining chores and prepare morning reports. When it was time for breakfast, most of the patients were more interested in finding out about Kramer. Even private physicians had difficulty with their morning rounds as every patient who was able to speak, and some who couldn't, wanted to expound on their theories rather than talk about their own cases; some of the doctors were also so inclined. Television and radio sets could be heard from the hallways, waiting for the morning news to come on. Some patients in the coronary care unit had to be heavily sedated because their physicians worried that the excitement might aggravate heart attacks. Word was also beginning to spread that the police had gotten a photograph of the assailant from WGN Studios. . . .

Security remained tight throughout the building. Policemen were positioned on every floor with instructions to check everyone who entered, which became a real annoyance to those physicians who had patients situated on different wards.

Outside, crowds of spectators were again beginning to gather. Some had stayed through the night, hoping for good news or watching out of mere curiosity. Others had gone home for a few hours' sleep and were now returning to continue the vigil.

Reporters had converted the hospital lobby into a gigantic bedroom, using nearly every available couch and soft chair. The air held an aroma of old tobacco, and the carpets were littered. Disgruntled sweepers were just beginning to clean up the mess, cursing beneath their breath as they worked.

Most of the television personnel had replacements coming, but the radio and newspaper men did not have the same luxury. As one impatient line began forming outside the only public bathroom, another quickly formed in the cafeteria. The last report issued on the Secretary's condition was at midnight—it gave his condition as critical. Since that time, only rumors had drifted down, and most were inaccurate.

At 7:00 A.M. a day nurse entered to check Kramer's vital signs again. He had a peaked, drawn appearance, much like a corpse, and was barely responsive to any stimuli. The only movements detectable were his shallow respirations and an occasional muscle twitch. Although a breakfast had been delivered to his suite and was waiting unattended outside the door, it was obvious that an error had been made and it would be sent back to the kitchen.

As the nurse began pumping up the blood pressure cuff on Kramer's left arm, Fitzgerald stood up to stretch. He had managed to stay awake, but his mind felt as though it had been stuffed with cotton and his mouth had a dry, unpleasant taste. Absolutely every muscle in his body hurt. The intern Wheelin, who had joined him during the last hour, was sound asleep, slumped over in a chair on the opposite side of the room, and didn't waken until Fitzgerald began opening the curtains.

The nurse reported that Kramer's blood pressure was stationary at 100 over 62, but his pulse was thready and racing at an incredible rate of 160 beats per minute. When she went to retrieve the thermometer, the mercury had pushed past the 106 mark. As Fitzgerald immediately asked her to recheck it with another thermometer, Wheelin ran out of the room and to the kitchen, where he dumped out a wastebasket and filled it with tiny ice cubes from the ice machine. By the time he returned the repeat temp was also 106. He first looked to Fitzgerald for his approval, then dumped the ice cubes across Kramer's chest and between his legs.

The Secretary's son was still waiting outside, frightened by Wheelin's dramatic exit and frantic return. He moved closer to the door to see what was going on and finally entered. Fitzgerald moved to stop him but he was too late. The boy had gotten a good look at his father. As he stood motionless now, acutely aware that death was imminent, his aunt came in behind him, took a quick glance and pulled him back out into the hallway.

In a corner of one of the laboratories, Stecker and his eager medical student, wholly unaware that daylight had come, were caught up in their last-ditch attempt to identify a short chain protein molecule that Mickey had earlier noticed on his electrophoretic strip. The work was Stecker's meat. It was an easy chemical to separate out for identification, the type of analysis he'd done as an undergraduate in quantitative chemistry. The fact that Kramer's blood sugar had fallen so precipitously suggested to Stecker that they might be dealing with a type of long-acting insulin, and as the two, with growing excitement, hurried through each step, one result after another confirmed his suspicions. There was only one drawback, which they both temporarily chose to overlook in the seductive pull of at least the promise of a positive result—the fact that the electron microscope report had indicated the presence of a virus.

Next door, Ryan and Dressner were talking about this new report. Ryan, not surprisingly, was extremely angry that Waxman had talked the group—himself included, though against his better judgment—out of testing for viruses. When they now went to locate the professor, thinking he might be sleeping, he was nowhere to be found and no one had seen him.

Downstairs another officer from the Twelfth Street Precinct arrived with a sealed manila envelope for Inspector Pritchard. It contained a copy of a 5x8 photograph of a gray-haired man identified as a passenger during a recent plane hijacking in Miami involving the black revolutionary Madison. Thomas had also identified the man as the same person who had run off through the subway tunnel with him.

It didn't, of course, take long for Pritchard to recognize the face. When he handed the photograph to Nissen, the surgeon, first startled and then shocked, found himself insisting that a mistake had been made . . . it *must* be a mistake . . . At that moment neither he nor Pritchard was aware that the professor was missing. When they went to the laboratory, Ryan told them, which clinched it. It was also, for Ryan, final vindication of his virus theory, but he did not comment on it. The awful implications of where this now left them . . . left Kramer . . . were too overwhelming. Stecker, when Nissen told him that Waxman was the assailant, was less subdued. "That son of a bitch . . . I should have known when the stain came out darker on the newer blood that somebody had been monkeying around. I bet that bastard's been giving Kramer insulin somehow. He knew just how to fool his own computer, and he managed to do a job on us too. *I* should have known! Of course it's a virus. God knows *which* virus. He's been heading us off all night so we'd work on the wrong stuff. . . ."

"But how could he have given him insulin?" Pritchard said. "Dr. Fitzgerald's been in the room all night—"

"I don't know, that's your job . . . All I do know is that now that we know it's a virus, we don't have time to identify it. Not with that fire and all . . ." Stecker's voice drifted from outrage to quiet frustration. Then . . . "But *Waxman*, my God, Dr. Louis Waxman . . . *Why?* Sure, he's sort of a pacifist, I hear, but so what? So am I . . . Why *this*, and what the hell would he have to do with a bunch of murderers? . . . I don't get it . . ."

After Stecker had finished saying what they all were thinking, Nissen, shaking his head in disbelief, asked the Inspector to follow him back upstairs. The surgeon went straight to the emergency supply room, where he began squirting the contents of the pre-loaded syringes into cotton balls. After each one, he stopped to smell the cotton and soon noticed that the syringes for meperidine, a narcotic used for Kramer's pain, didn't match up. In fact, the contents of one syringe had a slightly different tint to it. From there he began to scrutinize the room. After several minutes of searching he found a partially used bottle of insulin hidden under some papers in the trash. His only comment was that Waxman had once told him that it wasn't safe to leave loaded syringes out in the open, and that he should have listened. . . . Waxman . . . Like Stecker he could only wonder why . . . and more importantly, when—if at all—they'd get the promised antidote. He knew the convicts' release had been set in motion and so the antidote was supposed to come by noon . . . but that was over four hours away. Even if it came on time, would it be in time for Kramer? . . . Close . . . it would be very close. . . . .

Once Pritchard relayed Waxman's identification back to Twelfth Street, an APB with his name and description was put on the air and a squad car was dispatched to his recent hotel room in Evanston.

As radar in the Edmonton control tower began picking up the second plane, carrying Millitz, word reached Canadian officials that the third plane had been diverted by the Arab prisoner and apparently was heading due east. Akubar was reported to be sitting in the cockpit with his revolver aimed at the co-pilot, not at all interested in flying to Canada.

At 7:45 A.M. the second plane requested permission to land. Unlike its predecessor, its passenger compartment was still pressurized. Once again, police took up their assigned positions as the plane touched down, and the pilot was instructed to remain within the confines of his cockpit.

It seemed nearly a rerun of the first landing, the only difference being a later hour and more sunlight. Once the plane came to a halt at the end of the runway, the panel truck traveled the same path out onto the field and parked near the rear of the airplane.

Millitz was watching from one of the windows as the truck approached, then quickly disappeared inside. He was a man who lived on tranquilizers—the phenothiazines prescribed for him, and others acquired through the prison underground—and having been without them all night, he was beginning to decompensate. With the building onset of an acute paranoid incident, the soft tap of the metal ladder settling against the rear door triggered in him the odd delusion of a plot of giant killers coming after him, to punish him, and this time far from the protection of his "home" in California. Well, they would pay . . .

A moment later the hatchway began creaking open. Millitz

177

rushed to the back of the plane, yelling, paranoia now fullblown. When the officer raised a hand in a gesture trying to calm him, Millitz let fly a barrage of pistol shots close range. The policeman fell hard to the wet ground. One bullet had skimmed across his cheek, ripping part of his ear away; another furrowed a jagged wound over the bridge of his nose, then penetrated into his skull. He died instantly.

The second officer immediately went to the far side of his truck and lobbed two tear·gas grenades through the small rectangular opening. Seconds later Millitz, gasping and choking, stumbled back to the center of the plane and began grappling with the emergency exit. As he began pushing it open he was struck by bullets from the terminal building. He instantly crumpled to the floor of the plane, his gun falling outside and plopping into the snow.

An ambulance now sped out to the plane, and as it did the last jet, bearing Giovanni, radioed in for permission to land. It was placed in a holding pattern until the second jet could be removed from the runway.

A call was also placed from Edmonton airport authorities to Ottawa, explaining the extreme provocation that had forced their hand against Millitz before going through the prescribed procedure of requesting and getting explicit authorization. Ottawa understood—they'd half-expected it. They doubted the U.S. people would be equally tolerant. They were right. The doctors still had not identified the poison and it seemed most unlikely they would by the twenty-four hour deadline of noon, when the antidote supposedly was to be delivered. Millitz, because of his self-acquired medical knowledge and considerable raw I.Q., had been a prime suspect as the key man among the five convicts. If indeed he were the one, his death would doubtless cut off the delivery of the antidote—some prearranged signal must have been set up that would not be activated if the convict in question were not safe and able to give it. Millitz was dead.

So would Kramer be if Millitz were the man.

Chapter XVI

Waxman waited at the Polk Street El station, keeping his back toward Presbyterian Hospital two blocks away and his eyes on an approaching train, as if willing it to come faster. When the elevated subway train finally did arrive, he had to wait for several passengers to disembark.

Once the passageway cleared he hurried on board, took a seat on the opposite side and glanced in the direction of the hospital to see if he could spot anyone following him—he suspected they must have noticed he was missing by now and begun to wonder . . . he had no idea, of course, that he'd been positively identified. He studied the other passengers; none of them seemed particularly interested in his presence.

The train turned east and traveled down the center of the Eisenhower Expressway to the edge of the Loop, where it slowly descended into a dark tunnel paralleling Dearborn Street above. When it reached Washington Avenue seven minutes later, he got off, walked down the center stairwell and hurried through another underground tunnel used by commuters to change trains for downtown. Halfway through, he spotted a crippled beggar playing "Easter Parade." For no apparent reason the beggar stopped his accordion playing, stood up and as Waxman approached began heading in the same direction. Waxman shrugged this off, though it did strike him as somewhat odd. He had no time, however, to linger. He was in a hurry to catch a northbound train and moved now toward the far end of the ramp. His mind was preoccupied with the antidote. He knew all too well that time was short. Kramer had gotten worse sooner than he'd expected . . . its performance, of course, was still only generally predictable. The timing had been further complicated by his having to wait until the last possible moment to leave the hospital and thereby risk drawing suspicion on himself. . . . When the train arrived the beggar followed him on board, entering the car by a different set of doors. He found a seat that strategically faced the professor from the opposite end of the train, and arranged his dog and accordion back against the window side of the bench before sitting down himself.

The plane carrying Giovanni was forced to circle Edmonton Field four times before given permission to land. Meanwhile Canadian police, stunned by the brutal killing of one of their officers and under orders to do everything possible this time to avoid a confrontation, changed their tactics. An effort would be made to talk the prisoner out of the plane rather than approach him directly.

During the three hour flight from New York Giovanni had remained somewhat confused by the earlier interrogation involving Kramer that had ended with a free airplane ride and loaded revolver. Ever since his imprisonment he'd been looking for some angle while his lawyers continued to appeal his case, but, after thinking it over, this was much too easy. His people were good at working miracles, but this? . . . and without warning . . . ? By nature and experience he was a suspicious man. He already knew the trip had *something* to do with the attack on Kramer . . . could it be he was being set up for a frame . . . ?

Giovanni's fears intensified when the plane came to an abrupt stop at the end of the runway and a moment later he heard the click of the cockpit door locking. There was silence as he went from window to window on each side of the aisle. He wanted to break

180

through one of the emergency exits and start running. He stopped to try to analyze the situation, but he was too nervous to think straight. He only knew he wished that he'd refused to board the plane in the first place. In his panic he didn't see the panel truck making its third trip out on the runway.

As two new police officers connected a portable microphone to the truck's batteries to explain the procedure for his "escort," authorities at Miami International Airport were preparing a completely different and untried approach. Akubar's plane crew had already radioed ahead that they would be landing for fuel . . . and by his hijacking action diverting the plane from Edmonton they were now reasonably certain Akubar was a kind of supernumerary with no direct involvement in the trade deal.

Because Miami was a jumping-off point, key to the Caribbean as well as several Mideast countries and there had been several hijackings—including Madison's attempt recorded on the telltale newsclip reviewed by Thornton and Pat—initiated elsewhere but refueling in Miami, the police had formulated a new plan and were anxiously waiting for an opportunity to try it. The man responsible for the plan was a biomedical engineer from Jackson Memorial Hospital who had once been hijacked himself. He lived only fifteen minutes from the terminal and had already been called.

Before their night's journey had begun, Madison and Lawson hardly knew each other. They lived in different cell blocks and worked at unrelated jobs. Although Madison's political fanaticism equaled Lawson's religious fervor in degree, and both men had demonstrated they would kill for their beliefs, there was little else they had in common except their life sentences.

There was friction from the moment they were put on the plane. Lawson resented the grueling interrogation and accurately blamed the much smaller Madison for his present predicament. Madison, nonetheless, realized he needed another black man as a decoy and became angry when young Lawson refused to speak or cooperate with him. After several failed attempts to pose as his friend, followed by threats, he managed to grab Lawson's revolver and sat down across the aisle from him to watch every move he made.

After an hour in flight Madison flipped on the intercom and demanded to know the plane's time of arrival. The pilot considered lying, couldn't see the point in it, and proceeded to report forty-five minutes. The intercom was then turned off again.

Madison put one gun into his back pocket and pointed the other directly at Lawson, ordering that he put on a parachute—he never had any intention of coming this far and landing into a double-cross, or simply trusting to his luck in getting by the Canadian authorities at Edmonton Airport to the prearranged connection . . . hence the original request for the parachutes, which normally weren't carried on commercial airplanes. A moment later the two were standing at the rear of the plane. Madison quickly undid the hatch and literally booted the hulking Lawson out into empty darkness. Lawson could be heard screaming as he fell. Then, with some last minute reluctance, Madison followed convinced he could master the technique without previous experience.

The chutes opened at altitudes where the oxygen was thin and temperature below freezing. Both men had considerable trouble catching their breath, and as they glided downward a strong wind carried them ten miles to the southeast, separating the two chutes by almost a half mile. Neither man, as might have been expected, had good control of his descent. Madison soon found himself plummeted into a wooded area. His chute was ripped into shreds as it crashed through the branches and finally knocked him to the ground, fracturing his left leg in two places.

Lawson was considerably luckier. He landed feet first, without a bruise or scratch, in the middle of a small field. While struggling to untangle himself from the straps he watched Madison's silhouette in the distance, but once he was free and had hidden the chute under a nearby bush he headed in the opposite direction. He was pleased with the new-found freedom and decided, after finding some food and warm clothing, to sneak back to Chicago and his mother. Even from this distance Madison appeared to be injured . . . well, good on him . . .

Madison could see Lawson going off and tried calling out to him but there was no response. He seemed to have pain everywhere. His leg was the worst, but his face was on fire with a crisscrossing of superficial cuts, his hands were bloody from gashes and scrapes, and his chest hurt whenever he took a deep breath. He didn't think that he could ever get up, but as he lay on his back the cold wet snow beneath his torn uniform began to soak in. He turned on his side and tried standing, but the injured leg wouldn't support any weight. He knew he couldn't stay where he was, looked around and spotted one of the newly broken-off branches a few yards away. Using his forearms to support his weight, he dragged himself across the ground. Every movement sent lightning pains down his back into his legs. He even considered forgoing his half of the deal, but there was too much money at stake . . .

Madison reached the crooked branch and somehow managed to pull himself up with it. As he did, the sharp autumn wind chilled his lightly clothed body. He began limping in a direction away from the rising morning sun, leaving a twisted and bloody trail behind. It was too much trouble to gather the remains of his parachute.

As the subway train wound through the corridors beneath Chicago's near North Side, Louis Waxman found himself staring at his own reflection in the smudged window next to his seat, becoming, in fact, fixated on it, and as he did so the awful tension of the present began to dissolve back once again to the time and place it all started, the installation in Arizona he'd been so summarily called to . . . and from which he'd at first demanded to be removed from when it became apparent that it involved a Department of Biological Warfare project. General Russell at first tried arguing against Waxman's resistance, reminding him that his principles should give way to the fact of two scientists' lives being in extreme jeopardy and his being the man with the best chance of saving their lives.

Waxman was hardly unaffected by this argument, but he also remained intensely aware that if he found the antidote, the possible use of the rabies virus might one day jeopardize the lives of millions . . . . Finally the general shrewdly persuaded the professor at least to look at the two men, who were being kept in a special isolation unit down the hall. Surely, Russell said, he wouldn't mind giving some suggestions for their immediate care until, perhaps, someone else could be found . . . Waxman could hardly refuse, and thereby entered a nightmare whose bizarre complications he could not possibly have imagined.

Both scientists, the general told him, were recent graduates of Dartmouth, in their early thirties, with families. One of the men, who was paralyzed from the waist down and delirous with fever, had a picture of his wife and three girls on his bedside table; as Waxman began his examination, he could hear the man muttering his wife's name. The other man was not nearly as confused, although his fever was only a tenth of a degree less, but he too was becoming paralyzed and when Russell introduced the professor he gratefully thanked Waxman for coming.

What had begun as a definite refusal became increasingly compromised. Waxman truly hated this project that had already brought two of its participants near death. He had been working and talking for the banning of such projects, which presumably were against the official policy of the U.S. government. He was surprised, in fact, that he'd been called at all, considering his well-known position on the matter, and assumed that in a way it was testimony to his special expertise—a testimony he devoutly wished the general had spared him. And yet, when it came down to it, he knew he couldn't just let these two men die without trying . . . . Every rationalization became increasingly weaker. He tried to tell Russell that an antidote would probably require months of research and would surely be too late for these men . . . until the general reminded him that his people had been close to a solution to the antidote. Finally Waxman acquiesced, planning in the back of his mind to destroy the research papers if and when he should ever find the cure. If the men died before he should succeed, he would immediately quit.

Waxman now unpacked his bag and spent the remainder of the night mulling over piles of research papers and studying the deadly virus under various chemical conditions, familiarizing himself with its properties and sensitivities. At the beginning he was able to get some information from the second less affected scientist, but the material was sketchy at best and the patient soon lapsed into a semicomatose state like the first. Nonetheless, the group's written notes were unusually meticulous and quite legible—indicating, as reported, that they had been close to finding an antidote themselves.

Over the next five days Waxman worked around the clock with the help of two highly trained assistants, stopping only when human necessity demanded and racing against time as the two men's condition steadily worsened. The paralysis was an ascending type, beginning with the lower extremities and slowly working its way up each man's body.

On the sixth day Waxman managed to extract a crude antiserum, but before he could properly purify it for human use the first scientist died. On the night of that same day Waxman hastily injected his antidote into the second scientist, who was barely holding on. There had been no time to test the material in laboratory animals, and it could well have made him worse, but by the next morning his vital signs had shown a significant improvement and within forty-eight hours he had become alert and oriented. Unfortunately the paralysis lingered, leaving him bedridden for life. Waxman reasoned that there might well have been a complete cure if the antidote had been available considerably earlier—

After ten minutes and three stops underground, a blast of fresh air hit the cabin as the tracks rose above ground to follow an overhead viaduct, momentarily bringing Waxman back to the present and the thought that Kramer, if all still went as planned, should certainly escape such drastic consequences. The train stopped at Fullerton Avenue, waited a few moments for a smattering of commuters to board and then slowly pulled away, rumbling along through the backyards of shabby brick buildings whose individual colors were charred with Chicago soot, past vacant lots that were littered with garbage, behind schools whose barred windows were cracked by vandals' rocks and whose walls were decorated by the local graffiti. As the El gained momentum, Waxman's thoughts kept pace, finally once again dissolving back to Arizona, to the night before he left . . . .

Now that the army had an antidote, the nerve toxin would be added to their arsenal. Adding to his dismay, Waxman realized his plans to burn his notebooks had been made irrelevant by the fact of his two capable assistants, either of whom could reproduce everything significant that the three of them had accomplished—and very probably would be ordered to do so unless the project were shut down and the program abandoned.

In the press of the moment, his thoughts were racing for a response that had at best only a general outline. But it did occur that if to destroy his notes and records would no longer destroy knowledge of this poison and its antidote, perhaps their potentially horrendous consequences could at least be neutralized by moving in the exact opposite direction . . . if the dangerous knowledge could not be eliminated, then perhaps its widespread availability might be the answer.

So rather than destroy all notes and records, it was important first of all to insure that he could preserve and take them and all other pertinent materials away with him. He quickly now took advantage of an empty office full of research books and other materials to xerox copies of his laboratory notes—which he knew would soon be stamped as classified—as well as the project's original protocol, a thick official document with a two-page table of contents that included instructions for the capturing of the West Indian bats, methods by which safely to extract the rabies virus from their saliva and excrements, and a step-by-step analysis of the procedures necessary to isolate and fractionate the specific neurotoxins. It was a most unaccustomed piece of larceny, and his perspiring hands seemed to be moving in slow motion as he waited for each rotary turn of the machine . . . and as General Russell, in the next room, spoke to a superior in Washington about his accomplishment.

Russell's enthusiasm was an obverse of Waxman's depression. But their degree of determination was shared. Russell's had helped get him what he wanted. Waxman's was now devoted to stopping any possible eventual use of the Z-3 poison. The outlines of a plan were already beginning to fill in. . . . He had scientific contacts throughout Europe, particularly Geneva . . . in neutral Switzerland . . . and *neutralized* was what needed to be done to the Z-3 toxin—politically neutralized, that is, so no one country or group would be tempted to use it. An international scientific body of some sort, with the kind of responsible scientists he knew, seemed a reasonable approach. He was no naive political dupe—he had no intention of turning it over to a rival superpower or the U.N. with its politicized General Assembly and even special agenices. No, this would be a matter of full disclosure coupled with real control by men who understood Z-3's deadly potential and were sufficiently worldly to use their knowledge as responsible leverage to protect, inform, educate and eventually perhaps dissuade. Meanwhile, the very fact of responsible parties having the knowledge of the poison and its antidote would tend to make its usefulness as a threat by one nation or group against another pretty well obsolete.

Of course, Waxman realized, such a course was drastic and he would not pursue it until he'd exhausted all other remedies available—including going to Russell's superiors, to the Secretary of Defense himself if necessary, and attempting to persuade them to go along with him. . . . Just now, though, the immediate order of business was to get off the general's premises. He managed to pull the last Xerox sheet and stuff the uneven pile between a hurriedly assembled stack of books at just about the time Russell hung up and came into the room, smiling. Waxman picked up the books, nodded briefly and headed for the door.

"Looks like a lot of heavy reading for one night," Russell said, pleased with his pun, "especially after all your long hours—"

"Well, I suppose it's all in the eyes of the beholder," Waxman said with what he hoped was more cool than he felt as he passed through the doorway and quickly headed for his own quarters, where he'd also hidden two small vials—one with a minute amount of the Z–3 toxin and the other with the newly discovered antidote. . . .

The antidote . . . the word seemed to explode in his consciousness as the train now reached Belmont Avenue. The fact of it, begun back in that Arizona desert, had grown into a life-size thing for him, life-and-death for Kramer . . . for Kramer, whose behavior, unwittingly of course, had made him a kind of passive collaborator. . . . His thoughts slipped back to his several trips to Pentagon offices appointed in varying degrees of plush according to rank, to the polite unsmiling headshakes as he attempted to argue his position and got precisely nowhere. He'd done his country a real service, they'd said, and that ought to be that.

When he finally requested an appointment with Secretary of Defense Kramer, it was politely refused. The Secretary's schedule was especially full just now, with campaigning as well as his departmental responsibilities, but "one of his chief deputies," a Mr. Jeremy Royce, would be glad to see Professor Waxman . . . Waxman, wondering how there could be more than one "chief," quickly accepted.

As it turned out, Jeremy Royce was a difficult man to dislike. Pleasant, soft-spoken, in his middle forties, he'd been with Kramer from the early days as district attorney in Chicago. While

188

he couldn't, of course, speak for the Secretary, he thought he knew the Secretary's views quite well and would attempt to be as responsive as possible to Professor Waxman, whose reputation and recent contribution to the country he was, of course, aware of.

Waxman nodded and got right to it. "I'm afraid I don't consider it a 'contribution,' Mr. Royce. I'm glad, of course, that I was able to help save a man's life, but the price will be altogether too high, I believe, if the substance that poisoned him and killed his colleagues, as well as its antidote, are not destroyed and all reference to them *permanently* eradicated, with a standing directive that they never be reproduced or used in any way—"

"Professor Waxman, as I said, I can't speak for the Secretary, but it's my impression that such substances are not intended to be used. They are only—"

"Yes, yes, I understand the good *intentions*, but that hardly argues against my point. Mr. Royce, I've never met Secretary Kramer but my impression is that he is a reasonable and decent man, although I believe we disagree in numerous areas. It's precisely to those qualities of reason and decency that I'm now appealing, through you, when I tell you that this material could paralyze an entire country. Leave nothing but invalids, if they survived . . . it's not like tear gas or mace or—"

"Or nuclear weapons?" Royce said, still in his equable tone.

"I understand the point, but I disagree with it. The fact that *so far* we've not resorted to ultimate destruction hardly argues for adding on another awful, even if short of ultimate, weapon to the growing tinderbox."

"Professor, surely you don't think we're the only ones who make guns, or bombs, or—"

"Of course not, but I believe it unlikely that anyone else has isolated the poison in question, or devised its antidote. And lacking evidence to the contrary, I say as a civilized people it's hardly up to us to invent new and uglier ways to kill millions of people . . . Mr. Royce, please, you've *got* to convince the Secretary that this thing be stopped now, right *now*." He punctuated the last words by slamming his fist on the desk.

"I respect and admire you for your feelings, professor, but, if you'll forgive me, I must say I honestly believe *you* are missing the point. I told you, that I don't speak for Secretary Kramer, and I don't. But I've been around here a long time and I think I know some of his thoughts in these matters. Let me try to give you a few. As you said, he's a decent man. He's also a man of the world, literally. As a lawyer, he could put his trust in the courts. As a man whose job is to see that the country is protected in the world—and I'm almost quoting him now—he's operating in a sort of no-man's land where there is no court or police force—and where your law is your arsenal . . . including anything necessary to keep the balance of power within a policy of détente. . . ."

So damn plausible, Waxman thought as he listened. So reasoned and calm . . . and no doubt sincere. It was truly terrifying. . . .

"I'm not trying to persuade you, professor. Somehow I doubt that would be possible. But I did want you at least to hear our side of things, to understand, perhaps, a little better why we feel as we do. As I said, I don't expect to make a convert of you, and so, along with our gratitude for what you've done, I must also remind you that the project was and is classified top secret, and that you as well as the rest of us are legally bound to keep it that way."

He stood up then and started around from his desk to shake hands. Waxman, however, had quickly gotten up and was already walking out of the room. There was no longer any question in his mind. He'd tried his best. There was nothing left but to take Z–3, its antidote and the papers to Switzerland. . . .

Switzerland. A long way, a very long way from Chicago, from a Chicago elevated train taking a sharp ninety degree turn and stopping at Sheridan Avenue and opening its doors. No one got on or off. Waxman, rubbing his eyes, could make out Lake Michigan rimmed by high rises off in the distance. As the train started once again, passing over a shopping center, Waxman felt again his anger after leaving Royce's office, and afterward wondering more than once whether if only he'd been able to see Kramer he might not, somehow, have persuaded him. . . . Kramer . . . too busy, running for office, to grant an audience . . . Kramer . . . Secretary of Defense, would-be Vice-President and . . . who knew? . . . one day President . . . Kramer, the man who was the object of his frustration, who was to have such an unexpected role to play in the equally unexpected plan he suddenly found himself forced to devise and put in motion. . . .

It began on a 747 jet, bound for Geneva. It had taken Waxman three days after his abortive meeting with Jeremy Royce to make initial arrangements with his scientific contacts in Geneva and book passage on Swissair from Kennedy Airport in New York. He had barely settled himself in his tourist-class seat when a commotion broke out in the rear of the plane. Assuming it was an argument with some disgruntled passenger whose seat was taken, Waxman ignored it until three black men suddenly made their appearance, announced that the plane was being hijacked and that, providing everybody behaved themselves, they'd be safely unloaded at Havana, Cuba, the new destination. The men had managed to get on board by climbing the fences near the terminal shortly before boarding and merging with the rest of the passengers, thereby avoiding the normal scanning mechanisms. Their leader was a George Madison—a member of the Black Panthers who two days earlier had killed a policeman during armed robbery of a liquor store, been arrested and had escaped en route to the Tombs.

When he ordered the pilot to change his flight plan for Havana, the pilot shook his head and asked him where he'd been lately . . . didn't he know that Castro had gotten tired of taking in the U.S.'s rejects and was no longer granting hijackers sanctuary? Madison said that sounded like crap to him and that if the pilot didn't shape up and fly right to Cuba he'd have to start messing people up. He waved a hand gun toward the passenger area to make clear who he meant. The pilot nodded, banked and headed south.

Madison, apparently satisfied and leaving one of his men behind

191

to make sure radio silence was maintained, went back to the passenger compartments and with his other accomplice began a survey of passengers' personal possessions, taking whatever struck his fancy. When he got to Waxman, whose briefcase was upright on the vacant adjacent seat, he demanded to see the contents of the briefcase. Waxman, beside himself, at first refused, then argued with more courage than he felt that all he had were some technical papers that would mean nothing to Madison but were his notes for a speech he'd intended to give in Geneva, at a meeting of a fraternal scientific group he belonged to. Madison, vaguely intrigued, bent over to take the briefcase and see for himself when Waxman, finally desperate, grabbed for it and nearly pulled it back. Very interested now . . . who the hell would risk a bullet in his head for some lecture notes? . . . Madison moved his gun close to Waxman's head, leaned over and took the briefcase away. A short while later Waxman heard Madison joking and laughing in the rear with his friend, and sandwiched in their conversation the words . . . "some kind of official papers . . . ought to be worth something to somebody . . . did you see the old guy freak out when I lifted them . . . ?" Waxman realized they must have seen the "Top Secret" stampings on the papers. My God, how would he ever get them back . . . ?

Madison, despite his high over managing to capture the plane, had some nagging misgivings about what the pilot had said. Well, even if it weren't crap, he'd rather take his chances in a rinkydink Cuban jail than a maximum security slammer in the U.S., or spend his life in exile in some Arab paradise . . . he'd had enough of Mecca during those six months in Algeria. . . . He decided he'd better go up front again to check personally on the pilot and crew when he noticed some white stuff flying by outside. Several of the passengers had also noticed it and began murmuring and speculating among themselves. Telling them to "stay cool," Madison hurried into the pilot's compartment and demanded to know what was "going down, man." "Nothing much," the pilot told him, "except half the supply of jet fuel—that white stuff was the fuel hitting the sub-zero atmosphere. And *that* isn't crap," he added. Neither was the fact that Miami was the furthest they could now go before refueling. "Don't blame your buddy," the pilot told him. "No way he could have known what we were doing."

Madison was not a fool. After forcing the pilot to show him the fuel gauges, and inspecting them carefully, he was sufficiently convinced that the pilot was telling him the truth. Suppressing his rage and desire to waste the man on the spot, he ordered him to go ahead and land in Miami, but to be very careful what he said. Just say he was off-course or something and had to make an emergency fuel stop.

Some two hours later, when the plane landed in Miami, the police and F.B.I. were waiting, having been alerted by a simple code previously worked out for all pilots to use in just such an emergency when radioing in for routine landing instructions. Unlike previous bloody episodes, nobody made a move to take over the plane. After some routine exchanges about the need to double check the fuel gauges now, two mechanics were allowed on board by Madison. Shortly thereafter, when Madison's attention was momentarily diverted, they drew their guns, quickly had him in cuffs and went after the other two men. In the exchange one of them was killed, and not a single passenger was injured.

It was a masterful operation, much praised and appreciated by everybody involved except Madison and his surviving accomplice, who were quickly removed, after being separated from whatever passenger belongings they had on their persons. These and all other belongings were quickly restored to their owners, including Waxman's briefcase. All that was required of him, as it was of the other passengers, was to sign an acknowledgment of receipt of his property. He was, to put it mildly, delighted to do so.

By then it was too late in the day to catch another flight to Geneva, but the airline was gracious enough to provide him with a booking for the following day and a hotel room for the night. After a quick lunch, he went to poolside, hoping to relax but nonetheless taking his books and briefcase with him . . . he had no intention of ever letting them out of his sight. Thoroughly exhausted from all he'd been through, he retired early.

Around ten o'clock, shortly after he'd fallen asleep, there was a knock on his door. Startled awake, he called out inquiringly and a voice loudly announced that it was the police and they were sorry to disturb him but they needed to ask him some questions about the hijacking. Waxman could hardly refuse . . . especially after avoiding all attempts to interview and question him at the airport. He worried, though, about them looking at the contents of his briefcase. At first he thought of hiding it and then realized that would be a panicky reaction. After all, he was Dr. Louis Waxman, a scientist with some rather substantial credentials. His friends in Switzerland had said they would handle customs there, but alone in a Miami hotel room . . . There was another loud knock on the door, and quickly tying a robe around him, he took a deep breath and went to open it. When he did so, he found himself looking directly into the barrel of a gun held by a man who bore no resemblance to a police officer.

Actually he was a close old friend of the hijacker Madison, named Lucas Marion, and he immediately backed the professor into his room and signaled for him to sit on the bed.

"I hear you made quite a fuss a little while back about some papers in that briefcase, man. Top secret or something, right?" Lucas nodded toward the leather case sitting in plain sight on the bureau. "We figure we oughta be able to do some business—like, say, my buddy Madison for these papers." He walked over now to the briefcase, unlatched it, took out the papers and began flipping through them.

Waxman sat silently on the bed. He couldn't believe that it was happening to him again. "Madison? . . . I don't understand . . . I thought they arrested or shot—"

"Well, so they did, Dr. Louis Waxman"—he noted Waxman's

194

surprise that he knew his name—"but even hijackers got to have their rights. George got a lawyer down there right quick, laid it all out to him in a few minutes of private lawyer and client chit-chat, I was called and the rest, like they say, is history . . . . By the way, don't look so spooked, doctor, your name is right there on your briefcase. Also on the hotel registry. Also this is the hotel the papers said all you victims was being put up in. Piece of cake, doctor."

Waxman would gladly have had the opportunity to do something about Lucas's insufferable smugness. The old World War II line, "Wipe that smile off your face, soldier," came to mind. He was, he realized too well, hardly in the position to do so. "But I don't understand," Waxman said, terrified that he did indeed, all too well, understand, "how you could possibly expect me or anybody to —"

"Well, now, hold on, doctor. Let me help you out. Those papers are some kind of government secret stuff—even a poor uneducated type like me can tell that. You damn near got a bullet in your head, way I hear it, when my friend Mr. Madison was about to separate you from them. Okay, fine, you want your papers, we want Mr. Madison. Let's do business . . ."

Waxman shook his head, and now his voice began to rise uncharacteristically—the last time was at the end of the meeting in Royce's office—as he said, "Those papers are no good to you, you've no idea what they are and—"

"Well, you're right about not knowing what they are, and we couldn't care less, probably more secret stuff to blow up the world with. Fine and dandy, that's out of our league. The more you talk, though, the more convinced I am that they can be a lot of good to me, and to Mr. Madison. Now let's get to it, Doctor, let your people in Washington or wherever it is know what we got and what we want." He was backing toward the door now, briefcase in hand. "Like the man said, 'Don't call us, we'll call you—' "

"It won't work," Waxman persisted. "The government would

195

never consider such a deal. Maybe they should but I guarantee you, they're much too stubborn . . . I know . . ."

"Well, maybe so, but you just convince them, doctor. You're a smart man, they'll listen to you—"

"They *won't* listen to me, those papers are stolen, they don't even know they're missing . . ." Waxman blurted it out in desperation, sat back down on the bed, his head in his hands.

Lucas Marion looked at him and almost laughed. "Well, I'll be damned. And I bet I just got me a good notion who did the dirty deed." He shook his head. "It just goes to show what I've been saying all along . . . you white folks get tired of stealing from us black cats, you going to start in on yourselves. For shame, a nice respectable gentleman like you . . ."

Waxman barely heard him. . . . "I'll give you twenty thousand dollars for them. You can have anything I own for security —" He hoped the money might make the man forget any promise he'd made to Madison. He would have made it more, but it was all he figured he could possibly raise on his few securities. He prayed it would be enough . . . the last thing he wanted was for Lucas to go to the government. . . .

"Well, well, but what about my buddy? No, man, he's counting on me to get him loose. No deal unless he goes with it—"

"All right," Waxman interrupted. "I'll manage it somehow. I'll get him out, I'll—"

"Well, that's good to hear, Doctor. And I'll tell you what we'll do. You get half the money right away for me. I keep the papers until Mr. Madison is free like a bird. Then you give me the other half and I give you your loot and you go peddle it any old place you want. You white gentlemen got your games, we got ours. Well, I guess that about wraps it up for now. And remember, don't try to find me. I'll be in touch. . . . You know, I got a notion it's going to be real comfortable-like, doing business with you, Doctor. After all, in a way you're one of us."

196

He was out the door then, and Waxman, still sitting on the bed, heard him laughing as he walked down the hall to the elevators. It was, Waxman realized, a terrible deal. One-sided, but he was hardly in a position to bargain when he looked at the options. For a moment, shaken by the cool presentation of Madison's emissary and the notion of the secret of Z–3 being in his possession, he was tempted to give up, to put in a call to Royce, or even Russell, and tell what he'd done and risk the consequences. And then his analytical impulses came into play. He realized he not only was being pointlessly self-sacrificing, he was both betraying what he'd believed in—and still did believe in—and overlooking what he already knew about both the government people and Madison and his friend. Suppose he did contact the government? First, there was an excellent possibility they wouldn't believe him, that they would assume he had stolen the toxin and antitoxin and now after second thoughts wanted to return it and had concocted the story of the theft and Madison as an ingenious if seemingly far-fetched cover. Their minds moved in the ways of supersecret intrigues—as recent revelations of the intelligence agencies had indicated—and this might make sense to them. He might well end up arrested for theft of secret government documents and materials, or worse—lose his samples and, of course, fail to recover the documents that Madison's people had. So, dismissing that impulsive notion, he returned once again to analyze the situation he was left with by Madison's friend, First, he was fortunate that the man had little inclination to set up the deal himself for a trade with the government, and, whether he knew the reason or not, he was probably right. No doubt the government—providing they believed Madison's people at all—at best would attempt to recover the papers, and somehow not follow through on the release of Madison. Whatever the reason, Madison's people had no trust in or desire to deal with the U.S. government, which put Waxman in a strong position—at least to the extent that they considered him a

197

directly interested party and the prime one to deal with. At the moment, of course, he hadn't the slightest notion of how he would go about securing Madison's release, but even if he were to hit on a substantial plan, he worried about the lure of the second $10,000 being sufficient to insure their bothering to hand over the documents once Madison was free. Except for two important considerations: they rather clearly had little interest in attempting to deal for the documents themselves, apparently feeling this was too risky, and they were right; and the money was obviously of paramount importance—hadn't the newspapers said Madison had held up a liquor store, committed a homicide, for money? For a man in his position, $10,000 was a very considerable amount, and there was also the interest of Madison's friend, who obviously—he'd already demanded $10,000 in advance be paid over to him—set considerable store by another $10,000. Waxman wished the sum he could offer were higher, but that was all he could manage on his own, which was the only way he could conduct this business and hope to maintain the secrecy needed until he could fulfill his own purpose of getting the samples and documents to the scientists in Geneva.

Having at least put his thoughts in some order, Waxman flew to New York City the next day. He sold enough of his securities to raise the first $10,000 and kept the money in the form of a cashier's check while he waited to hear from Madison's go-between—he still didn't know his name—and to devise some scheme for securing Madison's release; hopefully the scheme would develop before he heard from the intermediary.

At first his mind turned to wild and foolish notions, including subornation of jurors, armed assault on Madison's jail, and other fantasies as dramatic as they were impractical. Finally, as when he overcame his impulse about confessing all to the government, his disciplined and sophisticated organizational training as a professional researcher took over. He needed a program that, regardless of how unusual or unlikely it might seem on the surface, would

198

have a built-in reasonable chance for success. He was dealing with an unfamiliar field—crime. He would investigate it.

At first he began studying books on criminal investigation, accounts of unsolved crimes, particularly those involving kidnappings, hostages and the like—after all, his Z–3 papers were being kept hostage, weren't they? . . . Nothing seemed even remotely helpful. He spent hours in his library at home, skipping lectures, making up excuses of illness. The pressure kept building—especially when the phone calls from Madison's friend Lucas (he'd finally told him that one name) began to arrive almost daily with increasingly blunt inquiries—and it showed in his increasingly irritable behavior with friends and family, who became concerned for his health. . . .

Health . . . illness . . . and the thought of it took him to the memory of the two victims of the Z–3 virus, of its harrowing effect, and of the refusal of the government people to destroy it and all records of it and its antidote so that its effect could never be perpetrated on any people, accidentally or otherwise. And with that memory, the refusal of Secretary of Defense Kramer to see him when his underlings had refused to go along, and the final, so reasonable and well-intentioned position of the Secretary . . . Secretary Kramer, now would-be Vice-President Kramer. Parallels began forming in his mind, parallels that had an inherent symmetry of form and content as well . . . Madison for the Z–3 papers was the proposal that had been put to him. That outrageous proposition rested on the refusal of a man named Kramer to see him, to consider and act on his request that the stuff be forever destroyed and proscribed. It was not only neat, but appropriate . . . Kramer for Madison, which in turn would mean the return of the papers to him. Madison and the papers in this equation were interchangeable, indeed they were synonymous—in more ways, ironically, than one. But how in the world actually to manage the kidnapping of the Secretary and holding him until Madison's release? The notion really involved too much potential violence,

199

strong-arm, literally, which was neither his style nor, he was sure, within his capability. Kramer was certain to be surrounded by unusual security now that he was a candidate. The idea of accomplices was entirely too risky, out of the question. The most likely outcome of any attempt by him single-handedly or otherwise actually to kidnap Kramer would be his death or capture.

Still, the notion of Kramer being somehow a centerpiece in this affair would not leave him, and he found himself acutely aware of the Secretary and everything about him that appeared in print and on TV, almost as though the world had somehow focused in on the man, and he, Waxman, had developed a tunnel vision leading to him and excluding all others. It was at this time that he noted the brief story in the *New York Times* about the sudden death from an apparent heart attack of Mr. Jeremy Royce, an aide to Secretary of Defense and now vice-presidential candidate Kramer . . . It startled him, the man had seemed so calm, but he knew of course that frequently those under considerable pressure maintained facades, and were prime candidates for sudden and surprising heart attacks. Royce's death also depressed him, invoking as it did his intense feelings of angry frustration as he left the man's office that day.
. . . Somehow he now felt his attention even more focused on Kramer. Suddenly and increasingly he noted stories about Kramer meeting with foreign opposite numbers, conferring with the President, making campaign statements; and on the nightly newscasts Kramer the candidate appearing about the country on the campaign trail. It was on such a newscast with a film clip from Boston that, watching Kramer, he realized how the man increasingly these days was stepping from behind his podium and going into the crowds to shake hands, in pressing-the-flesh fashion of such gregarious types as the late President Johnson and Bobby Kennedy. It struck him especially by its contrast with Kramer's behavior in his own case when he'd tried so hard to see him without success. Kramer the candidate was clearly more accessible than Kramer the keeper of defense, and with that thought came another, startling, frighten-

ing, but exciting at the same time as it finally pointed to the direction of a solution to his quandary about what approach to use to somehow make Kramer a hostage for the release of Madison and thereby secure the recovery of the Z–3 papers.

Kramer could not be isolated, immobilized as a hostage by conventional methods, but he might well be by others uniquely within his, Waxman's, world . . . and so become a *medical* hostage. And the method would be a substance to immobilize the Secretary, under control, for a reasonable period during which the safe release of Madison and confirmation of same could be made, followed by the transmittal of the necessary information about the immobilizing agent, its antidote, and so forth, to restore the Secretary to normalcy. The time would depend partly on the agent, but at least twenty-four hours seemed indicated for all that would need to happen and yet keep the project in a sufficiently concentrated period of time to heighten the impact and sense of seriousness for Kramer and those around him.

Waxman's mind began rushing ahead now, into technical areas he was fully at home in. The agent to be used . . . that was the next consideration . . . . He made lists of various immobilizing substances that were accessible, and then methodically eliminated those that struck him as being subject to easy identification by a reasonably competent medical laboratory or the experts that the government was certain to call in . . . . He even considered combining two or three to confound and confuse those seeking to detect and identify, but that would mean an untested mixture that might turn out to be fatal, and, despite his anger and frustration which he laid to the Secretary, he certainly did not want that . . . . Unable to hit on the right substance to use, his thoughts turned to a much more solvable problem—the method of transmitting it. A preloaded syringe could easily be concealed in one hand, and its silent use would insure that a minimum of attention would be attracted to him. He now proceeded to buy several different types from reputable supply houses and determined that a 5 cc syringe, greased with glycerin and activated by a metal spring, took less than a second to inject its contents—much like, say, the syringes carried by those allergic to bees, who might die from a sting without an immediate injection of adrenaline.

Still very much in mind of Kramer's penchant for handshaking in crowds, he decided he would be one of those to grasp the Secretary's offered hand—as he was not able to do when he had made his numerous attempts to meet with him in a less public forum. After a short time he was able to devise a method for strapping the loaded syringe to his wrist, but the homemade gear struck him more often than it struck the rubber ball he used as a surrogate hand. Almost every position that he tried had a significant flaw, leaving his hand painfully dotted with needle marks. Finally, after days of frustrating experiments, he borrowed some plaster of Paris from his hospital and made a long arm-cast that kept the syringe far enough away and yet could easily be triggered by a short string looped around his thumb.

The next step was to plan the logistics of the actual— But first, and he had to catch himself up short—he needed to return to what had been eluding him, or to what he had been avoiding . . . he wasn't entirely sure which, perhaps both . . . . He had to settle on the agent to be used, especially now that he had the device to transmit it. All right, the three desired characteristics that were basic and inescapable were: 1) an agent that would in effect immobilize a man and whose effects would be reversible within a reasonably predictable period of time; 2) an agent that would not likely be detected by trained and skilled technicians and scientists, at least not until the release of Madison and the transfer of the Z–3 papers had been accomplished—for this, it occurred to him, it would be helpful if he could actually be on the scene at some point when this detection process was going on . . . he would, of course, be in the area of whatever hospital they would take Kramer to, but at the moment he didn't see how he could simply ring up and volunteer his expert services without possibly becoming suspect himself, nor was he sure how well he would hold up under such circumstances in any case; 3) and following directly and logically from 2, an agent whose properties were almost uniquely within *his* knowledge, and one for which the antidote, also known almost uniquely to him, would be especially likely to resist the best efforts of scientists and technicians . . . .

It had, he suspected, been in the background of his thoughts right along, or at least for some time, but he hadn't really wanted to confront it. There was now an inescapable logic to its selection—the agent that fulfilled all three stipulations was, of course, the Z–3 toxin, of which he had one vial, taken from the lab in Arizona, in the wall safe in his home, and whose antidote he had managed to discover in time to save the life of one of the scientists working on the secret project in the government installation there. That scientist had been infected by the virus for several weeks before Waxman had been called in and was able to develop and administer the antidote. He'd become paralyzed, but within only a 24-hour time span, the results, while predictably acute, would also predictably not only be reversible but reversible with the reasonable likelihood of total recovery. Of course there would be risks, especially for Kramer, and for himself too . . . but there was the larger objective as well, and, having come this far, its importance hardly paled—on the contrary, it became even greater and more insistent. The danger of admittedly well-intentioned, sincere and self-convinced men like Kramer and Royce was hardly diminished—especially with Kramer now moving toward a position that might well put him, as they said, only a heartbeat from the presidency. In fact, as he'd seen, so-called decent men could be the real fanatics, worse than the cynical opportunists who rode with the prevailing winds, especially when they were wrong—as Waxman and many other responsible scientists and, indeed, statesmen and ordinary citizens believed they were. Their convictions, hardened by a sense of being reasonable and "right," became even more difficult to turn aside, and they to dissuade from their policies. Only the accident of circumstances had brought him to this position that actually involved some potentially serious physical danger to another human being. He hated this, despite his personal feelings toward Kramer, but he would not panic and lose sight of the larger purpose; rather, he would do his best to reduce the risks and accomplish what he felt was essential.

And it was essential . . . he was, indeed, convinced of that. If this made *him* a kind of fanatic, well then, perhaps in a sense he was. He was a scientist. He knew, most especially, about the inherent, awful dangers of the substance he was attempting to remove from his country's weapons arsenal. He had no illusions about single-handedly reversing the course of traditional official thinking, however enlightened, relatively speaking, it might be on the subject. But he at least might contribute to some movement in a positive direction, and he could do something in this specific case about this specific substance and its really horrendous potential for mass paralyzing illness and death. Too often in the past, he felt, scientists, all good men, had subordinated their consciences and larger responsibilities to the men of the so-called real world, as though having skill and knowledge somehow exempted one from reponsibility in the world. To the contrary, having such knowledge, he'd come to believe, heightened one's obligations to take a position, to take a stand. It was a long road, looking back, from those early unconcerned days just after medical school to now, but it was one that had brought him to this admittedly harrowing point. It would be a denial of all that had come before to turn back now. . . .

He came back now to the stage in his planning that he'd abruptly left earlier—the working out of the actual confrontation with the Secretary. It would have to be at one of his open public appearances, a political rally where a large crowd would act as camouflage and where the man would likely indulge his observed habit of moving among crowds to shake hands. There would have to be more than one escape route . . . . If he were apprehended, he could use the antidote for bargaining . . . though that again would involve convincing authorities of his entire story, and might well frighten off Madison's people and jeopardize the likelihood of ever recovering the Z–3 papers. Still, his method of attack, which nobody could be expecting, and the acutal injection itself that would neither involve noise such as a gun shot nor any large commotion nor even an especially dramatic reaction on the Secretary's part . . . all these factors would make excellent the prospect for his escaping the area undetected. He considered, momentarily, the notion of some disguise, a beard, for example, and decided against it: first, though reasonably well known in the scientific community, especially in his specialty, he was hardly likely to be recognized generally, even if cameras were full on him—the interview at the Miami airport had proved that; nobody identified him in the papers after he'd refused to give his name. Second, though it had always been something of a curse to him in earlier years, he had what he felt was actually a rather nondescript face, one that now could be confused with any number of other middle-aged men who looked somewhat older than their age. His was a face, he suspected, that might even defeat a police lineup. And then, so thinking, he felt the whole notion of a disguise such as a false beard was altogether too theatrical, distinctly not his personal style, and one which would make him feel uncomfortable, unnatural and heighten the unease that was sure to accompany the inherently melodramatic act he would be involved in. He'd wear some longish coat with a collar turned up, and that would be it. Better depend on relative anonymity than the shaky security of a stagey disguise. . . .

This decided upon, he needed to refine matters further to select the actual place for the confrontation. He carefully scanned the papers for news of Kramer's itinerary, and to supplement this he called Kramer's campaign headquarters in ten major cities, representing himself as a long-time admirer of the Secretary and asking for whatever dates and places they might have for his appearances in their respective cities. He learned that Kramer had some eighteen speeches planned for six major trips to Philadelphia, New York City, Boston, Los Angeles, San Francisco and Chicago—the last of which, being Kramer's home town and where he'd gotten his start as a district attorney, was expected to draw the largest crowd. Also, by somewhat closer questioning, he found out, or rather had confirmed what he'd already observed on newscasts, that the rallies were accompanied by midday motorcades—to take advantage of potential lunch-time crowds. The big Chicago rally certainly looked especially promising. Waxman had been to Chicago on numerous occasions and considered how "right" for his purposes would be an attack that could take place near any one of four subway stations, whose underground passageways always struck him as resembling a rat maze. In such a situation he could with relative ease get to the hospital involved, perhaps get a sense of the impression there of the extent of the injury to Kramer, and most crucially, manage to leave a note that would get to the Secretary, or his doctors and staff, announcing the twenty-four-hour deadline for releasing Madison if they wanted the Secretary to survive the assault he'd just experienced . . . . Whether he would actually mention Madison's name in this instruction, he wasn't sure . . . perhaps that should come in a second communication . . . . Also, the details of how he'd actually leave the message weren't entirely clear, but as he thought about this it seemed likely he'd be able to use the messenger station, which he knew in most hospitals was usually cluttered and periodically unattended—a condition that was almost certain to be intensified with the fluster and furor that would be attending the Secretary's arrival. Yes, the Chicago site was by far the most promising, but he couldn't count on it alone; he'd need to make duplicate plans for the other cities as well . . . .

The idea of mentioning Madison's name in the original note continued to bother him, and as he thought about it, he realized why . . . . Actually identifying Madison as the subject of the trade increased the likelihood of the police and other authorities being tempted to "cheat" on the arrangement, to try to renege somehow on the release of Madison once they had secured the antidote. And of course if this should happen it would mean the papers most definitely would not be returned, thereby defeating the objective of the entire operation. To divert and confuse as much as possible those whose job it would be to save the Secretary and frustrate the release of a rather notorious murderer, he decided it would probably be necessary to add names to the ransom note. This would also make less likely Madison's being recaptured before the papers could be returned.

During this period while he developed his final plans, the calls from Lucas not only became more frequent, but more demanding as to details of whatever the "good professor," as he persisted in calling him, had worked out. Lucas told him the time was getting short—Madison was an impatient fellow and might try something foolish on his own, which would be the end of the professor's chances for a trade for his precious papers . . . right? Dig?—and maybe he'd just have to call the deal off and send the professor's precious papers to the cops with a little note about the crooked professor . . . .

To appease Lucas, and to convince him of the serious progress he was making, Waxman filled him in on his thinking, including the consideration of using more names for the ransom note to protect Madison. When he heard this news, Lucas delightedly contributed a long list of his friends that he wanted included, and it became extremely difficult to convince him that just any name wouldn't do, and most especially, Waxman pointed out, close associates of Madison were risky because they might be traced back to him. Lucas, impressed if disappointed by the consequences of the professor's logic, finally concurred, but insisted that he be kept up to date on the professor's choices . . . .

To search out the additional names he needed, Waxman spent two days in the New York Public Library main branch perusing back issues of the *New York Times*. By the end of the second evening he had selected twelve prospects, eleven of which were serving life sentences—most for capital crimes. His final select list was in line with his purpose of confusing the police, thereby protecting his subject as much as possible. He chose prisoners from different parts of the country, each of whom would be a plausible suspect—both for his compelling reason as well as a potential means for setting up the crime. He didn't much like the idea of using such men, guilty of extreme crimes, but to pick men guilty of lesser offenses would leave Madison too easily pinpointed as the one with the most obvious reason for going to such extremes to be released. Also, he did try to mitigate this somewhat in his own eyes by telling himself there was a reasonable chance that most, perhaps all, of them would eventually be recaptured . . . .

Dr. Gerald Weisberg was the first name chosen. The Miami Beach physician was a perfect fit—he'd actually used poison to kill his wife. Muhammed Akubar was his second choice. The newspapers had tied him in with a Palestinian terrorist group known to hate American government officials for their identification with the cause of Israel and fanatical enough to risk almost anything to help an imprisoned comrade escape. The fact that he was imprisoned at Soledad on the opposite coast from Weisberg was a plus. Third choice was Louis Anthony Giovanni, at Attica in New York state. Although the mobster was neither smart nor knowledgeable enough to be taken seriously as the brains behind this plot, he would believably have excellent contacts who could be, and therefore he could not be eliminated as a suspect.

Several names were debated for the fourth pick, but he finally decided on Carey Millitz, who was at San Quentin in California. Millitz, a paranoid schizophrenic, unusually well informed for a layman on medical subjects, seemed to lack obvious outside contacts but shaped up as being likely to be capable of devising the assault. Ernest Philip Lawson was at Joliet State Prison in Illinois, which in itself provided a kind of further insurance against the identification of Madison as the primary convict involved. At the same time, his temperament and religious fixations hardly made him a likely candidate to be a partner of Madison—in short, he could stand on his own as a possible suspect . . . .

Now came the question of how much of this could be on the original note to be left at the hospital, how much later and in what form. Thinking on it, he decided the first note at the hospital should be a plain shocker, to get their attention, to be followed by a second that would set forth in relatively easy, decipherable form a superficially cryptic message that would spell out the trade—the antidote for release of the convicts. The "Aunt Dotie" for antidote, a crude sort of pun-and-anagram construction that he felt might reasonably be taken to have been concocted by most any of the men selected or their allies, was inspired by memory of an actual Aunt Dorothy, his mother's sister and an especially doting one at that. It also depended for its effectiveness, once deciphered, on the hospital people having understood that a poison had been somehow injected into the Secretary—which the first note and their own deduction should establish rather speedily. If mention of this, even a hint, was missing from press and television reports, he would risk a further communication, but the fewer of those, obviously, the better. The only time, he hoped, that it would be necessary to use the telephone would be a call to direct attention to the personal columns of the appropriate newspaper, which in turn would depend on where he finally made the connection with the Secretary—he'd need to put the same ad in a newspaper of each of the major cities on the Secretary's itinerary.

The final decision was to establish an escape route for the convicts, and for this he indeed did need Lucas's input. Lucas had never given him a number to call, but there was not long to wait for his next importuning call. Lucas was at first surprised and then pleased to hear that now his help was actually solicited, and promptly suggested that they now meet to set the details. He chose an east-side Manhattan restaurant called the Madison, in the east Eighties, where he and Madison had recently met to concoct the ill-fated liquor store heist after going to a former lady friend of Madison in the area who had once been chicly radical about his Black Panther association and, after his flight to Algeria, had considerably cooled in her ardor. At the time they'd thought the name of the restaurant, just around the corner from her apartment building, was a good omen. Hopefully, Lucas thought, it would prove to be one now, the second time around. Lucas even forgot his sardonic tongue as he came up with a former draft evader turned drug trafficker, a brother, now operating just south of Edmonton, Canada. Word would be gotten to him to be expecting Madison; he was also a possible back-up to Madison for making the call to Lucas confirming Madison's safe arrival, thereby putting into effect the exchange of the papers for the remaining $10,000 and Waxman's release of the antidote for the Secretary. "I assume, professor. that air travel arrangements can be made to Edmonton," Lucas said. "Complete, I'd think, with parachutes, so my friend can drop like a bird from the bird if it should run out of gas, or something . . ." He carefully avoided mentioning the possibility of Madison ditching the plane in any case before arriving at the airport, to avoid itchy-fingered guards dumb enough to blow the deal for Kramer's life, or too cynical to think it mattered, that Madison and his friends wouldn't bother with their end of the bargain. Lucas figured what the professor didn't know . . . "We'll fix us up a nice message for the Secretary's friends, and I'll be the one to deliver it just as soon as we know it's the time. I expect you'll give me the word when the deal is on, or the gentlemen of the press will . . . right, professor?" Later, on his own, Lucas would add words to the message requesting a revolver . . . .

When the train jolted to a halt at Granville Avenue, and a single passenger boarded, Waxman's gaze went up to the route map fixed above the doors. He already knew that he was on an A-line train and saw that Morse Avenue was only a few stations away. So close

now, if everything continued to go as planned . . . Not daring to
think about it, he thought instead about the long process that had
taken him to this point, beginning with placing the Aunt Dotie ad in
the *New York Times* and *Chicago Tribune* for the appropriate dates
provided by Kramer's headquarters—he'd decided that he'd have
to restrict himself to the two most promising sites, that it would
simply be physically impossible for him to sustain for more than
two attempts all that would be involved. The New York rally in the
downtown Wall Street area was impossible; he'd never gotten even
close to the Secretary. Chicago, the big State Street rally, had
found him carried along in a crowd right up to the front of the
platform from which Kramer launched his now habitual campaign
practice of moving off into the crowd for direct contact. All had
gone smoother than he'd dared hope, and the Chicago subway
system had worked to his advantage just as he'd expected, spilling
him out close by St. Luke's-Presbyterian, where he could with
relative ease gain access to the hospital, leave his note on the
Secretary's CBC at the messenger's station, unattended in the
flurry of activity, as he'd anticipated, and walk unobtrusively out
and back to his hotel. Only later, as he waited for the time to make
his call about the classified instruction, had the near self-hypnosis
begun to wear off and the reliving of what had occurred begun to
sink in, together with his awareness that something was now in
motion that he could only partially control. After he'd made the
call, he worried that the meaning of the ad would escape them,
although before he'd been so confident it would not, and then when
he was contacted by Dr. Nissen he'd been at least reassured that
they understood it was a poison they were up against, and yet he
panicked momentarily at the notion of having to be on the scene,
although that did, as he'd considered at the start, have its advan-
tages for him—and likewise its dangers if he became too obvious.
He worried about getting away at the appropriate time to make the
final rendezvous trip he was now on, but he also realized that in any
case there was no way he could reasonably turn down Nissen's

211

request. He almost smiled now as he recalled how, ironically, it was in a way fortunate that he had never actually met the Secretary, never gotten that much-requested appointment to argue his case against Z–3. Otherwise he might well have been recognized by the Secretary at the hospital—never mind counting on his delirium from the virus—and together with his previous argument and the presence of a mysterious poison, it well might have been over for him before it had started. Ryan had been a problem . . . he was a good man and Waxman felt badly despite their past differences about having had to deceive him, maybe one day he'd be able to explain . . . . Once it became known that the government had made the decision to go along with the trade, it was imperative to get out of the hospital in time to do what was necessary to meet the deadline mentioned in his note for the trade, and to make it and provide the antidote before Kramer's condition deteriorated even more than it had . . . he had already gotten worse, it seemed, than could reasonably be expected in that short period of time, on the basis of Waxman's experience with the stricken scientists on the Arizona project. Of course, it was impossible to know with certainty the depth of the injection or other variables that could determine the rate of its impact—it was, after all, still a relatively experimental substance, which he'd considered when first choosing it but felt that the great difference between a relatively few hours and several weeks—which it had taken the Arizona scientists to be so severely affected—would insure a safe margin. Once the final message about the planes and Edmonton had been delivered by Lucas—after his call to him—Waxman's concern about the time factor increased to the point where his complex charade with his medical colleagues and awareness of the deadlines had his stomach in a turmoil unlike any other time since those days at the front during the war watching young men's innards being patched up . . . .

And so thinking, he was reminded once again of the horrific consequences that would magnify times beyond comprehension

212

those scenes he'd witnessed if Z–3 and its successors were allowed to take their place in conventional arsenals of "defense." . . .

Morse station, he noted, was two stops away, and soon he'd finally know if the planes had arrived safely, or rather, most importantly, Madison's had, and whether the convict had survived and given the word to Lucas, who would be waiting for it at a pre-designated phone booth, from there to join Waxman to make the exchange of the money for the papers . . . the money, and for the first time in hours he thought of it, and hoped fervently once again that its importance would have motivated Madison to follow through on the plan. . . .

It took longer than usual to gather all of the doctors in Schaeffer's office for another meeting. Everyone was tired and frustrated. Their purpose now was to streamline their attack. Too many people were working on too many different projects, and there was still, despite the agreement to the trade, no guarantee that they would get the antidote in time . . . indeed, at all. As they began attempting to put together new plans, two police cars arrived at the front entrance. Pat and Thornton were in the first car, and as they were being escorted through the milling crowd in the lobby, other reporters, some of whom knew Thornton, swarmed about for anything he might have for them, assuming as they did that arriving with this sort of official escort he must be on to something.

The second car, pulling up moments after Pat and Thornton's, carried the professor's personal belongings, confiscated from his hotel room. The most striking item was a long plaster arm-cast with a 110-degree bend at the elbow, split open longitudinally. On its outside were three loose leather straps, one at the wrist level and the other two on each side of the bend, and on the inside of the hollow shell was a glass syringe with a two-inch needle, held in place by a clamp within the plaster. The loop of string which had once acted as the trigger appeared like a small hangman's noose. In addition to a valise with Waxman's clothes, the police brought along an empty medicine vial.

Dr. Ryan was the first to examine the vial. As he passed it to Dressner, he commented that the outside markings had been scraped away, but also suggested that there might be microscopic traces of the poison inside. Dressner agreed, adding that the size and shape of the container were too common to provide any clue. As it was handed around the room, Ryan warned everyone not to open it.

By 8:00 A.M. every television and radio station in the Chicago area was broadcasting Waxman's picture and name. It was too late to make that morning's papers, whose headlines dramatically stated that the Secretary's condition continued to worsen. The UPI teletype began with "Kramer near death . . ."

Meanwhile Inspector Pritchard was back on the telephone. After notifying the President of the newest developments, he called his own office, requesting as much information as was available on Waxman. Arrangements were also made to send FBI agents to Waxman's home.

Kramer's press secretary was sitting outside the executive suite waiting for his latest vital signs. He was now taking his instructions directly from the President and had been told to avoid answering any questions about Waxman until more could be learned about him.

On the other side of the door, Kramer's temperature was "down" to 104 degrees and the ice bath was being wiped away with towels. His body was covered with goose bumps and his lips had a bluish-white discoloration. He remained in coma, unable to move any part of his body and unable to control his normal bodily functions.

The result of the latest set of blood tests had come in, indicating that his sugar was still below normal, the white count remained elevated and the anemia was worsening.

Hematology Laboratory
CBC
Time Drawn: 07:00

Test	Result	Normal Values
Hemoglobin	11.0	14-18 gm/100ml
Hematocrit	32%	42-52 ml/100ml
Red Cell Count	3.72 million	4.6-6.2 million/cu mm
White Cell Count	17,540	5-10,000/cu mm
neutrophils	81%	54-62%
bands	10%	0-5%
lymphocytes	4%	25-33%
monocytes	3%	3-7%
eosinophils	2%	1-3%
basophils	0%	0-1%
metamyelocytes	0%	0%
promyelocytes	0%	0%
MCV	89	82-92
MCH	30	27-31
MCHC	33	32-36
Platelets	260,000	2-300,000/cu mm
Sedimentation Rate	58	less than 15 mm/hr

RBC Morphology: occasional fragmented cells

Chemistry Laboratory
Electrolytes
Time Drawn: 07:00

	Result	Normal Values
Sodium	141	132-142 mEq/L
Potassium	3.5	3.5-5.0 mEq/L
Chloride	103	98-106 mEq/L
BUN	17	10-20 mg/100ml
Sugar	58	60-90 mg/100ml

VITAL SIGNS

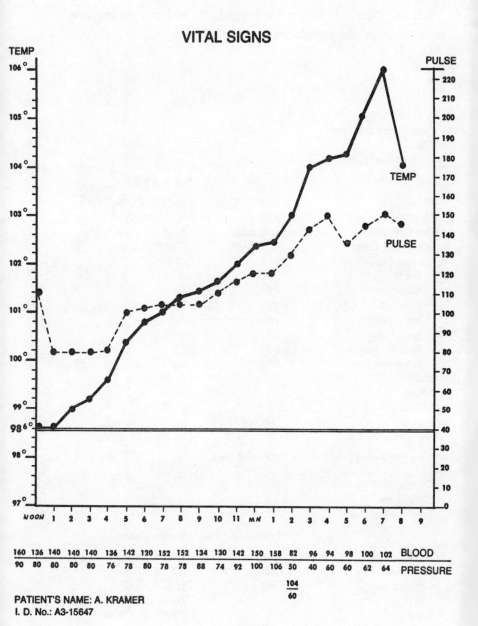

PATIENT'S NAME: A. KRAMER
I. D. No.: A3-15647

216

Chapter XVII

It was 10:00 A.M. Eastern Standard Time when the airliner diverted by Akubar landed along the eastern runway at Miami for refueling, while at Edmonton Giovanni had surrendered without a fight—still somewhat confused about exactly what happened. No one, however, expected the same relatively easy results in Miami. It was a bright sunny day, temperature in the mid-70s, as spectators and airport personnel alike were quickly cleared from the immediate area. New anti-hijacking procedures were in place. So, too, as back-up, were police sharpshooters, who now took up strategic positions around the empty airfield. . . .

The last note of the instructions had said that if the dispatch of planes carrying the convicts named in the classified notice was initiated in one hour, the antidote would arrive by noon—the close of the twenty-four hour period originally stipulated in the scrawl left on the Secretary's first CBC report. Going literally by that, authorities might have decided it was within the rules of the game to do everything thereafter to stop the convicts or recapture them immediately. Such a reading, however, was clearly not consistent with the careful instructions negotiated by the U.S. authorities, including the President, himself, with the Canadian officials at Ottawa. The main objective, after all, was the safety of Secretary Kramer, which depended on his receiving the antidote in time to save his life, and since this depended on the safe release and shipment of the convicts, nothing foolish or vainglorious at the last

217

moment was to be risked that could jeopardize the Secretary's chances, however remote they might be. In this context, only because of the extreme provocation was Millitz killed. When it was discovered that Madison and Lawson had parachuted from their plane, one, or both of them, seemed almost certainly the convicts for whom this whole elaborate operation had been devised, while the others, pretty obviously now, had been included to throw the authorities off the scent. From the first it was speculated by some, in fact, that the request for parachutes in the planes meant that they would indeed be used, while the others thought it a sort of gratuitous gesture, the indulgence of somebody who would never think of jumping unless the plans failed or was about to crash. With Madison and Lawson clearly having parachuted from a plane in no operational trouble at all, they became the prime suspects. The notion of a trailing plane was debated, and finally one was sent to observe but not impede such a jump. By the time it arrived, however, Madison and Lawson had jumped, but there was no sign of their chutes in the snow-covered landscape below.

The fact that no word had been received since the death of Millitz or the capture of Giovanni that the trade was off tended further to confirm that it was Madison or Lawson or both that all this was for. The further significance of this was that Akubar was almost certainly *not* the man, and therefore attempts to frustrate and capture him in the process of his hijacking adventure were in no way likely to jeopardize the trade and the Secretary's life.

After Akubar's plane had come to a stop several hundred yards from the main terminal and the noisy engines were turned off, a large Shell Oil truck rolled onto the field, approaching the plane as if this were a routine refueling. Following closely behind the cumbersome yellow truck was a nondescript Volkswagen camper bus. Its driver was Harold Wennings, a heavy-set man in his late forties with a receding hairline and darkly tinted glasses. He was wearing street clothes, brown slacks and a flowery short-sleeved shirt that fit tightly across his midline. In the back of the camper were four small tanks of compressed nitrous oxide, a sleeping gas often used in operating rooms. The other two men in the first truck were both airport employees.

Although the two vehicles parked next to the plane's fuselage, the camper positioned itself on the far side, using the tanker as a partial shield. As the two attendants connected their fuel pump to the jet, Wennings quickly slipped beneath the plane's belly, making certain that he wasn't being watched from above, and quickly unlocked the luggage compartment. Once he was able to raise himself up inside and confirm that the ventilation pipes overhead were accessible, he returned to his camper to unload the tanks. Because each one weighed over forty pounds, he had to make four separate trips. In the interim, Miami police tried to distract the hijacker by making repeated demands over the radio, threatening to shoot out the plane's tires if he didn't give himself up. Akubar thought their efforts humorous and old-fashioned, and did not respond.

Wennings worked as quickly as possible once all four tanks were on board. Using special leather straps, he fastened each one to the metal support rods toward the back of the luggage area and afterward cut into four separate pieces some long plastic tubing that had been coiled in his back pocket, using the first three segments to connect the tanks in tandem. The last strip was used to connect the fourth tank to a pressure valve on one of the inlet pipes. After rechecking his connections, he opened the pressure release valve and listened for the flow of gas. A moment later he could hear the hiss, and quickly jumped to the ground, shutting the luggage compartment behind him, and hurried back to his camper. Akubar heard the doors slam and assumed that the sound came from the refueling truck. Wennings then put on his headlights to signal that the nitrous oxide was hooked up. Approximately ten minutes were needed for the gas to take hold.

In a few moments, however, Akubar's patience became frayed. He began demanding that the refueling be halted and threatened to shoot the co-pilot if the plane didn't take off immediately. The control tower was silent. Those on the outside knew more time was needed, that if the plane made it into the air now it was certain to crash.

Akubar repeated the demand as if he sensed some unknown danger, and finally the pilot signaled the ground crew to disconnect their lines and back away. Once the trucks were driving toward the terminal building, the pilot came back on the air and requested permission to take off. Tension escalated as the authorities sought some means to delay them.

At first there was no response from the control tower and soon the pilot made another pleading request. He was not aware of the sweet but colorless gas that was beginning to diffuse throughout the plane's interior. After a third request he threatened to leave without permission, but before he could start his engines the traffic controller responded. It was an order to wait for an American Airlines jet that had lost one of its engines and was about to make an emergency landing.

The radio was quiet as six more minutes dragged past and the wounded plane didn't show. Akubar, increasingly nervous, raised his gun, aimed at the co-pilot. Without a word, the pilot started his engines. The gas had now permeated the plane. The three men in the cockpit were beginning to feel its effects, without knowing the source, and were fighting to keep their eyes open.

The plane began taxiing toward the end of the runway as the control tower continued to importune them not to take off, which moved Akubar to swing the butt of his revolver about and smash the radio set.

The plane slowly turned around, lined up imperfectly with the long asphalt strip. A last-minute check of systems was sleepily made, the engines roared, the plane began to roll . . . and then slowed as the pilot, in an instinctive gesture of self-preservation as he sensed his control was lost, extended his arm and just managed to switch off the engines. Quiet. An overwhelming feeling of drowsiness laved them all, crew and Arab terrorist alike.

The control tower, testing, tried to raise an answer.

Two officers from S.W.A.T., wearing gas masks, carrying shotguns, entered the rear of the plane. Moments later, they came back into view, signaled the all-clear. The crew was found asleep in their respective seats. Akubar was discovered slumped against the cockpit door. His revolver had fallen to the floor. His unseeing face wore a bemused scowl.

The northbound A-train was coming to a stop at Loyola University on Chicago's far North Side. Only a few people were waiting, and when the doors opened two noisy freshmen boarded Waxman's car and sat at the opposite end, near the beggar and his dog.

Just below the elevated station, Madison's friend Lucas Marion waited inside a telephone booth. He was adorned in a purple outfit with a long-sleeved polka-dot shirt. The Z–3 papers taken from Professor Waxman were casually folded and stuffed into his back pocket, as if they might have been yesterday's newspaper. The call confirming Madison's safe escape was late, and as Lucas heard the train pass above he speculated that Waxman might well be on board en route to their rendezvous. He was most anxious to get the transaction over with, but he would have to wait for the designated meeting point, which was the next stop north.

As the train began to roll once again, the old beggar kept his eyes fixed on Waxman, his stare camouflaged by his dark glasses. Nondescript as Waxman might have always considered himself to be, to the sharp eyes of the beggar, an experienced people-watcher of long standing, he was almost instantly recognizable as the man who'd run by him on the subway platform in the commotion after the attack upstairs the day before. He smelled remuneration now, and all the booze it could buy. He could hardly wait to make a phone call, and had already checked his pockets three times to confirm that there were sufficient coins inside.

221

At Presbyterian, Dr. Ryan had carried the mysterious vial, recovered from Waxman's apartment, across the street to the university's laboratories as Nissen returned upstairs to relieve Fitzgerald. When he arrived he found the other doctor standing over the bed. Kramer appeared to be sleeping, his eyes were shut and his breathing seemed somewhat labored. The only other sound in the room was the continuous cardic monitor, rapidly firing its electrical complexes above his head. The new intravenous bottle was half empty.

After Fitzgerald gave him a brief summary of the last hour, expressing his pessimism, he washed his hands and left. Nissen proceeded to check Kramer's reflexes, and found that his body was still limp. He pulled up a chair and began rereading the Secretary's thick chart. It was unbelievable to him that although just about every test known to medical science had been done, each had failed. Added to the dismal picture: Kramer was anemic from the massive bloodletting alone.

The rumble of the subway train made it impossible to hear the conductor, but Waxman easily spotted a large black and white sign announcing Morse Avenue. He was at the exit as the train slowed, and once the doors had swung open he quickly headed across the platform before the beggar could drag his frightened dog onto the wooden planks. Within seconds Waxman was down the steps, through a side turnstile and out of sight. When the beggar finally made it to the bottom of the steps he found himself confronted with three possible exits. He arbitrarily chose the one going to the main street, but when he reached the sidewalk there was no sign of his quarry.

Madison's pace was not nearly so fast as Waxman's or the beggar's. He had managed to find a dirt road that wound through a thick forest, and after following its twisting path for a half mile he came on an isolated farmhouse. A two-tone station wagon was parked out front, and gray smoke billowed from a brick chimney. He stopped for a moment to check that he still had both revolvers, then proceeded. Each step was a struggle for him, he was freezing from exposure and his hands and feet were fast becoming numb.

In the same time that it had taken Madison to travel his short way, Lawson had covered five miles in the opposite direction, where he found a two-lane highway. Using it as a guide, he turned south and soon passed a sign for Moose Jaw.

The Washington report on Waxman was brief. Most of the information seemed routine biography. Born in Philadelphia, attended the University of Pennsylvania for undergraduate work, Harvard Medical School and Columbia for postgraduate. Served two years in the Army during World War II, received honorable discharge. He'd received three separate grants from the National Institute of Health totaling $60,000, and had worked as an advisor on several government ecology projects, the last of which was in Arizona. Present salary was $30,000; $25,000 mortgage on a three-bedroom house; maintained savings account of approximately $10,000; had another $20,000 invested in securities, half of which apparently were sold recently—although no large purchases or bank deposits had been recorded. Wife's name, Margaret; married for over nineteen years, two sons. Eldest, an insulin-dependent diabetic. No record of membership in political party; claimed to be an independent, no known affiliation with any left-wing organization. One arrest: a misdemeanor during an anti-Vietnam War march; given a small fine. Considered expert on infectious diseases, particularly viruses. Traveled abroad on several occasions; passport recorded no visit to an Iron Curtain country. Hobby, chess; considered an expert.

Pritchard was struck by the fact that Waxman had recently sold some of his securities, but ascribed it to his need for money to escape the country. There was, of course, no record of the Arizona Project. Even the President was unaware of it—actually he'd issued a directive earlier banning such projects in the future. The Arizona one, certain Department heads observed, was, at the time, in the present. Jeremy Royce might have thrown considerable light on the question of Waxman's motives, but he had only recently died of a ruptured cranial aneurysm, not uncommon in his family—he'd also had a heart problem ever since a childhood bout of rheumatic fever, which led to the newspapers' error in reporting his death as due to a heart attack. All that seemed clear was that Professor Louis Waxman seemed to have harbored a most powerful and peculiar rage against Secretary Kramer—one that, most improbably, had somehow gotten him linked up with one or more murderous convicts. Improbable as well was a reasonable, pacific man such as Dr. Waxman being subject to such passion, or a likable man such as Secretary Kramer being the victim of it.

When FBI agents confronted Mrs. Waxman with the news that her husband had been Secretary Kramer's assailant, she refused to believe their statement, just as she had the television reports, and demanded to see a search warrant before she would permit them to enter her house. They'd come prepared, but after an hour's search through the Professor's voluminous papers and personal belongings, they were unable to find anything of use. His wall safe was empty. . . .

Meanwhile the gigantic electron microscope was slowly scanning a sample taken from the empty vial. Every millimeter was studied. Dozens of photographs had already been taken and were being developed as rapidly as they could be transported to the darkroom next door. Dust particles loomed like huge boulders, and chips of glass seemed like jagged mountains of ice. Fingerprints with their rolling hills and deep valleys obscured many of the shots, interfering as they did with the light refraction.

Edmonton airport remained closed to the public all morning as planes assembled, awaiting a report that the antidote had been delivered so that they could begin a coordinated search for the two convicts who had parachuted. Numerous reports of mistaken identities were already flooding police stations in the area, but no action was to be taken until the word came. They waited.

Madison, on the dirt road, was determined to make the phone call confirming his escape. More than ever now he'd need the money that Lucas would collect from the professor, who, he had to acknowledge, was some kind of cat to have pulled off this little operation. Yes . . . the money tree was damned bare, especially since his pretty white lady friend had given him the gate— apparently old Black Panthers were no longer "in" on Madison and Park Avenues. The ten thousand Marion had gotten on account would go fast for forged passports and the rest. He needed the rest of that bread. . . .

He was particularly cautious as he approached the farm house. He could see that the curtains were drawn, but elected to use the blind side, where the chimney was situated, for his approach. A few minutes later he was listening at the back door.

Inside a young woman was vacuuming. Her husband had left an hour previously with their pickup truck to borrow some equipment from their closest neighbor four miles away. She appeared to be in her early twenties and slightly overweight, wearing levis and a checkered shirt tied at her waist and unbuttoned through the braless cleavage.

Madison could hear the hum of a vacuum cleaner and after glimpsing the lone housewife, felt relieved. Almost home free . . . He tried the doorknob, but when he tried to force the door open his hands began to hurt badly. Frustrated, he finally located a bedroom window that could be pried open with a thin piece of shale

225

he'd spotted on the ground. Nonetheless the window was tight and the cracking sound woke the baby inside; a baby whose cries were either ignored or not heard by his mother in the next room.

Waxman hurriedly approached a small relatively inconspicuous espresso shop at the intersection of two one-way streets, a block north of the Morse Avenue El station. The beige store-front lacked a marquee, but there were two handwritten posters sitting in one of the windows, one announcing an upcoming local chess tournament and the other merely "ESPRESSO SHOP."

After Waxman entered and closed the door, whose center plate was lined with stained glass, he hesitated a moment to allow his eyes to adjust to the dimly lit interior. Along each side was a short row of picnic-type tables, each with its plastic black-and-white chessboard awaiting players, and with an unlit candle for a center-piece. Directly across from where he was standing, just a few paces away, was a long-haired young man grinding coffee beans on a wooden counter. To his far left was a single customer whose eyes were trained on the chessboard in front of him; the pieces, however, were untouched and still in their starting positions. Waxman's contact.

The pressure on Waxman seemed to have slackened for the moment: he was off the street, where he might be spotted, and it was doubtful that many customers would be entering the shop in the next half hour. He proceeded to hang his trenchcoat on an old-fashioned coat rack, and then ordered a cup of espresso, and silently joined the other customer, whose expression did not change until Waxman moved the white king's pawn to king four. The man responded with king's knight to king three. The prear-ranged signal was completed, and the man introduced himself as Thomas Bahnheim, a friend of Dr. Carl Reinhart, a retired profes-sor of biological sciences living in Geneva. Then, without further word, the game continued as the two men waited for the secret documents to arrive.

Inspector Pritchard once more reviewed in his mind the roster of convicts. Weisberg had been eliminated because of his refusal to travel. Giovanni seemed honestly confused by the morning's events, and was steadfast in his denials. Akubar would have had little chance to contact Waxman once he'd hijacked the airliner, and more to the point, Pritchard doubted such an act was part of the plot—it lacked the detailed planning that had characterized matters so far. Millitz could not be entirely eliminated, but he was dead and that was that. He would have been much more concerned about Millitz if Madison or Lawson did not seem so much more probable, especially after their use of the parachutes, requested in the last note of instructions. They were the *only* ones to use the parachutes.

Assuming that one of the two was responsible, it was also likely that the contact confirming escape and releasing the antidote would be made by telephone, and Pritchard immediately made arrangements with the telephone company to trace any calls to Chicago initiated within a five-hundred-mile radius of Edmonton. The police department was still on full alert, and squad cars were dispersed throughout the city with a special radio frequency band kept open.

The crippled beggar continued his door-to-door search along Morse Avenue, pulling along his dog, who was attempting to give attention to each and every parking meter they passed. Some people found it rather strange . . . an apparently blind man peering intently into each window; the old man, indifferent to their amused comment, did not overlook a single store, going directly inside and inspecting the premises whenever he felt the need. On several occasions his patronage was less than appreciated. One of the larger restaurants used his dog as an excuse to evict him, but not before he'd made certain that he had inspected the face of every customer. Next door, in a would-be-exclusive men's store, a prim salesman actually took him by the collar and led him back to the sidewalk. As if to offset this, an old bearded tailor invited him in to stay for morning coffee. It was against his nature to decline, but he managed.

The results of his search were depressing. Nobody questioned had seen the man he described. The last store on the north side of the street was a small florist shop, and when the beggar left the premises with the same response he now began to consider the two new high-rise apartment buildings he could see a bit further down the street, fearing that his man might have gone into one of the apartments and would therefore be impossible to trace. He forced that horrible thought from his mind and, being an established optimist, crossed Morse Avenue and began working his way back toward the El station. In his haste, he failed even to realize that he didn't know the name of the reporter he planned to contact once he'd located his target. He also continued to overlook the fact that he was supposed to be blind, using his white cane as a walking stick, not a blindman's guide, and moving along the sidewalk completely oblivious to the attention he was attracting.

At Presbyterian the research work continued at its accelerated pace, as some technicians stopped to nap and others from the day shift took over their workbenches. Everyone was aware that time was running out, yet some personnel who had worked all night were simply too exhausted to continue.

When the third set of photographs from the electron microscope reached Dr. Ryan, they revealed the remains of a few empty viral particles, similar to those spotted earlier in the Secretary's wound biopsy. He had difficulty finding a complete virus, but the structures seemed to be rodlike, resembling a small caliber bullet, flat on one end and rounded on the other; each had a thick capsule covered with hundreds of tiny projections. None of the capsules had a nucleic acid core as might be expected with a viable virus. Judging by the magnification, he estimated each viral particle's size at 60 to 70 angstroms across the cylindrical base and 200 to 250 in length.

Ryan studied each photograph, searching for an intact particle, but there was none to be found and as a consequence he was unable to make a positive identification. Dressner had the same problem when he reviewed the films.

Finally Ryan decided to telephone the lab at M.I.T. once again. He requested that they resubmit Kramer's symptoms, add the virus description and delete any symptoms that could have been caused by the insulin.

Waxman moved his queen to the far side of the chessboard and soon lost it to a bishop that was waiting in plain sight. He was, understandably, having trouble keeping his mind on the game, and two moves later Bahnheim declared an easy checkmate. It was just past nine. The worries he'd mostly been able to suppress about Lucas and a doublecross now surfaced full blown. He reached into his coat pocket to reassure himself with the presence of the envelope containing the second $10,000. Bahnheim, setting up the pieces for a new game, now swung the board around, and after moving his white pawn forward, waited for the professor to respond. The two men continued to be the only customers.

The last store on the south side of Morse Avenue was an appliance store which throughout business hours, which had just commenced, promoted itself by leaving every television set turned on and aimed at passersby. The beggar had entered a few moments earlier and paused to catch his breath and watch the barrage of television screens . . . which just now were going to black and interrupting the program with a news bulletin. Immediately after he was looking at Roger Thornton's face on every screen. It was an on-the-scene report, and before reporter Thornton began speaking, an announcer proclaimed his name in reverberating stereo.

Seconds later, Louis Waxman's face appeared on the same screens. With a start, the beggar realized it was the same man he

229

was trailing. He quickly studied the faces inside the store, then hurried outside to continue looking on the other side of the viaduct, armed with Thornton's name and feeling increasingly excited about his prospects.

Once Madison had managed to pry the window loose, he set the crutch against the outside wall and struggled inside. The vacuum cleaner was still running in the living room, but the baby's cries had faded into the slow, deep respirations of a sleeping infant. Once inside, he quietly reached back out to retrieve the broken branch, then cautiously made his way across the bedroom toward a closed door.

With each step his eyes studied the child intently, hesitating whenever the wooden boards creaked beneath his feet. He started to turn the doorknob, but heard the telephone ring and quickly stopped. He tried to listen, but the woman's specific words were inaudible, which reinforced his imaginings that it was someone warning her about escaped convicts. He tried opening the door a crack to eavesdrop, but his makeshift crutch got in the way and slipped onto the polished floor beneath. Within an instant the sound of the crutch banging on the floor brought the child awake, and screaming. The mother, who actually was speaking to her husband about a new job prospect, immediately dropped the receiver and rushed into the bedroom. A moment later the husband heard his wife scream and then . . . there was a click on the telephone. When he tried calling back, the line was busy.

The first monitored call from Canada came from Calgary, a town 150 miles south of Edmonton. When the word was relayed to Rondowski, he became excited, thinking that it was an ideal spot for Madison or Lawson to make a contact. Several squad cars were immediately dispatched to an apartment building near Oak Park and a few blocks from the Eisenhower Expressway. Once the brick structure was surrounded, two men from Special Weapons, wearing bulletproof vests and armed with automatic rifles, broke down the door, unannounced. They discovered that the flat belonged to two elderly widows, one of whom was still on the telephone and almost had a heart attack.

The second, and more promising, call from Canada followed a few minutes later. The telephone company traced the local terminus to a pay booth at the Loyola El station, and again squad cars began converging. By the time the first car arrived, the booth was empty and the train Lucas barely caught had rounded the bend and disappeared from sight. Nonetheless, they were able to get his description from a high-school girl working behind the newspaper stand, though she was unable to say in which direction he had gone. An immediate APB was put out, and cars were dispatched to search the neighborhood and to check every train stop north and south of Loyola.

There were only a few stores on the other side of the concrete viaduct, and within a short time the beggar had managed to check each one. This time he returned to the El station and headed north along a deserted one-way street. He noted an espresso café in the distance and planned to return to the high-rise apartments once he'd checked it out. This idea was speedily abandoned once he peered inside and focused on a man who surely *resembled* Waxman —it was a profile and in the darkness it was impossible to be certain. He decided to go in, but barely made it past the doorway when the young man who worked behind the counter started toward him. He quickly pulled his cup from his coat pocket and approached the two men at the chessboard. Waxman started to reach into his pocket for change, but the young proprietor grabbed the old man by his sleeve and led him back to the entrance. It didn't matter. The beggar had gotten a good look, and although he made a

231

point of complaining about the manager's bullyboy tactics, there was a wide grin threatening to take over his saturnine face at any moment.

Once back outside he hurried painfully across the street—his infirmities were beginning to take their toll with all this activity —and went to a row of pay phones he'd passed earlier. The names Thornton and station WGN kept racing through his mind, and as he tried to shut the folding door of the booth, he almost cut his trailing dog in half. The extremely cramped space once he got the dog and his accordion in the booth with him was only a slight deterrence. He literally smelled paydirt.

The phone book pages were torn and filthy, but the W's were relatively unscathed. His education a third grader's, he at first had trouble finding the station's number. Finally he located WGN. Keeping one finger on the page, he dialed with his other hand, having let the leash drop to the floor of the booth. Once he got the operator at WGN he immediately asked for Mr. Roger Thornton. The switchboard operator connected him to Thornton's empty office and allowed the extension to ring some twenty times. Finally, when she returned to the line, the beggar was frantic, alternately pleading and screaming at her to find him. The girl, apparently immune, cordially connected him to the newsroom, where an impatient voice told him that Thornton was at Presbyterian and not in the studio. Before the beggar could get the hospital's number the man hung up.

For just a moment he considered calling the police. Presbyterian was a big hospital, maybe he'd never get hold of Thornton . . . but then he dismissed the notion, reminding himself that the chance of a reward from the police, for someone like him, was not too good. He dug deep into his frayed trouser pockets, but the only coins left were two pennies and a shiny quarter. The idea of using his last quarter offended him. There was no *guarantee* that the reporter or his paper would reward him either, and he needed fare to get back downtown. He hesitated for a moment, then decided that he could work Morse Avenue later if he had to.

232

He dropped the quarter into the largest slot and dialed "O." Followed by a ring and an operator's voice intoning to him that the telephone company could not give change. The old man promptly began screaming that this was an emergency and he needed Presbyterian Hospital immediately. Unexpectedly, the coin returned as the phone on the other end began ringing, but his instant smile of relief was wiped away by her request the he reinsert his coin. As he glanced about, waiting for the hospital to answer, he saw but hardly noted a black man wearing purple bell-bottoms walking past on the other side of the street and entering the espresso café.

When the operator at the hospital finally answered, she at first thought that Thornton was a patient's name and spent several precious seconds skimming through her rotary file. The old man hollered that Thornton was a reporter and that his call dealt with Kramer's life. She then immediately connected him to Schaeffer's office, where Pritchard answered the phone. The beggar, however, refused to speak to anyone except Thornton. Pritchard immediately placed him on hold and went to look for the reporter. . . .

At the same time another call was coming through the hospital switchboard for Dr. Ryan. It was his return call from M.I.T. The computer had been unable to give them a precise answer, but did provide a list of viral possibilities: parainfluenza, respiratory syncytial, Newcastle, distemper, rinderpest, rabies, vesicular stomatitis virus, Hart Park virus, coccal and sigma viruses of insects and three varieties of plant viruses. Both Dressner and Ryan were stymied by the list. Some of the viruses were new to them and others would take too long to prove out. . . .

While they debated about how to proceed on what seemed an impossible task, Canadian police, as a result of the monitoring and tracing of calls from the Edmonton area to Chicago, were closing in on a small farmhouse south of Edmonton. There was only one access route, and as the police came cautiously down the dirt road they spotted a station wagon beginning to pull away. Madison, inside, was having trouble with the car's stick shift and floor pedals. Assuming that he'd never be able to drive away from them, he pulled out his gun and began shooting; a shotgun blast in return smashed through the car's window and distributed part of his head across the front seat. A moment later the husband sped past the squad cars with his accelerator floored. Inside the house he found his wife tied to a chair, shaking from fright, and the baby wailing in the other room.

Actually, Madison had come close to getting away. Not until word of the monitored conversation came through, indicating a go-ahead in the trade, were Canadian police allowed to move toward the farmhouse where the call had originated. But when they got there, if there was any doubt, they were not to interfere with Madison . . . providing, of course, that he was still there. If Madison had been able to maintain his cool, he just possibly could have limped away free . . . at least for a while. His friend Lucas Marion would likely have managed rather better. . . .

Thornton finally made it to the phone.

"You met me yesterday," the old beggar was still hollering.

"Yes . . .?"

"In the tunnel, by Dearborn. Ten dollars, remember? I seen him again, he's right across the street—"

Thornton urgently signaled for Pritchard to listen in on the other line. "Where are you?"

"At Lunt, by the El. He's in the coffee shop and he ain't goin' to be there long, I'm guessin'."

That was all they needed. Thornton understood he was talking about Waxman; details could wait. Pritchard immediately contacted Rondowski, who in turn put out a call for cars in the Rogers Park area to proceed to Lunt Avenue. Included was a warning *not* to shoot, or indeed harm, Waxman under any circumstances. The antidote came first. Kramer was not expected to live more than a few more hours. The three men hurried downstairs to the captain's car, which was parked in the front of the hospital.

Inside the café Waxman, Bahnheim and now Lucas Marion were attempting to conclude their business. Lucas's colorful garb

234

momentarily startled the sedate Bahnheim, but went unnoticed by Waxman as he focused in on the primary object—the exchange that all his planning and delicate and, yes, daring maneuvering had pointed to. For once Lucas kept his humorous cool in check as he joined the two others at the chessboard. He barely nodded, extracted the papers sticking out of his rear pocket, as though yesterday's newspaper, scanned them casually and put them in his lap, covered by the edge of the table. He looked at Waxman, who removed an envelope from his coat pocket and placed it under the table in Lucas's lap, then removed the papers from Lucas's lap and stuffed them into his coat pocket that had contained the money envelope. All that was left now was to transfer the papers to Bahnheim and deliver the antidote to the hospital. The arrangement for this had been worked out by Waxman and Bahnheim before Lucas's arrival—Waxman had no intention of allowing the antidote to be another potential hostage for Lucas. Once his business had been transacted with Lucas, Waxman would proceed alone out of the café. Bahnheim would follow. Once they were certain Lucas had cleared the area, Waxman would give over the papers to Bahnheim—eventually to find their way to Switzerland via diplomatic pouch—as well as the vial containing the antidote. This last was necessary because it was now confirmed by Lucas that Waxman could be identified. He could no longer risk the final stage himself; instead Bahnheim, reluctantly, would take his place. This would involve going to Presbyterian and to its bank of public phone booths on the ground floor. He would dial the hospital, ask for Dr. Nissen and inform the surgeon that the antidote was in one of the booths. The normal activity in the booths should make it highly unlikely that he could be pinpointed later as having been making a call in this bank at this time. Once he'd made the call, he would leave the vial in its white envelope provided by Waxman, mingle with others making calls, entering and leaving the booths, walk toward the hospital entrance and attempt to confirm by sight that the vial was actually retrieved. This last would depend on the circumstances, of course. If necessary he would proceed out of the hospital and take the one last slight chance that somehow in the moments between the call and the certain instant response to it, something might happen to the vial. The possibility of this, however, seemed extremely remote. Altogether, Waxman felt he was doing everything possible to insure that Kramer would now receive his end of the bargain. . . .

When the beggar hung up he saw that three men were now standing inside the café and apparently preparing to leave— the two white guys had been joined by the black man that he thought he'd seen walk by his phone booth. He quickly grabbed his dog's leash and got across the street as fast as his crippled body would allow, brandishing his white cane to slow down an oncoming city bus. Once he reached the café he threw his dirty coat onto the ground in front of the doorway and sat himself down on it. A moment later he was playing his accordion, although he found himself too short of breath to sing along.

Waxman was the first to reach the door, but when he tried pushing it open the beggar leaned back with all his strength. Waxman, startled and confused, gave another shove; the only response was increased volume from the accordion. Enraged, his nerves taut as wires, Waxman actually began shouting at the old man and turned to Bahnheim and Lucas for help. As he did so, the flashing blue lights of a police car approached the café. Panic finally set in. The three men made a rush for the rear exit. A moment later the front of the building swarmed with police cars. Waxman and Lucas managed to escape into an alleyway before the police could make it around back, but Bahnheim remained behind in the café, where he was immediately taken into custody.

As Lucas and Waxman ran eastward between two rows of houses and their empty garages, Waxman could barely comprehend, certainly not accept, the awful, sudden unraveling of all that he'd worked for. The papers and the antidote were still in his coat pockets. How would he ever get the papers to Bahnheim, or the vial to Kramer . . . ? He had no idea whether Bahnheim had gotten away or not, and he looked back now for an instant to see if he might be following. He was not. . . . Ahead was Lucas, several yards ahead. . . . The squad car pulled into the opposite end of the narrow passageway. Waxman darted through an open gate, nearly losing his balance as he stepped on a child's discarded skate, then made it out of sight between two houses. Lucas, however, had gotten too far ahead, and when he turned back toward the gateway, he found himself trapped by a second squad car approaching rapidly from the other end. He immediately tried scaling an eight-foot fence as one of the officers jumped from his car, rolled to the ground, positioned himself and fired a warning shot. Lucas continued his scrambling upward. As he cleared the top, a volley of shots sent him toppling backward. He lay unconscious, bleeding from his flank and chest. There was a pained expression on his face, as though he'd been robbed.

Waxman, meanwhile, was now running in a daze . . . running for survival. . . . Not familiar with the neighborhood, he felt his only chance was to make it to the beach, which he knew was a few blocks away. From there he at least could not be followed by the cars. . . . After he made it between two more houses, he found himself back on Morse Avenue. From there he ran across the street and found another small pathway threading between two stores and into a second alleyway. He turned eastward again.

By now he was becoming extremely short of breath, and there was a dull ache in the left side of his chest. He couldn't stop, he told himself, but he realized his pace was slowing anyway. . . .

A few moments later he found himself at Sheridan Road, a major north-south throughway. and ran directly across and in front of the late morning rush hour traffic, which included a pack of police cars, among which was Rondowski's. Rondowski immediately pulled over to the side of the road, and along with Pritchard and Thornton took up the chase.

At first Waxman was able to keep his distance, but his chest pain was getting worse, changing from the dull ache to a sharp, jabbing pain. Pritchard and Thornton were less than fifty yards behind him, calling to him to stop. Ignoring them, Waxman found another alley and headed down it toward its end. The sandy beach was now in sight, but as he neared the end of the alley his pain became excruciatingly severe, radiating up to his jaw and down his left arm. He could not catch his breath and soon his pace slowed to a walk. Finally he collapsed, drenched in perspiration and over-whelmed with pain. The Z–3 documents that had been hastily stuffed into his pocket now fell out and were scattered over the gravel in the immediate area.

Thornton was the first to reach him, immediately loosening Waxman's collar and feeling his pulse.

"Pain," was the only word Waxman could manage as he strug-gled for air. His lips were turning blue and his pulse was becoming weaker.

Pritchard now came running up as Thornton called out to Ron-dowski, who had lagged somewhat behind, to get an ambulance. Pritchard immediately began questioning Waxman about the anti-dote, demanding it. Time was, after all, extremely short.

Waxman, unable to take in enough air to speak, seemed to understand. His hand moved slowly toward one of his coat pock-ets, and as it did he attempted to speak once again, managing to get out only something that sounded like "zee three . . ." Pritchard, paying no attention, quickly reached inside the overcoat pocket and retrieved a plain white envelope. Inside was a small vial.

Pritchard now quickly scooped up the papers that had tumbled out of the professor's pocket when he fell. Then motioning to Rondowski, the two men ran to the police car and proceeded to the hospital, sirens blaring.

Thornton, meanwhile, put his ear to Waxman's chest. Not detecting a heartbeat, he immediately began external cardiac massage—the only thing that he learned in the army that he considered useful—rhythmically pressing on the professor's chest and stopping intermittently to breathe into his mouth. He stopped this procedure only when the ambulance arrived and its two paramedics had connected the professor to a heart monitor. The recording was a lifeless straight line.

Chapter XVIII

Professor Waxman's body was taken by the ambulance to the county morgue, where it was later claimed by his wife and son. Both seemed in a state of shock, and refused—then and thereafter —to grant interviews.

Thomas Bahnheim, thanks to credentials from the Swiss Embassy and several transatlantic calls, was subsequently recalled to Switzerland. His letters to Waxman's widow and son attempted to reassure them about the late professor's inherent decency and dedication to world science, but being under orders not to give details, his efforts seemed bland and banal, and were, not unreasonably, resented more than appreciated.

Ernie Lawson was taken into custody in Moose Jaw, not far from a school playground.

The other surviving convicts shared nothing more than before —except their uncomprehending involvement in Waxman's plan. Giovanni, a patient man, would wait for his family to try another time, another place; he had decided that they were behind the escape attempt, and would think of something else soon. Akubar, not a patient man, read with satisfaction of the growing international prestige of his terrorist leader and was certain that even his maximum security prison wouldn't long hold him. And Dr. Weisberg, who had assumed that well-intentioned if misguided friends had interceded in his behalf, was hopeful that they would not try again. A certain tranquility that he had found in prison had become his preferred way of life, until death. Thou shalt not kill was his people's injunction, and it came back more strongly to him the longer he remained in prison. He did not wish to disrupt his expiation.

The antidote taken from Waxman and rushed to the hospital was instantly administered to Secretary Kramer, who recovered slowly over a forty-eight hour period, though he was left with a permanent paralysis in his right hand. Remaining viral cultures, photographs and laboratory animals were in the first instance confiscated by Pritchard in behalf of the FBI and subsequently destroyed.

So, also, at Secretary Kramer's personal instructions were the records and all the plans for further development and storage of Z–3 and its antidote—including the duplicate papers Pritchard had retrieved after Waxman's collapse. Waxman would have been pleased.

Thornton persisted for a time in attempts to decipher the meaning of "zee three," the last words uttered by Waxman, but he ran into unyielding blind alleys and dead ends.

The crippled beggar was first arrested for loitering on Lunt Avenue, but was released when Thornton paid his fine. Thornton also slipped him a twenty once they were outside the precinct station. The subways of Chicago did not see him, or his raffish dog, or hear his cacophonous sounds, for an entire week.